KISS OF REDEMPTION

TOGETHER WE STAND - BOOK ONE

MAGGIE COLE

PULSE PRESS

This book is fiction. Any reference to historical events, real people, or real places are used fictitiously. All names, characters, plots, and events are products of the author's imagination. Any resemblances to actual events or places or persons, living or dead, is entirely coincidental.

Please note. May contain situations that may be sensitive for some readers.

FREE GIFT FOR YOU

Dear Romance Addicts,

A while back we had Team Week. This was in my Romance Addicts group (click to join if you aren't a member and want to have some fun or go to https://www.facebook.com/groups/maggiecole/) At the time, only four books in my All In series were published.

Team Tom and Liv took the gold! But Teams Meg and Collin, Jack and Maddie, and Blake and Laura all gave them a run for their money!

The combination of teams created these specifics for me to create a story around:

Characters: Dakota Jinx and Logan Alexander

Theme: Brother's Best Friend

Five Props: Tattoos (important to character), Journal, An important heirloom (not jewelry), Pantyhose (40's vintage style with the line up the back), Ice

Location: Montauk Point Lighthouse, Long Island New York

Click here for your freebie short story just for fun!

XOXO -

Maggie Cole

PS - Make sure you check out the Sneak Peek for Sins of Justice, book two, of the Together We Stand series, after the Epilogue.

To my readers,
May you fall in love with the Brooks family as much as I have.
XOXO
Maggie Cole

PROLOGUE

Beckett

REDEMPTION OCCURS BY CLEARING YOUR DEBT. ABSOLUTION FOR A sin that isn't yours can turn you into the exact opposite of what you once were. At least, that's my personal journey through hell.

"Beckett Brooks, do you feel that you've rehabilitated over the last ten years and are no longer a threat to society?" the lady wearing a navy-pinstripe suit and blue glasses, whose nameplate says Judge Filmore, asks me.

Society. What do I know about society anymore? How much has changed on the outside?

"Yes, ma'am. I wish to live an honest life of peace and contribute to my community."

"Is there anything you would like to say today to your victim's family?" She points behind me.

I didn't do it, and I wish you could know the truth about what happened.

I spin behind me. My mouth goes dry and pulse increases. The last decade inside hasn't given me anyone to look at, and most of my memories are faded and gone regarding any of the teenage girls I ever felt anything for. She looks familiar, but I've surely never seen her before, and it's as if God himself opens up the gates of heaven and says, "Here's your reward for going down for a crime you didn't commit."

Long black curls frame her porcelain, flawless skin. And eyes like the ocean—at least what I remember of it—drill into the depths of my soul. But not the darkness of the sea. The bright blueish-green color you'd find in the Caribbean or off the shores of some parts of Florida. I'd seen those eyes in the past on only one person, but she is dead. This woman has a mouth so lush, I can't help but stare at it until her lip begins to shake, ripping me out of my trance.

Get your head out of your dick and remember where you are so you can get out of this hellhole, Beckett.

She is blinking back tears.

My heart breaks, watching her experience her pain.

Who is she? Why have I not seen her before? Where are Clay's grandparents?

"Ma'am." I nod at her and take another deep breath. *She hates me. Understandably so. She thinks you killed her loved one.* "I'm truly sorry for the involvement I had in your..." I turn to the parole panel. "I apologize, but I've not seen this woman before. What is the relation?"

Judge Filmore says, "Sister."

My head snaps back to her, and the blood draining from my face gives me the chills. "Mia? You're alive?"

She wipes at tears streaming down her cheeks, and I blink back my own.

How is this possible? They told me she died.

I would give anything to comfort her and tell her what happened so she no longer hates me. But I can't.

What do you know anyway? You thought they murdered her, too.

"Please make your statement or turn back around. And

address the victim's family as ma'am or miss," the judge instructs me.

I swallow hard, scanning her eyes. "Ma'am, if I could have a do-over, I would. I cannot tell you the remorse I have in my heart regarding your brother's death. Not a day goes by that I don't think about that night and not one will."

I will her not to hate me, to somehow magically know that I did not kill her brother. I expect to see a disgust for me in her eyes, but all I see is her pain, and it shatters me to the core.

How old is she? She was only thirteen and would have been fourteen in the fall...

The judge clears her throat. "Mr. Brooks, please face me."

I turn around, the chains on my legs clashing against each other, reminding me why I am standing in this room.

Focus, Beckett.

"Is there anything you would like to say, Ms. Crimson?"

I keep my head straight even though I want to look at her again.

"No," she says so quietly I almost don't hear her, but her voice drips honey and everything sweet.

The judge addresses me. "Mr. Beckett Brooks, the State of Florida is granting you early release for good behavior. It is my sincere hope you do not make us regret this decision. In the next forty-eight hours, the paperwork will be filed, and you will be a free man, with time served for your crime. More information will be given to you regarding the steps to stay in good standing with your parole requirements. Do you have anything further to say?"

She's letting me out?

"Thank you, your honor. You will not regret this."

"I hope not." She bangs the gavel, and an officer takes my arm to escort me back to prison.

On my way out, I glance over at Mia. Tears pour down her porcelain cheeks.

How is she alive? Does she know I didn't do it? Why is this the first time she's been here? Who knows she's here?

The guard tells me, "Look where you're going, Brooks."

Through the doors we step, and the slamming of the metal echoes behind us. The muggy Florida weather fills my lungs, reminding me of the stale air I've breathed within the prison walls for the last ten years.

I'm led to a police van where the half-hour journey back to hell begins.

Only forty-eight hours, and then you're a free man. You can put all of this behind you.

It's a lie. Warnings have plagued me for the past decade, reminding me of what's next. They will surely know I'm out.

I need to get to them before they get to me. And now they will be after Mia.

My vengeance is waiting for me on the outside.

1

Mia

MEMORIES LACED WITH HAPPINESS AND PAIN CONFUSED ME FOR over a decade. Beckett was only a boy just having turned seventeen when he went to prison. My brother Clay and I lived with our grandparents. Our mother was sixteen when she got pregnant with my brother then twenty with me.

We never met our father, and my mother never told us or, to the best of my knowledge, her parents his name. He came in and out of her life, responsible for both pregnancies. It seems he was another one of her addictions.

When I was ten, my mother died of a drug overdose, and my grandparents became our sole guardians.

In some ways, nothing changed. We already were living with them, and my mother wasn't the maternal type. She partied so much, days, sometimes turning into weeks, would pass without her coming home.

But it was still painful. As absent a mother she was, she still was Clay's and my only parent. I thought I had cried all my tears after she died. And then Beckett murdered Clay. At least that is what my grandparents told me before they sent me away to a boarding school run by nuns on the Upper Peninsula of Michigan.

When I turned eighteen, my grandparents sent me to a private college attached to the boarding school. I only moved buildings. Anytime I asked to come home, the answer was always the same. "It's not safe."

They wouldn't tell me why it wasn't safe. Clay's killer was in prison. *How was it not safe?* But no matter how many times I asked the question, I never received an answer.

My grandfather died of a heart attack when I was in the middle of earning my bachelor's degree on an accelerated course. My life consisted of classes and limited acquaintances. I threw myself into studying from the time I arrived at the boarding school through my master's, putting up a wall and making sure I didn't get too close to anyone.

No one knew my story, and I wasn't about to tell them. I could only imagine the conversation with the gossipy girls in my classes.

Drug-addicted mom who overdosed, no-name father, and a brother murdered by his best friend would have been the talk of the school. So I kept to myself and didn't get close to anyone.

My grandparents couldn't travel much, and when my grandmother called to tell me about his death, I wanted to come home. She wouldn't let me, and I didn't have any funds to disobey her.

Last year, she died as well. I inherited all of their assets—the small house in the seaside town of Anna Maria Island, a smaller stock account, and bank accounts. I wasn't rich, but it gave me enough to move back to Florida after finishing my master's degree.

They never told me why I needed to stay away.

And I am tired of hiding.

Ten years have passed. I still have nightmares and hear sounds of bullets and my brother's voice. A man always yells, "Get down, Mia." I always think it's Beckett, but they told me he shot and killed Clay.

When my grandparents told me that, I swore it wasn't possible. I remember Beckett and Clay being tight throughout all their childhood. They played sports together and went on double dates and did all the other things boys their age do.

I had a crush on Beckett. But besides being his best friend's quiet little sister, he didn't know I existed. And why would he have? Teenage acne covered my face and, the metal braces on my teeth didn't scream "Pay attention to me." Sure, he was kind to me and would tease me with Clay at times, but his mind was on all the girls who chased after him.

And Beckett had his pick of the town. He ran his hand through his thick, sandy-colored hair often. When he laughed, displaying his perfectly straight white teeth, his deep-brown eyes lit up. Unlike most boys his age, he wasn't just cute—he was beautiful.

Being captain of the football and basketball teams didn't hurt his popularity status, either. Girls constantly threw themselves at him. Clay and Beckett took advantage of the nearby beaches, and I'd hear them after each trip, rating which girls they thought were hottest in their little bikinis.

They were like brothers.

But Beckett has never denied it. Over ten years have passed, and not once has he claimed his innocence. So the confusion that plagues me is constant.

It's May, and I just graduated. I'm planning on moving back to Florida, but I move my timeline up when two days after school is out, I'm opening my mail and receive the notice of the parole hearing.

I stay up all night, packing my few belongings into my small SUV and drive through the night and the next day until I reach the house I grew up in and inherited.

Throughout the drive on I-75, I can only think of one thing. *I have to know why he did it.*

I arrive three days before the hearing. The island town of Anna Maria has grown considerably since I left. Houses have been torn down, and new, exquisite ones replace them. But the little cottage home I grew up in until I was almost fourteen is still standing, and when I step through the doors, memories flood me.

I see my grandparents and Clay. But mostly, I see Beckett.

He's giving me a nuggie while Clay tickles me.

He's eating dinner with all of us.

He's playing video games on the brown leather couch.

Emotion overcomes me, and I blink back tears. *Why did he do it? How could he have done it?* The questions plague me, ripping my heart to shreds as raw as the day I learned Beckett pulled the trigger.

I wake up the day of the hearing and take a shower. No one ever showed me how to put on makeup, so I wear very little. I dry my hair, plug my curling iron in, and decide to fight the humidity.

Looking at the few items of clothing I own, I debate but decide I should look nice going to court. The nicest thing I own is a sundress I bought the previous day at one of the stores on the island. I only went in to buy a hat to shield my face from the sun but decided to buy it because my clothes are warmer from living in the Upper Peninsula.

I put the dress on and look at the time. There's one hour until the hearing. My stomach is in flutters, knowing that I'm going to face Beckett today.

Deciding that traffic is unpredictable, I leave for the courthouse and get there thirty minutes early. I sit in my car, breathing in and out, trying to calm my nerves.

It's useless. Ten minutes before my time, I get out of the car and enter the courthouse, go through the metal detector, and a guard nods to the correct courtroom.

The room is empty, except for the panel of four professionals who sit at the front. A woman whose nameplate says Judge Filmore says, "Can you state your name so I can verify you're in the correct hearing? These are closed proceedings."

I clear my throat. "Mia Crimson."

She looks at her file then back at me. "You are Clay Crimson's sister?"

"Yes, your Honor." Her sympathetic expression only makes my nerves oscillate faster.

"And you are the only living relative?"

I nod, unable to talk as a thick ball forms in my throat.

There's no one but me left.

"Please, have a seat, then." She motions to the seats.

Do I sit at the front or the back?

The back. The farther away from Beckett the better.

Several minutes pass, and I tap my foot and twist my fingers together in nervous anticipation.

The doors finally open, and a guard stands between a man in an orange jumpsuit and me, guiding him to the front of the room. His hands and ankles are chained together.

My heart beats faster in my chest. I swallow hard, looking at the back of him.

He's different—filled out, full of muscle, no longer a boy. His hair is darker than ten years ago, and he has a thin goatee. I can't see his face, but when the judge asks him questions, his voice is the same one that yells in my dreams, "Get down, Mia."

It's deeper than ten years ago, but it's his voice.

"Is there anything you would like to say today to your victim's family?" The judge points to me.

Beckett turns around. My insides quiver hard and I blink back tears. The boyish grin he used to carry is gone. His chiseled jaw is now a man's. Eyes that used to be full of happiness are full of sadness, and...hardness?

Surprise fills his face, almost as if he doesn't know me. He opens his mouth to speak then closes it, turns to the judge, and asks her who I am.

He doesn't remember me? Is this some kind of sick joke?

When she tells him that I'm Clay's sister, he spins to me. "Mia? You're alive?" The blood drains from his face.

Confusion once again fills me. *Why does he think I died?*

His remorse seems genuine, but he doesn't deny killing Clay. His eyes bore into mine as if he's trying to tell me something, but I don't know what.

He killed your brother. Don't let him fool you.

But he couldn't have.

Then why doesn't he deny it?

The judge tells him to turn back, and then she says, "Is there anything you would like to say, Ms. Crimson?"

Tell her to lock him up.

But he yelled for you to get down the night of the shooting.

I came to tell her to keep him in jail. That ten years isn't enough for my brother's life. I am here to plead with her to keep him locked up forever. But I can't. Instead, my social anxiety overpowers me and, to my surprise, I barely get out, "No."

The muscles in his back tense, and the judge tells him she is releasing him. In forty-eight hours, he will be free.

I'm sorry, Clay. I've failed you.

Tears stream down my face. He will be free in two days, and my brother will still be in the ground. The last ten years of my life will always be a decade of grief and loneliness due to what Beckett did.

But he gets to go free.

As the officer escorts him out of the courtroom, he locks eyes with me, his jaw clenched.

On the outside, Beckett Brooks is still as beautiful as I remember, except now he's a man. But I won't ever forget the ugliness that must reside inside him.

2

Beckett

"SIGN HERE," THE GUARD SAYS.

I sign my name on the line, and he slides a plastic bag to me. An orange swimsuit, blue flip-flops, and a Florida Gators baseball cap are the only contents in it.

"Go change over there. There is a laundry basket for your shoes and jumpsuit." He motions to a changing area.

"Are you serious?"

"Do I look like I'm joking? We aren't at the mall. You leave with what you come in with. Be happy you got paroled."

I take a deep breath and go to the corner of the room that has a shower rod bolted in the wall and a flimsy curtain for privacy.

The swimsuit is encrusted with salt from ten years ago. There are splatters of blood on all three items as well. I take off the only outfit I've worn for over a decade and stare at my old clothes before tugging the firm fabric of the shorts over my legs. The shorts are tight, at least a size too small, no doubt from the muscle I've gained from spending any moment allowed working out.

Sand still cakes the soles of the flip-flops. I put the hat on my head and the sandals in the plastic bag. I tap them against each other to get as much sand off as possible.

I toss the jumpsuit and prison shoes into the laundry bin, throw the plastic bag in the trash, and slide the curtain back then stand in front of the guard's desk.

He looks at me. "You're free to go."

"That's it?"

He folds his arms over his chest. "Try not to come back."

I open the door. The glaring sunshine blinds me, and I put my hands over my eyes for a second. The air isn't quite as thick as a few days ago when I left court, and I take a few deep breaths.

Now what?

"Beckett! Oh my God, Beckett." My little sister Gabriella comes flying at me, tears in her eyes. Her blonde ponytail is swinging in the air.

She embraces me in a hug, the first one I've had in over a decade. The visitation in prison didn't allow contact. If you touched your visitors, they lost privileges to come back.

Don't cry, Beckett. You can't afford to go soft now that you're on the outside.

I hug her back. "Thanks for coming to get me."

"Like I would miss this. Mom wanted to come, but she had to finish her shift first. She couldn't get off."

My older brother, Ryland, smacks me on the back, and I turn around. He embraces me as well. "Trying to show off your six-pack?"

Ryland and I resemble each other but, unlike me, he's got dark hair and eyes.

I snark, "Note to you both: don't get arrested in your swimsuit."

"Noted. Let's go," Ryland says.

Gabriella hops in the back, and I get in the front of Ryland's truck.

"How does it feel to be free?" she asks.

"I just got released. Give me some time, and I'll let you know."

"Everyone is coming over tonight. Mom's been cooking up a storm the last two days," Ryland tells me.

I groan. "Please tell me Mom isn't throwing a 'my son just got out of prison' party."

Ryland's lips turn up.

I groan again and look out the window.

Ten years. A decade of change. Everything looks the same but different.

Throughout the drive, Gabriella is yapping about something I don't understand or care to ask about, my brother keeps giving me glances, and I continue to stare out the window.

The only thing that grabs my attention is when Ryland says, "I thought you were going to get out since there was no one to contest your parole this time." Five years ago, Clay's grandmother gave a big speech to the parole board about why I needed to stay in prison. After that, I didn't get my hopes up.

"That's not true."

"What do you mean? Both of Clay's grandparents died," Gabriella says.

My head snaps toward her. "They did? Why didn't anyone tell me?"

She winces. "Sorry. We must have forgotten."

I look at Ryland.

"Didn't seem like pertinent info on our visits," he states.

"But I knew you'd get out since no one was there," Gabriella claims.

"Mia was there."

"Mia?" Ryland questions.

"What? She's alive?" Gabriella cries out.

The curling in my stomach I've had since seeing Mia intensifies. "Apparently, she didn't die. Her grandparents lied."

"Then where has she been?" Ryland asks.

"I don't know. But she is alive and was at the hearing."

"What did she say?" Ryland furrows his brow at me.

"Nothing."

"So, she didn't try to stop your parole?" Gabriella asks.

I shake my head.

Ryland whistles. "That must have been her car I saw parked outside her grandparent's house. I assumed someone on the island finally got their hands on it and rented it out."

She's staying on the island. You know how to find her now.

Do not find her. Stay away. Nothing good can come of it.

We cross the bridge to the island, and both sides of my vision fill with sparkling turquoise water. *That's the color of Mia's eyes.*

Mia's face comes into my mind along with the pain I saw she carries. My heart beats faster, and I close my eyes, thinking of her tear-stained cheeks.

What does she remember about that night? Does she know I didn't do it, and that's why she didn't contest my parole?

Since seeing Mia and learning she is alive, all I can think about is her.

Where has she been all these years? Why did they tell me she died? Why was she at the hearing alone?

My only possible answer to any of those questions is if they wanted everyone to think she is dead, then they assumed I would come after her. They must know about them. They thought I was a part of them.

Who is protecting Mia?

The hairs on my neck stand as the idea of her alone and unprotected makes me shudder.

We merge onto the island. So much is different. "What happened?" When I left, the island real estates consisted of tiny, older, Florida-style houses. Everything now looks new and bigger. There still aren't skyscrapers lining the beach, but everything is updated.

"We've had a lot of construction. The island has had a boom."

I peer out the window as Ryland drives us down the island near the pier. We're nearing Mia's grandparent's house, and my gut starts to flip. There's a lineup of cars on the island, and traffic is crawling slower than the thirty-five mile-per-hour speed limit. We're stopped two houses away from Mia's when she walks out and down the driveway to the mailbox.

My pulse increases. She's wearing cutoff jean shorts and a tank top. Her hair is in a messy bun, and she removes her mail and steps back, shuffling through envelopes.

"Beckett, is that Mia?" Gabriella asks.

"Yeah."

The passenger in the car in front of us catcalls out the window. Anger bubbles through my veins. She's lost in thought reading and doesn't seem to notice. We creep closer.

How did she become so beautiful?

The car in front of us is now directly in front of Mia, and the passenger leans out the window and seizes her around the waist.

Mia's mail goes flying. Before I can think, I jump out of the car as Ryland and Gabriella both scream my name. I get to Mia as she's attempting to escape the guy's grasp.

He's drunk. I can smell the alcohol before I get to him, and I grab him by the throat and squeeze. He releases Mia and tries to pry me off him.

"Beckett!" Mia screams.

"What the hell, man, get off him," the driver shouts.

"Your friend needs to learn some manners," I bark.

"He's drunk and having fun."

"You call assaulting a woman fun?" I growl at him and continue squeezing his friend's neck.

The offender is turning purple when Ryland pries my hand from his throat.

Mia is shaking and I pull her against my body.

"I better not see you around here again," I snarl at them and shake Ryland's grasp off. The cars ahead of them have moved, and they inch as far up the road as possible, which is only a few houses.

Gabriella is collecting all the mail that flew out of Mia's hands. I'm still holding her tight to me.

Cars start beeping. "Get back in the truck, Beckett."

I ignore him. "Are you okay, Mia?"

A few tears stream down her face, and I brush them away with my thumb.

The air fills with the blare of horns.

Ryland puts his hand on my shoulder. "Beckett, let's go."

I turn to Ryland. "Go without me. I'll meet you at home."

"Beckett—"

"Go," I sternly say, still clasping Mia to my body.

He scowls and angrily shakes his head.

I snatch the mail out of Gabriella's hand. "You, too."

Prison changes you in lots of ways. One of the things you learn to do is block memories, and I tried to forget about Gabriella hanging out with Mia. But the truth is that they were as good of friends as Clay and me.

A tear drips on my forearm, and Mia shakes more, staring at Gabriella.

Ryland pulls up and yells out the window, "Gabriella, time to go."

"I'm glad you're alive. I was devastated about losing you." Gabriella wipes her eyes and climbs in.

"Beckett, come on," Ryland tries again.

"I'll see you at home." I guide Mia into the house.

As soon as I set foot in the door, I freeze. It's like stepping back ten years ago. Pictures of Mia and Clay line the walls and crowd the tabletops.

I haven't seen an image of Clay since the trial, and grief floods me. He was my best friend. We did everything together since we met in kindergarten.

I clench my jaw. *Don't cry.*

"You should let me go," Mia whispers, and I realize that I'm holding her against my bare torso, and I'm still wearing the too-small bathing suit with Clay's and her blood along with crusted ocean salt on it.

My heart is pounding, and I scan her eyes but don't release her. The scent of her skin, a clean floral aroma, flares in my nostrils. Time stands still as my growing erection presses against my already skin-tight shorts.

Her lip shakes harder, and I don't think. I keep my arm tight around her and using my free hand, brush my thumb over her trembling mouth, then cup her cheek. *Her skin is like soft butter.* "Did he hurt you?"

"No. You did," she whispers as another tear escapes.

But I didn't do it.

"You don't remember, then?"

"Remember what?"

She doesn't know. She thinks I killed Clay. "Why didn't you contest my parole if you don't remember?"

"Remember what?" she repeats.

I can't tell her. If she doesn't remember, she can't know. I tear my arm away from her.

Slowly, she steps away from me. I instantly feel the loss of her warmth and regret releasing her.

"Why did you lie about being dead?"

She glares at me. "I never claimed I was dead."

"Where have you been all these years?"

"Why did you say you didn't know who I was at the hearing?"

"They told me you were dead. You don't look like the Mia I used to know. There's a resemblance, but you're a woman now." I swallow hard as I say it, cursing myself as my gaze wanders down her body.

"How could you kill Clay?" she quietly asks as her chest rises and falls faster.

I swallow around the thick knot in my throat. "I loved Clay like my brother."

"Then why?" she whispers.

I can't answer. If I deny it, she's going to want to know why I took the fall. Instead, I ask, "Who's watching over you?"

"I don't need anyone. I can take care of myself."

I take another step into her house and check the windows.

"What are you doing?" she angrily asks.

"Seeing how easy it is for someone to break in."

"Is this what they call casing the joint before the act takes place?"

I jerk my head toward her. "I'm not a thief."

"Who said I was referring to you stealing anything?" Pain and sadness darken her eyes.

She thinks I'll murder her, too?

I step toward her and she steps back. I keep moving and she keeps retreating until she is up against the wall, my body inches from hers.

Her head tilts up at me, her lip is shaking again, and I play tug-of-war with my mind, holding myself back from kissing her.

I finally say, "I will never hurt you."

"Is that what Clay thought before you stole his last breath from him?"

I bite my tongue not to tell her the truth.

As I grapple with myself, a surge of energy shoots through my veins as her finger begins to outline the side of my waist.

"C.C. & M.C. You have a souvenir of your kill," she blurts out in horror and rips her hand off my tattoo.

"Not a souvenir. A reminder for vengeance," I blurt out, not thinking about the consequences of my words.

"Vengeance?"

I turn to inspect her back door. The handle is loose, and the lock barely works. I spin, surprised she's only a few inches behind me.

My breath rises and falls faster.

She's so damn beautiful. I've not seen a real woman in over ten years, but I didn't even know what one was when I went inside. My numerous sexual activities with teenage girls in my class are now faded memories. And Mia is stunning. There is nothing ordinary about her.

"Tell me what you mean," she pleads.

"I can't. I want to, but I can't."

"Then tell me why you killed him. Please," she cries out as new tears fill her eyes. "I have to know."

I cup her face with both hands. "I can't tell you about that night. I want to, but I can't."

I'm cursing myself for hurting her and telling her too much already, when she whispers, "If you killed him, why did you yell, 'Get down, Mia?'"

I scan her eyes. "So, you do remember?"

Tears drip onto my fingers. "It's in my nightmares. Your voice is in my nightmares. I know it's you."

"What do you remember about it?"

"Nothing. I just hear gunshots, you yelling at me, and I see my brother bleeding to death." Anguish fills her face. "You should have let me die. I wish you would have let me die."

Ten years of learning how to hold my emotions and not cry, and the moment I embrace Mia, tears flow down my cheeks. "No. Don't say that."

She sobs into my chest. "You ruined my life. You should have let me die."

I hold her tighter, tears falling on her head. "I'm so sorry. I wish I could redo that night."

She shoves me away. "But you can't."

I'm not able to deny it. "No."

She closes her eyes as if in further pain. I kiss her on the top of her head and leave. I no longer am seeking vengeance for myself, or Clay. I vow to get it for Mia.

3

Beckett
10 Years Ago

"THAT'S HER." CLAY GAZES AT A BLONDE GIRL WITH A SMOKING-HOT body and a tan to match.

I whistle. "Now, that is the type of girl you go back for seconds with."

Clay laughs. "Don't worry. I'll be getting my next round in soon. Already stocked up on condoms."

I snicker and give him a fist bump.

"She's coming over, so zip it."

"Hey, Clay." She bats her eyes.

"Hey, Veronica. Tonight still good?"

She flips her blonde hair behind her shoulders. "Eight o'clock, right?"

"Yep."

Her friend comes up behind her. She looks like a replica of Veronica but with darker hair.

"This is Stacy," Veronica says.

"Clay."

"Beckett." I give her the signature expression I've reserved just for hot girls like her and let my eyes wander down her body then back to her face.

She blushes. "Hi."

"We're going down to Coquina tonight for a bonfire. You want to come, Stacy?" Veronica asks.

"Sure." She glances at me then quickly looks away.

Hook, line, and sinker. I'll be banging her tonight.

"Well, Beckett and I have to get to our workout. See you tonight," Clay says.

"Nice meeting you both." I check Stacy out one more time then wink at her as we leave.

When we get to the parking lot, Clay arches his eyebrows. "Stacy looked good."

"Yep. I'm claiming her for tonight." I open the passenger door and get in.

Clay opens his console and tosses me a strip of condoms. "I think I owe you."

"Nice." I throw the strip in my gym bag on the floor.

"We need to make a quick pit stop."

"Where's that?" I ask.

"The Kmart parking lot."

I groan. "It's going to take forever to get across the bridge."

"I know, but it has to be done today."

"What does?"

"The errand."

"For Skates?"

"Yeah."

"Dude, I told you not to be running errands for him. He's bad news."

"I only have to drop off some items to the restaurants on the island. He doesn't want to deal with traffic."

I suspiciously glance at Clay. "What kind of items?"

"All legit. Napkins and shit."

While Skates is an avid skateboard junkie, the rumor is he got his nickname because he always skates close to the edge of going to prison. I don't like Clay anywhere near him.

"Dude, really not a good idea."

"Listen, I just need to do this one job. I don't have time to get hired anywhere with our pre-season football workout schedule coming up, and I can't keep asking my grandparents for money. Mia's braces cost an arm and a leg, and I heard them stressing about it. What Skates is going to pay me will be a month's worth of flipping burgers."

"For one job?"

"Yep."

"Doesn't that seem a bit odd to you?"

"His time is valuable. You know how crappy it is to sit in island traffic during season. He's got better things to do."

"I have a bad feeling about this."

"Beckett, you worry too much. Chill out. I always have your back on all your shit. Let me earn some cash."

I take a deep breath. He's right. He always has my back. "All right, man."

We spend the trip talking about girls and sports. The Kmart isn't far off the island, and Clay turns toward the back of the parking lot.

"Where is he?"

"He'll be here," Clay insists.

"How many of these have you done now?" I ask him.

"I don't know. A handful. It's easy money."

Uneasiness fills me. "Promise me you'll be done after today."

"Dude, stop freaking. It's paper products."

Anger flares through my bones. "You're playing with fire."

A black Cadillac Escalade with tinted windows and chrome wheels arrives.

"Jesus. He screams drug dealer," I mutter under my breath.

"Chill the fuck out." Clay gets out of the car.

The window to the passenger side rolls down. Skates has leathery skin from too many days in the sun, blond hair, and blue eyes. A scar runs from his right eye down to his mouth. A tattoo of a twisted heart on a skateboard adorns his forearm.

The two of them slap hands, and Skates motions to the back of the vehicle.

Over the next two minutes, Clay moves boxes between Skates' and Clay's vehicle then the Escalade takes off.

Clay gets back in the car.

I try to contain my rage. "Dude, how the hell did you get hooked up with that guy?"

He turns on the engine and drives through the lot. "He watches our practices. Haven't you ever seen him?"

"No. Should I have?"

"I've talked to him quite a bit."

"Where have I been during these talks?"

"Probably behind the bleachers licking some girl's pussy."

I chuckle and shrug cockily. It's possible.

"So, he came up to you and asked if you wanted a job?"

"No. We talked several times, and he asked if I was from Bradenton, and I told him I live on the island. Then he asked me if I would be interested in helping him out."

"Was this before or after you knew he was Skates?" Skates had a reputation around the area.

"I didn't know until my first run when his driver called him Skates."

"What did you think his name was?"

"He introduced himself as Jimmy."

"Jimmy?"

"That's his actual name."

"Jimmy what?"

"Cline."

My eyes widen. "Cline, as in Casey Cline?" Casey owns half the restaurants on the island.

"Yep. He's his dad."

"Shut up."

"Yeah, I was surprised, too. But he's involved in his businesses, and that is why he needs me. It really is easy money, and it's just paper products," Clay insists.

"Have you ever looked inside the boxes?"

Clay jerks his head at me. "Why would I do that?"

The hairs on the back of my neck stand up. "God damn. Sometimes you're an idiot."

"Dude. My job is to deliver paper products, not open boxes."

"Pull over."

"What? No."

"Clay, pull over now," I demand.

He sighs and parks in one of the spaces on the causeway. The turquoise water sparkles, and people are riding horses along the shore.

I open the door and get out.

"Beckett. Don't be fucking with their stuff."

"Dude. I bet you a box of condoms there is something illegal in here."

"Going to Casey Cline's restaurants? No way. You know Casey. He runs legit businesses."

"His son is Skates. You don't know shit. Open the trunk."

Clay rolls his eyes but complies.

The boxes aren't even taped shut. They are folded in so anyone can open or close them.

I open the box in front of me.

"See, told you. Paper products," Clay says in an annoyed voice.

I remove bundles of napkins.

"Don't mess their shit up," Clay says.

I'm removing the last stack of napkins when I feel it taped to the bottom. Shaking my head at Clay, I hold the bundle out to him and turn it over.

"Fuck sake!" I yell out. "Is that heroin?"

The blood in Clay's face drains. "Put it back, now."

"You fucking idiot!"

He picks up a pack to put back in the box and stops. "Shit." He turns it over to see a similar package taped to that one as well.

As we turn over each bundle, we find every one has heroin attached to it.

"Put it back in the box." I pack everything the way it was and shut the box and trunk.

"Fuck. Beckett, this is bad."

"No kidding. Did you really believe this wouldn't have anything illegal in it? It's Skates."

"Beckett, I didn't think. I just wanted to earn some cash so I wouldn't be a burden on my grandparents. You know I wouldn't have done this if I had known. My mom died from overdosing on this junk."

I take a deep breath and calm my voice. "I know, man. Listen, you need to get this stuff dropped off and be done with Skates."

He scrubs his face. "I'm done. After this, I won't ever do another job."

"Okay. Let's get this out of your car. Come on."

I go with Clay to all five of the restaurants. I wait in the car while he drops a box off in each place of business. When he finishes, he looks at me. "Beckett, I'm sorry. Honestly, I wouldn't have said yes if—"

I hold my hand up. "Dude, I know that. No more calls from Skates. No more jobs. No more talks on the sidelines."

"Okay."

I let out a deep breath and grin. "But you still owe me a box of condoms, and instead of the sidelines, you should focus on getting some ass in the bleachers."

He laughs and fist bumps me. "Done."

4

Mia

Present Day

Beckett Brooks' visit to my house only confuses me more. *Why did he jump out of the truck to come to my rescue? Why did he tell me to get down ten years ago? Why does he say he wants to tell me what happened that night but can't?*

Once he leaves, I pull myself together and go for a stroll on the beach. For hours, as the water rushes over my toes, I try to get Beckett out of my head.

It's not just the questions about my brother that plague me.

I'm attracted to Beckett. As much as I should hate everything about him, all I've done since seeing him at the courthouse is think about him and the way he looks at me. I've not been around many men. The boarding school I went to was all girls. The college as well. I've had little social life and rarely dated. I've never even had a serious boyfriend.

Being alone is more comfortable. I don't have to answer questions about family life. I don't have to create stories around why

I'm not going home for the holidays. I don't have to hide my past or worry about waking up in the middle of the night, screaming in fear, with someone next to me asking me to explain.

The presence of Beckett is like a never-ending hum of energy against all my cells. And that's without him touching me.

In his arms, fear and disgust should thrive. All I feel is safe and wanting more. And I hate myself for it.

The sun is setting, and I'm lost in thoughts about how Beckett's rock-hard body felt against mine.

He was wearing the shorts he wore the night he killed Clay. *Blood of your brother is on that swimsuit, and all you can think about is how much you want to be back in his arms.*

I curse myself for the millionth time and turn around to head back to my place. I'm passing a beach bar, and the smell of hamburgers and other food fills my nostrils. My stomach growls, and I try to think when I last ate. I realize it's been two days.

I amble up to the bar and choose a seat. There are tables full of families and friends laughing and enjoying each other's company. Children play in the sand in view of their parents.

As the tide crashes against the shore, my own waves of sadness pass through me. Family and friends—I had both once upon a time. I didn't realize it when I had it. Then, boom, everything changed.

No more friends. No more family. Just a life of loneliness.

"Ma'am, what can I get you to drink?" The bartender flashes a smile and puts a square napkin in front of me. Something seems familiar about him, but I push the thought aside because I don't know anyone here.

Well, at least not anymore. I used to know people.

I've never been much of a drinker. "Something fruity."

The bartender, whose name tag says Connor, eyes me up. "On vacation?"

I almost say no, but I decide it'll be easier to pretend. "Yes."

"Try the fishbowl, then. It's every tourist's favorite."

"Sure." I open the menu.

He makes my drink and sets it in front of me. "That's on the house."

"Thank you. Can I get a grouper sandwich, too?"

"Coming right up." He winks at me and punches the order into his machine.

I consume the fishbowl, which tastes like sweet Kool-Aid, a little faster than I usually drink. I had left the house hours ago and didn't bring any water.

Halfway into my cocktail, my sandwich comes, and I eat half of it. I whip some cash onto the bar and finish my cocktail.

"Another?"

I shake my head and stand up, wobbling, and reach for the bar to steady myself.

He chuckles. "Guess you know your limit."

I laugh, too. It feels good. I don't remember when I laughed last.

Connor joins me on my side of the bar. "My shift's over. I'm heading home. Where are you staying?"

"Off Pine."

"I'm going that way. Care to have some company?"

"Sure."

"I'm Connor." He holds out his hand.

I shake it. "Mia."

"Nice to officially meet you, Mia. I'm ready if you are?"

We leave the bar and make our way down the sidewalk.

"How long are you in town for?"

"I don't know. I'm staying with my grandparents."

He groans. "That's typical. The island is full of retirees. Where you from?"

I almost tell him Florida but say, "Michigan."

"That's typical, too. You here by yourself?"

"Me, myself, and I," I chirp, the alcohol having a good effect on my social skills.

"It's not really the season anymore. Are you just visiting your grandparents for the fun of it? Or are you here for another reason?"

What the hell. Just tell him you live here now.

"I'll tell you a secret, if you want."

Connor wiggles his eyebrows. "I'm all ears."

"I just moved here. I'm staying."

His grin gets wider. "Really?"

"Yep."

He does a victory pump in the air. "The island gets another young person. Yes!"

"It can't be that bad."

He raises his brow at me. "You have no idea."

"Maybe I should run while I can, then?" I tease.

"Tell you what, before you run, why don't you come to a party with me? Then you can meet some people and decide if you want to stay or not."

A party? Meet people? Hmm. Why not. I have nothing else to do.

"Okay. Your friends won't mind if I tag along?"

"It's actually a party my mom is hosting. Everyone should be feeling pretty good by now."

"Are they drinking fishbowls?"

"Probably not, but I have no problem making you one if that's what you want to drink."

I giggle as the alcohol hits me further. "I don't normally drink. I think I'm probably good for a bit."

He leans toward my ear. "Okay, then. I'll make sure I load you up on water or something else without any side effects."

"You won't leave me to fend for myself?"

His hand flies in the air. "Not a chance. Scouts honor. I'll stick by you all night."

"All right. I'll go with you."

"Awesome." He grasps my hand and maneuvers me onto the lawn between several houses. "Let's cut through."

"Is this the back alley of Anna Maria?" I tease.

He laughs. "Something like that. Stick with me, and I'll make sure you're safe."

"Good to know."

Connor leads me between several more houses, and we pop out into a backyard full of people, food, and music. A patio has become the dance floor, and a pool is lit with several people in it.

A mix of people, both younger and older, are at the party, and, sure enough, people seem to be feeling pretty good as Connor predicted.

Connor releases his grip on me then puts his hand on my back, guiding me through the groups of people, nodding and saying hello as we pass.

"Let's go inside so I can introduce you to my family. I don't see any of them out here."

"Okay."

We are almost in the house when a man with gray hair puts his arm out across the door. "Connor! Shot to pass."

Connor groans. "Dave, I swear you're still pretending you're at the frat house from 1970."

"Ouch." Dave pretends to beat his chest and be hurt then hands Connor and me a shot.

"You don't have to do that," Connor tells me as I throw it back. "Or you can." He downs his.

I grimace as the liquor burns the back of my throat and hand the glass back to Dave. He allows us to pass, and I hold the back of Connor's arm to steady myself as we make our way through the house.

"Honey, why are you so antisocial? Everyone has missed you. Go outside and mingle," a woman's voice says.

"Jesus, Mom. I'm not into your my-son-just-got-out-of-prison party."

My gut drops, the hairs on my neck stand up, and I suddenly have a hard time breathing.

"Do you know how hard it was to keep our friends after everything happened? Please don't be rude."

"Sorry you had to go through what you did, but I'm still not interested."

I freeze and dig my nails into Connor's arm.

He turns. "Mia, you okay?"

Behind the woman, sitting in a chair, is Beckett, and he's gaping at me.

I let go of Connor and start to move toward the front door.

How could I be so stupid? Connor Brooks. We went to school together. He's a year behind Gabriella and me. Of course, a Connor who lives on the island with his family would be him.

The house has been remodeled, but everything seems familiar in my drunken haze.

A chair crashes on the floor and Connor and Beckett call out, "Mia."

I get through the hallway and am almost to the door when I run into Gabriella. "Mia! What are you doing here?"

I stumble past her. The front door opens as more people come in, and I shove between them.

"Mia!" Connor and Beckett call out again.

I think I've made it outside when everything spins. I fall on the grass, and my hand slides into something mushy.

Get me out of here.

A burning sensation scorches my palm and forearm.

"Oh my God! Oh my God!" I scream in pain, holding my wrist.

"What's wrong? Did you break your arm?" Connor asks.

"Oh my God! Why is my arm burning?"

Beckett kneels beside me. "Shit. Fire ants. Connor, grab a bunch of ice and the first aid kit." Beckett rips off his shirt and swipes the ants off. In one graceful swoop, he picks me up as he stands.

Connor stares at him.

"Go!" Beckett barks.

Connor runs back in the house.

I'm gripping my arm and crying on Beckett's chest, but I still feel the beat of his heart as the burn moves into my biceps.

Beckett takes a step, but I cry out, "Don't take me back inside."

"Shh. I'm not."

Connor reappears with the first aid kit and an entire bag of ice like you would get at the grocery store. "Let me help you, Mia."

"How much has she drunk?" Beckett demands.

"A fishbowl at the bar and a shot Dave made her drink out back."

"Has she eaten?"

"She had part of a sandwich at the bar."

"Ow...ow...ow." Another bout of stinging heat flies through my arm.

Beckett takes the first aid kit and ice from Connor. "Have Mom fix a plate of food and bring it down to her house."

"How do you know where she lives?" Connor asks.

"Because he killed my brother," I slur.

"What?"

Beckett carries me down the street.

I curl up into his chest.

"Just do as you're told," he calls back.

"Beckett!" Connor yells.

"Connor, stop wasting time. Food, now." He continues down the street.

I'm whimpering. When I close my eyes, the world spins, so I try to keep them open.

Within minutes we are outside my front door.

"Where's your key, Mia?"

"I didn't lock it."

"You didn't lock it?" Beckett opens the door and steps into the house. He sits me on the couch, disappears into the kitchen, and returns with several towels and a big bowl. He sits next to me, puts the ice in the bowl, and opens the first aid kit.

"You can leave now," I insist.

He squirts something from a tube on his hands.

"Just go. I'm used to it. Everybody leaves me eventually." I try to get up, but Beckett holds me down.

"Well, I'm not everybody. I'm not leaving you." He clutches my arm and applies the cream.

"Ouch!"

"Shh. I'm sorry, I know this hurts."

I press my face into the couch as he finishes applying the cream then wraps the offended area with a brown bandage.

"Stay here," he instructs.

"Not sure where you think I'm going. This is my house, or did you forget that?"

"No, I didn't."

He brings several pillows from a bedroom, puts one behind my head, and props my limb on the other. He wraps ice in a towel and positions it on my arm.

He places the back of his hand and puts it on my cheek. "Do you normally drink?"

I shake my head.

There is a knock on the door. Beckett hesitates for a moment then stands and opens it.

"How is Mia?" Connor asks.

"She should be okay. I'll talk to you later," Beckett replies.

"Gee, Beckett. It's nice to see you, too," Connor snarks.

"I'm sorry, Bro. It is good to see you. And I promise we'll talk more tomorrow, okay?"

"Sure. We can talk tomorrow, but I brought Mia there, so why don't you go back and I'll stay here and take care of her. It is your party after all."

"No. That's not happening."

"Listen—"

"I'll be the only one taking care of Mia. Go back to the party. And we don't need to ever have this conversation again," he sternly says.

"Look—"

"Goodnight, Connor." Beckett shuts and locks the door.

He comes back to me with the food Connor brought, and I glare at him. "That was rude to do to Connor."

"He'll get over it." Beckett sits on the floor next to me. "Is the burning any better?"

I sniffle. "A little."

"Good." He unwraps a plate and holds a forkful of potato casserole to my mouth.

"I'm not hungry."

"You need to take an antihistamine, and you've been drinking. Eat."

I roll my eyes.

"You want the burning to go away?" He raises his eyebrow and holds the fork to my mouth.

I take a bite, chew and swallow. "My grandma used to make this."

"I remember. I think she gave my mom the recipe." He holds another forkful to my mouth and smiles at me.

Staring into his brown eyes, I eat several bites.

He puts the plate down and opens a bottle of water then holds it to my lips. "Drink this, Mia."

Wrapping my hand around his on the bottle, I drink half the bottle, thirstier than I thought.

Beckett turns the box of antihistamines and reads the package then removes the paper with all the side effects. When he finishes reading, he looks up. "I don't think you can take this right now. We need to wait till morning."

I'm struggling to keep my eyelids open.

He stands and scoops me up in his arms.

I freeze. "What are you doing?"

"Taking you to your bed."

Suddenly, I'm wide awake.

"I can go myself," I quietly tell him.

He carries me to my room and places me on the bed. "Let me get the ice."

My heart is pounding in my throat, and I've forgotten that I hate him.

As quickly as he leaves, he returns with the ice, towels, and bottle of water.

"Mia, what do you sleep in?"

I motion to the dresser. "Top drawer." If I hadn't been drinking, I would never tell him to open it. But I'm not thinking straight.

My top drawer has all my underwear, bras, and several spaghetti-strap nightgowns. I may not be wise to the world or experienced, but I've always liked sexy undergarments. Beckett opens the drawer and freezes. The muscles in his back shoulders flex.

"The pink one," I tell him.

He retrieves the satin gown, taking a deep breath. When he turns, the heat in his eyes creates a sea of flutters in me. "Let me know when you're done changing."

He hands it to me and leaves the room, and I quickly slip out of my shorts, tank top, and bra. Dressed in the gown, I call out, "I'm done."

Beckett stops in the doorway, gulps, and stares.

"Beckett, why are you still here?"

He comes over and replaces the ice packs on my arm. "I told you. I'm not leaving you."

5

Beckett

10 Years Earlier

"Get your ass moving, Crimson!" Coach screams at Clay.

"Let's go," I yell out and pat his back.

What the hell is up with him today?

The whistle blows, and we line up for another sprint. The next noise sounds off, and I run as fast as I can. I look to the left, expecting to see Clay, but he's several yards back.

"Crimson, do you have something wrong with your legs today?" Coach bellows.

Clay is breathing hard and looks like he's going to puke. "No, sir."

Coach blows the whistle. "Practice is over. Crimson, you better show up tomorrow ready to work."

Clay swallows hard. "Yes, sir."

I wait till everyone is moving off the field before moving to his side. "What's up with you today?"

He looks off in the distance. "Nothing."

"Then why do you look like you're going to throw up your breakfast?"

He palms his forehead.

I wait for a minute, but he doesn't move.

"Clay, what's going on?"

"If I tell you, will you promise not to flip out on me?"

I scan his eyes. "Okay. Tell me what's going on."

"Skates won't let me out."

The hairs on my neck stand up.

"Let you out? Of what?"

"He says I made a contract when I agreed to deliver for him."

"What?"

"I told him I couldn't do it anymore. Skates said I either do it, or there will be consequences."

"Consequences?" *Hell.*

Clay looks away.

I can only imagine what the "consequences" might be.

"That wasn't it though."

Chills run down my spine. "What do you mean?"

Clay blinks back tears. "He said he knows I went through the boxes."

"How would he know that?"

"One of the packages wasn't secure as it normally is, and he said that would only happen if someone shifted the contents."

"Shit. I'm sorry. That's my fault."

He shakes his head. "None of this is your fault."

"So he knows you went through the boxes, but nothing was missing."

"No, but he said I pried into his personal business, and he also said..." Clay stops and blinks harder.

I put my hand on his arm. "Clay, what is it?"

"He said I'm just like my mom. Nosy."

I jerk my head back. "What? Your mom?"

His face hardens. "He said if there was heroin, my mom could sniff it a mile away and I must be just like her."

I gape at him. "He dealt to your mom?"

Clay takes a deep breath. "I don't know...why would he say that? Could he be the one who killed her? He said she loved it till her last breath." A tear slips down his cheek.

Clay's mom died four years ago. We don't talk about it a lot, but I know it's painful for him.

"That's messed up."

"Well, now he says I made a contract with him, and contracts are for life."

"What? No way."

More tears slip down Clay's cheek. "I'm fucked."

"No. There has to be a way out of this."

"I don't see how. I'll be a dead man."

"Clay, let's go to the police. They can help you."

"Are you crazy? Skates will murder me if he finds out I did that."

"He won't find out. Let's talk to Henry. He'll know what to do."

"If anyone associated with Skates sees me going into a police station, I'll be a dead man walking."

"I'll call Henry and ask him to meet us at my house. He and my dad have been best friends forever and I'm confident he can help, Clay."

"But your parents will know."

"I'll have him meet us when they're at work. Henry will keep it on the down low."

Clay looks at me like he isn't sure.

"Just trust me."

Clay releases a big breath. "Okay, Beckett. If you think that will work."

"It will."

THE NEXT DAY, WHILE MY PARENTS ARE AT WORK, HENRY MEETS Clay and me at my house. I had asked him not to wear his police uniform or drive his cop car to my house. And I asked him if we could talk without him saying anything to my parents.

We all settle at the kitchen table. I hand Henry a Coke, and Clay and I each have a bottle of water.

Henry has red hair, a matching day-old beard, and green eyes. He's like a member of our family and in some ways, a second father to my siblings and me. "Beckett, what's going on that I have to meet you like this? You in some kind of trouble?"

"Not me, but Clay."

Clay and I have been best buddies for as long as I can remember, so he knows him, too.

"What is going on, Clay?" He looks concerned.

Clay shifts in his seat. "I got myself into something I don't want to be in."

"So get out," he says sternly.

Clay shakes his head. "I tried, but I'm not being given that option."

Henry sighs. "Tell me everything."

"I met a man after practice. For several weeks we talked. He found out I lived on the island. He offered to pay me to run errands for him."

Henry's eyes turn to slits. "What kind of errands?"

Clay holds up his hands. "I honest to God thought it was napkins."

"Napkins?"

"For the restaurants."

Henry's eyes close for a brief moment and he sighs. "Go on."

"I found heroin attached to the bottom of each bundle of napkins and informed the man I wouldn't deliver for him anymore, but he told me I had a contract with him."

"What kind of contract?"

Clay gulps. "A contract for life."

Henry glances at me. "You're delivering, too?"

"No. Only Clay."

"Good. Stay away from this, Beckett."

"I am. But what are we going to do to get Clay out of this."

Several minutes pass. "Who is the man?"

Clay says, "Skates. And the drop-offs are at the five restaurants his dad, Casey Cline, owns."

Sitting back in his chair, Henry taps his fingertips together and mutters, "Shit."

"I didn't know, I swear!" Clay insists.

Henry pats him on the back. "I know, son, but you have yourself in a right pickle."

I cut in, "Are you able to help us?"

He leans back and puts his arms across his chest. "Sure. Let me think about the best way to handle this. Give me a few days, and I'll tell you what we're going to do."

I sigh in relief. "See, everything is going to be okay."

Henry's eyes become slits. "Beckett, whatever you do, stay out of this."

"Yeah, no problem. I'm only here to support Clay."

"Good. Skates isn't anyone to piss off." He stands up. "Give me a few days, and I'll figure out the solution."

"Thanks, Henry."

"Don't say a word to anyone about this. You understand?"

We give him our word, and he leaves.

"Feel better, Clay?"

"I'll feel better when Henry tells me how we're going to solve this."

"Don't worry. He has our back."

6

Beckett

Sobriety is a condition of my parole. I'm not allowed to drink and will have surprise piss tests. But I went to prison at seventeen. I should have been starting my senior year of high school. Besides a few beers that Clay and I stole from my parents' fridge, I've never drunk alcohol. We were too involved in sports and girls to be interested.

Opportunities in prison to get into drugs and alcohol were constant. The dealers tried over and over to get all of us hooked, but I stayed away from it.

In ten years, nothing has changed. I don't know what I expected. My parents, along with the majority of residents on the island, are big partiers. Growing up, parties at my parents' house were the norm. Their home was a place everyone was welcome.

Having a son who is a convicted felon for murder should warrant their friends staying away. It should isolate my parents. The opposite seems to be the reality.

The entire night, I sit inside, keeping to myself and trying to avoid everyone. *Everyone is here to gawk at the murderer.*

I have five siblings. Ryland and Hudson are older. Gracie, Gabriella, and Connor are younger. Before the party started, I had dinner with my parents and all my siblings, except for Connor who is a bartender and couldn't get off his shift with such short notice.

My mom and I are fighting when Connor brings Mia into the party, and the fear and pain on her face creates a knife that slices through my heart.

Why is she here with Connor?

As soon as she sees me, she runs, and it's apparent she's been drinking.

Mia's had way too much to drink, and I want to kill Connor.

What was he thinking, letting her drink that much?

The quiet of her home, minus our little conversation, is a welcome relief after the loud party at my parents' house. I tend to Mia's arm and continue to ice it in twenty-minute periods.

In prison, I studied and passed my GED. I also took the offered college courses and obtained a nursing degree. Since I kept my head down and stayed out of trouble, they allowed me to work in the prison hospital.

Fire ants aren't new to me. Their sting creates a burning sensation, but the risk is for those who have allergic reactions.

I want to give Mia the antihistamine to be safe, but I'm worried about how much alcohol she's had, so I keep a careful eye on her arm throughout the night.

Her room holds a small closet, dresser, and bed. There is no chair, so I tuck her into the covers, put fresh ice on her arm, and sit on top of the duvet.

"You can go," she sleepily tells me again.

"Shh." I stroke her hair. "Go to sleep."

"You killed my brother, and they throw you a party," she mutters.

Is there anything else I can do to cause her any more pain?

I slide down on the bed until my face is next to hers. "I didn't want that. That is my mom's doing, and she doesn't mean it like that. I'm sorry."

"Everyone came to celebrate you." Tears come to her eyes.

I have no right to touch her, but I stroke her cheek. "They came to get drunk and see what a freak show I am. No one cares about me, nor is there any reason to celebrate anything about me."

"No?" She raises an eyebrow.

"No."

"You murdered my brother, and you still have all those people who love you."

"I'm sorry." She's right. No one should love me, based on my conviction, but my family ties are strong.

"I have no one, and you have everyone." Tears soak her pillow.

My heart bleeds. *How can someone so deserving be so alone?*

"I know how that feels," I admit.

"How?"

"Prison is lonely."

She scans my eyes. "But now you get to live, and everyone loves you."

I want to wrap her in my arms and tell her the truth. Allow her to see anything good that might remain in me from before that night—before inmate 4592 ever existed.

While I went to prison naive, I came out fully informed of the hell that can exist on earth. And the pieces that made me popular are now gone.

"People don't know me. They love what they remember of me. He no longer exists." I am not sure how the words flow out of me so easily after learning how to keep everything to myself and hardly speaking to anyone for a decade.

"I no longer exist," she whispers.

Her thoughts crush my soul. I played a part in her demise.

I stroke her cheek again, and, against my will, my thumb brushes over her lips. "You're beautiful, in every way possible," I murmur.

I shouldn't be touching her. My face is only inches from hers. The scent of her skin, the softness of her hair, and smoothness of her flesh are beckoning me, begging me to make her mine.

She stares at me. "Beautiful is misleading. You taught me that."

A few days ago, I thought the teenage girl Mia Crimson had died. A stunning, sensual, innocent woman now lies next to me. All I hear is the sadness, pain, and loneliness she's suffered.

She thinks it's all my fault. In some ways, it is. "I grieved for you," rolls out of my mouth.

Her head slightly jerks on the pillow.

"Every day I grieved for Clay, I grieved for you." For the second time today, to my surprise, a tear escapes.

"You thought you killed me, too?"

"No," I blurt out.

She squints. "Then who did you think killed me?"

Shit. I've said too much. I quickly look away.

The sound of ice hitting the floor coordinates with both her hands gripping my face and her body straddling mine. "Tell me who did it," she demands, her face inches from mine.

"I can't."

"You can," she cries.

One of my hands goes to her head. My other arm wraps around her back, and I roughly kiss her. I part her lips by shoving my tongue into her, greedily exploring what I've been dying to taste since I saw her in the courtroom.

She gasps then tears her head back, and I allow her to break the kiss but keep hold of her, gazing into her turquoise orbs. My breath is already labored as my lungs try to grasp any air they can.

She's a delicious piece of heaven I'm dying to devour, and no matter how much I've told myself not to make a move on her, it's like the devil himself is offering her to me.

Time stands still. She could move farther away but doesn't. I could release her body, but I don't.

What is she thinking?

I'm out of practice. Her lips felt like they belonged on mine, but what do I know? Maybe my kiss didn't do for her what it did for me.

That and the small detail she thinks you killed her brother. She hates you, Beckett, and now you gave her another reason to hate you more.

"I'm sorry. I want you so much. I...I..." I release a breath, but I don't let go of her and close my eyes, trying to figure out how to get her not to hate me more.

It's so faint, I'm not sure if I imagine it when her lips brush mine. When I open my eyes, she takes a shaky breath.

I knead my thumb on her skull, slowly tasting her, allowing her to taste me back, in a deep, sensual kiss.

Her hands slide from my cheeks then under my head, locking together, pulling me into her.

My fingers slip through her silky hair and slide under her nightgown, palming the cheeks of her ass that's circling on my cock in tiny movements.

I groan in her mouth, as she flicks my tongue, igniting my blood. My cock is hardening, and she shakes as her warm breath merges into mine.

Pulsing flesh, the heat of her sex penetrating the thin material of my shorts, and the glorious sounds of her whimpering make me feel alive for the first time in over a decade. I'm panting, my heart beating fast, my balls already tightening.

Fuck, I'm going to come in my pants.

I flip her on her back and move my lips across her jaw and down her neck. She grasps my shoulder and moans while bucking her hips up at me then crossing her calves around mine.

"You're beautiful perfection," I mumble as I release her straps and move my lips down to her breasts. My tongue hits her areolas, teasing them as they pucker and harden, my teeth gently nibbling between licks.

"Oh God," she whispers as I slip my fingers under her wet panties. I brush her slit and glide through her slick folds. She opens her legs wider for me and wraps her legs around my body, gripping her fingers on my back.

Crushing my mouth against hers then slowly inching my finger in and out of her, I groan at the mere thought of how tight she is and what it would feel like to be inside her.

Mia's chest heaves, her pert breasts warm, her fingers dig into my shoulders.

I circle her clit, and within seconds her body quivers.

Her hands trail down my back, slipping under my shorts. One hand cups my ass cheek and the other slips between us, rubbing my pre-cum and shimmying on my shaft. Heat scorches all my cells as my heart races.

"Mia," I breathe, closing my eyes and moaning as she moves faster, and I increase the pressure on her clit.

"Beckett, oh God...oh..." Her mouth forms an O, her cheeks flushed red.

"I have you, angel." I swipe her faster and rub my thumb harder, trying not to come all over her hand.

She unravels, eyes rolling, body trembling, moaning my name, and gripping my dick so hard, I lose myself and climax all over her.

We lie next to each other, gasping for air, skin full of sweat, mouths in each other's necks.

You just came all over her hand in under a minute: way to go, Beckett.

"Oh shit. I'm sorry, Mia," I mumble in embarrassment. "No one's touched me...oh God, I'm sorry."

She slips her hands out of my pants and wipes the one on the bed then cups my face. "Shh. It's okay."

"No. I'm—"

She smashes her lips to mine, drawing me into her world that's pure and good, giving me hope maybe life could have a do-over, and we could get past all the issues we have.

But I know better. I no longer am the naive boy I was the night of the crime, and I need to remember who I am and how far I've fallen. No one can save me from who I've become and what I'm willing to do, not even an angel like Mia.

7

Mia

I'VE SUDDENLY SOBERED UP. BECKETT TOUCHES ME HOW NO OTHER man ever has before. Besides a few guys I've kissed, I've never let anyone get close.

I don't know why I touch him. It's like an animalistic need to feel all of him. Without thinking or any agenda, I reach for him, stroking his hard-on, not even sure if I'm doing it correctly.

Within seconds of grasping him, he makes my head spin, creating an orgasm within me more intense than I could ever give myself.

As adrenaline spikes throughout my body, I grip him harder, and he cries out my name and ejaculates all over my hand.

Okay, you did it right.

I'm mentally patting myself on the back and trying to catch my breath when Beckett apologizes. I quickly realize that he's embarrassed and that he, while more experienced than me, hasn't had any sexual encounters for over a decade. At least, I'm assuming nothing bad happened to him in prison.

I may be inexperienced, but I'm not oblivious to the fact that I'm a twenty-four-year-old virgin, and that isn't normal. Any dates I have been on, I always felt anxiety due to my lack of sexual experience.

Once again, I don't think about how he killed my brother, or that he won't tell me who else was involved. My only concern is that I don't want him to feel shameful about his climax.

So, I kiss him, still breathing hard, my insides still slightly quivering, my arms tight around him.

Several minutes pass. Beckett hardens against my leg again but leans back. "I need to get you ice."

Reality crashes into me.

What did I just do?

He killed Clay.

But did he?

Part of me is convinced he didn't kill him, but he never denies it. He always goes around the question, telling me he can't explain anything to me.

You want to believe he didn't do it, and that is clouding your judgment.

Beckett pecks my lips and leaves the room. The only sound is him breaking up the bag of ice and my thoughts.

Go to sleep, Mia. You can't let this go any further, and he's too much of a temptation. Pretend you're asleep until you zone out.

Before Beckett returns to the room, I close my eyes. The scent of him, raw and woody, flares in my nostrils before he even touches me, but I keep my eyes closed.

He packs my arm in fresh ice, tucks me in, and kisses me on the head. "I'll get vengeance for you, angel," he says so quietly, I wonder if I'm imagining it.

I'm tempted to ask him what he means, but I know his answer will be the same. If I open my eyes, I'm afraid of what else I might do with him tonight, so I pretend to sleep, my loins wanting more but choosing my logic over my emotions.

CHIRPING BIRDS WAKE ME UP THE NEXT MORNING. I LOOK TO MY side, expecting to see Beckett, but he isn't there. His side of the bed is neatly made.

I feel a mix of disappointment and relief.

Back to me, myself, and I.

At least he isn't here tempting you to cross the line again.

What happened last night can never happen again.

My alarm clock says eleven.

Jeez. I never sleep this late.

Standing up, I make the other side of my bed, go to the bathroom, brush my teeth, and head to the kitchen to make coffee. When I get there, I freeze.

Beckett is fixing the lock on my back door. Connor and another man I don't recognize, but who resembles Beckett, have removed two of my windows. Four other windows are brand new and already installed with tape still across them.

"What are you doing?" I hurl at Beckett, and all the men stop to stare at me.

I realize I'm wearing my pink, satin nightgown and nothing else, as Beckett's eyes fill with the same heat I saw last night.

He jumps from his crouching position, scans the room, yanks the afghan off the couch, and throws it over me.

"What are you doing?" I repeat, but this time, it's more about him covering me up.

"Go put clothes on." He points toward my bedroom.

"Excuse me, but this is my house. You can't just come in here and tear it apart."

"We aren't tearing it apart—"

"Really? What do you call that?" I point to the empty holes where my windows once were.

"We're fixing things. Go put clothes on." His jaw clenches, and he points again.

"No. This is my—"

He picks me up and carries me across the room.

"Put me down," I demand and wiggle in his arms. But he has me tight to him, and I can't escape his grasp.

I hear snickering in the background.

When we get to my room, he puts me down, and the afghan falls off me. "Are you going to get dressed, or do I need to dress you?"

I glare at him. "This is my house. You do not have permission to be here nor rip anything apart."

"It's not safe. It will be when we're done today."

"That isn't your concern."

He raises his eyebrow at me and adamantly says, "It's my only concern."

My heart races as he licks his lips, and the only sound is the clock ticking. "I didn't ask to be your concern," I say quietly.

"You need to be more aware, Mia. Don't leave your house unlocked anymore. Windows, doors, everything gets locked."

Anger consumes me. "Is this another code for 'I know something that concerns you, but I'm not going to tell you'?"

"Mia," he groans in frustration.

"Get out of my room, Beckett."

He leaves and shuts the door.

I quickly change and return to the living area, stopping in front of the two holes in my wall. "Connor, what are you doing?" I ask, hoping to get more from him than what Beckett gave me.

He grins. "Hey, Mia. Do you remember our brother, Hudson? We're changing your windows. The old ones were falling apart."

"I don't mean to sound ungrateful, but I didn't authorize this. Please put my old windows back—"

Hudson cuts in. "Sorry, Mia, but the old windows fell apart when we removed them. This island gets some nasty storms. I'm surprised they didn't blow out before now."

I should say thank you, but I'm pissed they're tearing my

house apart without my permission. I don't need Beckett Brooks doing anything for me. He's already done enough.

"What is the cost?"

"No cost, Mia," Connor says, smiling.

I gape at him.

Hudson must sense my disbelief. "I own a construction firm. I had the windows from a job that was measured wrong, and we couldn't return them. They happen to be perfect for your cutouts. No cost."

I sigh from relief and frustration. "Thank you. What about your time?"

An amused expression crosses both their faces, and Connor replies, "No charge."

I should be elated that I'm getting all new windows and my door lock fixed, but I feel strange taking help from Beckett and his family.

"Mia, can you come here for a minute, please?" Beckett asks.

I approach him, and he says, "I need a four-digit code that you can remember."

"Why?"

"So, you can have keyless entry."

"I don't need that."

"Well, you're getting it, so pick a code."

"Beckett, this is so inappropriate," I tell him.

"Hey, Mia!" a familiar woman's voice calls out.

I turn to see Gabriella and another woman sticking their heads in the windowless hole. Ryland is standing next to them as well.

Why are the Brooks all in my house?

I spin to Beckett. "What is going on here?"

"I'm just fixing your door. You'll have to ask them."

"Seriously?"

He winces. "Sorry."

Someone taps my shoulder. A huge smile is on Gabriella's face. "Want to go to lunch with Gracie and me?"

Gracie. That's who the other woman is—Beckett's other sister.

"My house is kind of in pieces right now."

Gracie puts her hand on my back. "Exactly why you should go. Let them do their job, and you can come back after it's finished."

"Good idea. Go eat. Come back when it's done," Beckett instructs.

I glare at him, and he cockily grins. I have a flashback of him smiling like that with Clay standing next to him.

At first, it makes me happy, but as soon as joy comes, so does sadness. The pit in my stomach widens, and I blink back tears.

He stands up and takes both my hands. "Mia, what's wrong?"

I turn away from him. "Let's go, Gabriella."

She looks at me as if she isn't sure if she should ask what is wrong or not. We're out the front door when Beckett comes running after us. "Mia, wait!"

I turn around.

"I need a four-digit code."

I glare at him. "Four five nine two."

"Four five..." Pain crosses his face.

For a brief moment, guilt rears its head. I'm being so cruel.

You have nothing to feel guilty about. He's the murderer.

Is he?

Yes, and now you won't forget. It's another reminder not to fall into his arms again.

It's his inmate number. A reminder of who he really is and what he's done.

I blink back more tears.

His pain is replaced with hardness. Gone is any resemblance of who he was in the past. He nods and walks away.

8

Mia

10 Years Ago

"Everyone is going to be there. It's going to be epic," Gabriella gushes, flipping her long blonde hair, her blue eyes brightly shining with excitement.

"You think everything is epic."

"No, I don't."

"Don't you?" I tease.

She waves dramatically. "Anyway, all the high school guys are going to be there."

"And the high school girls," I point out.

"Yeah, but we're going into high school, so that's us now. We need to start acting like it."

"There is no way my grandparents are going to let me go to Coquina Beach. It's on the other side of the island, and they aren't going to drive around so late."

"Duh." Gabriella rolls her eyes at me. "That's why you're

spending the night at my house. Clay is, too. My parents are going to a party. We'll go with Clay and Beckett."

Beckett is going?

But he'll be with all his girls.

Still...

Gabriella looks at me impatiently. "You're never going to get a boyfriend if you stay home at night. It's time to live a little. Your grandparents will never know."

I sigh. "Are you sure they won't find out?"

"Yes. Stop worrying."

I open my closet then anxiously look at Gabriella. "I don't have anything cool to wear."

"Let's go shopping!"

"I don't have money for that."

She rolls her eyes. "Seriously, Mia. You need to get creative."

"What do you mean?"

She tugs on my hand. "Come on."

"Where are we going?"

"Relax, Mia. Watch and learn."

Gabriella leads me out of my house and down the road. When we get to her house, Beckett and Clay are in the kitchen, scarfing down plates of food, wearing nothing but swim trunks.

My heart beats faster like it always does when I'm around Beckett.

"Where's Mom and Dad?" Gabriella asks.

"No one is here except us," Beckett says.

"Good." Gabriella sits down between them. She slyly nods for me to take the other seat.

"Oh, hey, Mia." Beckett gives me his killer smile.

"Hey." I will myself not to turn red.

"What are you talking about?" Gabriella asks.

"None of your business," Beckett tells her.

Gabriella puts her hand on Clay's forearm. "Clay, can you give us a ride somewhere? Pretty please?" She bats her eyelashes.

My brother seems to have started to notice Gabriella. Over the last six months, she's developed boobs and looks like she's eighteen instead of fourteen. It's subtle, but I see the way he looks at her before he catches himself. And Gabriella seems to be able to get whatever she wants from him.

"Get your hand off my friend," Beckett barks at her.

Gabriella rolls her eyes at Beckett and puts her arm around my brother. "Aw, Beckett, you jealous that Clay's my friend, too? Clay doesn't mind, do you?"

Clay shifts uncomfortably, but she grasps him tighter and then sits on his lap. He glances at Beckett and laughs.

"Seriously, Gabriella. Stop touching Clay. You wouldn't like it if I touched Mia."

She smirks at him. "Wouldn't I?"

"Fine." Beckett yanks me off my seat and into his lap. "How do you like it now?"

Heat crawls up my neck, and butterflies explode in my stomach.

Gabriella arches her eyebrows. "You'll have to do better than that, Beckett." She leans into Clay's face. "So, can you give us a ride?"

His eyes move to her lips then back to her eyes. "Sure, Gabriella. Where to?"

Beckett's body stiffens.

"We're going to a party."

Clay looks over at me. "Grandma know about this party?"

I turn away from him, forgetting for a brief moment I'm on Beckett's lap, and almost run right into his face.

Beckett's lips tick up. "They don't know, do they?"

I shake my head.

"Then you aren't going," Clay says.

Gabriella puts on her pouty lip and runs her finger down his cheek. "Aw, Clay, I thought you were fun."

"I am fun," he says.

"You're not acting very fun."

"Gabriella, get off my friend," Beckett growls again.

She ignores him and puts her lips right next to his. "I'll owe you a big favor."

He licks his lips.

"That's it." Beckett stands me up and tugs Gabriella off Clay. "Do not touch my friend ever again."

"He doesn't seem to mind, do you, Clay?"

He glances between Gabriella and Beckett.

Gabriella smirks. "I'll make you a deal, Beckett."

He glares at her. "What's that?"

"Give us a ride tonight and forty dollars, and I'll never touch Clay again."

"Forty dollars? You're crazy." Beckett releases her arm.

Gabriella sits back down on Clay and puts her arms around him.

Beckett quickly tugs her off. "Fine. Done. It's in the drawer of my desk. Don't take a penny more."

"And the ride tonight."

He groans. "You're such a pain in my ass."

"But you love me," she coos.

He rolls his eyes. "Where is this party?"

"Coquina Beach."

"Mia, you aren't old enough to go to that party. You're thirteen," Clay tells me.

Usually, I don't lie to my grandparents or sneak off to parties. But Gabriella is right. I'll never get anyone, including Beckett, to notice me if I don't start acting like I'm in high school.

"I'm almost fourteen. And we're in high school now."

"Almost in high school," he reminds us.

I stand up, angry at him. "Stop acting like you're my father and being a hypocrite. You went to all these parties before you even got into high school."

"It's different. We're boys."

Gabriella looks at Clay and bats her eyes. "When I think of you, I think of a man, not a boy."

Clay's face flushes and he checks her out.

Beckett spins her into him. "Enough, Gabriella. Add in that you'll stop flirting with Clay, and it's a deal."

"Done," she sweetly says.

He releases her arm. "We're leaving at eight. Don't talk to me when we get there."

She snorts. "Please. As if I would want to talk to you."

"Don't think you're making this your new normal, Mia." Clay glares at me again.

"Whatever," Gabriella says. "Let's go, Mia."

We barely get out of the room, and Beckett says to Clay, "Seriously. Do you have to encourage her?"

My brother's voice is full of amusement. "What? I didn't."

Gabriella places her hand on my arm to stop and puts her finger to her lips.

"You didn't discourage her."

"Sorry, man, but your sister is hot."

Gabriella stifles a giggle.

"Dude, don't ever say that again," Beckett angrily says.

Clay chuckles. "Okay, but you should be more worried about everyone else who's going to be at the party and not me."

I STAND IN FRONT OF THE FULL-LENGTH MIRROR IN A HOT-PINK bikini with extra padding in it. "Oh, I don't know, Gabriella. This doesn't feel like me."

"Because your grandparents have you wearing boring clothes."

"My boobs look huge."

"They sure do!" she beams.

I groan. "The bottom doesn't even cover my butt cheeks."

"Another plus," she chirps then opens the curtains to my fitting room, wearing a black thong, string bikini.

I look between her curvy, tan body and mine that is pasty white and straight as a stick. "I look ridiculous."

"No, you don't! You look hot!" she gushes.

I cringe. "Really?"

"Yes!"

"Try on the cover-up, and I'll put mine on."

I throw on the black crochet dress that shows my bikini and body, and Gabriella comes over in the same one in hot pink.

She claps her hands. "This is perfect! You wear your hot-pink sandals, and I'll wear my black ones!"

"Don't you think we should wear clothes?"

"One, these are clothes. Two, it's a beach bonfire. Everyone is going to be wearing this. Clay and Beckett always go in their swimsuits."

Yeah, they have killer bodies like you do.

I sigh. "Fine."

We get changed, Gabriella buys the outfits, and we head back to her house. The entire way, Gabriella is talking about boys, but all I can think about is Beckett.

I wonder if he'll notice me tonight?

What if he thinks I look stupid?

"Earth to Mia." Gabriella waves her hand in front of my face, giggling.

"Oh, sorry. What were you saying?"

"We should start getting ready at six so I can do your hair and makeup."

GABRIELLA SPENDS AN HOUR PUTTING MAKEUP ON ME AND straightening my hair with an iron even though it's already straight. She claims it will stop the frizz. I'm not buying her logic, but I let her anyway.

She won't let me look at what she's done until I put on my outfit. I get changed and stand in front of her mirror.

"Ta-da!" she beams at me.

"Wow," I say in shock.

Gabriella has covered up all my acne. My black hair is shiny and straight, with no frizz.

"Your eyes are popping!"

I can't argue with her. For the first time in my life, minus my braces, I feel beautiful. And it's giving me the confidence to wear the outfit she picked out for me. It seems to work now that my hair and makeup is done.

Will Beckett notice me?

Gabriella does her makeup and hair, and, for the next hour, I barely pay attention to her gabbing. The more I think of Beckett, the more my nerves flutter in my stomach.

She finally finishes and looks at herself in the mirror.

"You look amazing!"

Her blonde hair is in waves, and her makeup is perfect. "Tonight is going to be epic! Let's go!"

The car beeps, and we quickly get outside.

"Jesus," Clay mumbles.

"What are you two doing?" Beckett barks, scanning Gabriella but then turning on me, and maybe it's my imagination, but he lingers longer than when he looked at Gabriella.

"What do you mean?" Gabriella asks.

"What are you wearing?" Clay jumps in.

"Stop looking at me like that. We're wearing more clothes than both of you." They are only wearing their swim trunks, flip-flops, and Florida Gator caps.

"Go change," Beckett orders.

Gabriella smirks and gets in the car. "No."

I climb in on the other side.

Beckett and Clay both shake their heads and get in the car.

"You'd better stay out of trouble tonight, Gabriella," Beckett warns.

"Whatever, Beckett. You go do your thing, and we'll do ours."

Since the tourist season has come to an end, traffic is light, and it doesn't take long to get to Coquina Beach. The sun has just set, and the only place to get food there has been closed down for the night along with the gift shop attached to it. A large group of teenagers assembles on the beach where there is a bonfire already lit.

Beckett turns around to us when Clay enters the parking lot. "I'd better not see either of you drinking."

"I don't drink," I tell him quickly.

He nods. "Good. Don't let my sister influence you."

Gabriella smacks him on the shoulder. "I don't drink, either, jerk."

His eyes turn to slits. "Well, keep it that way. There's going to be a lot of people offering you drinks tonight. Don't drink anything unless it's an unopened bottle of water or pop."

"Jeez, Beckett, you sound like Mom lecturing us not to eat the brownies at parties."

"Well, don't eat those, either." Clay parks the car.

We all get out and go down to the beach. The boys separate from us, but I keep my eye on Beckett. Gabriella knows more people than I do and introduces me to several guys, but I'm not interested.

Several hours pass. Girl after girl flirts with Beckett and Clay. Gabriella is surrounded by several boys.

I am over at the coolers to get water when I see Clay look at his phone.

When did he get a phone?

I'm about two hundred feet away from him, but I see him cringe and walk up to the closed gift shop and step inside.

What is he doing?

I'm about to go when I see Beckett follow him to the gift shop and enter it.

Why are they going inside, and how did they even get in when it's closed?

A bad feeling crawls through my body. I plod through the sand to the gift shop. I hear a sharp crack, but the music is loud. I faintly hear Clay and Beckett both cry out, and I open the door. It takes me a few seconds to adjust to the blackness. Clay is moaning in pain, and blood is seeping out everywhere.

Beckett turns. His eyes widen and he yells, "Get down, Mia," forcing me to the ground. I feel Beckett roll off me and see a blond blue-eyed man with a scar from his eye to his mouth aim a gun at me and shoot before I lose consciousness.

9

Mia

Present Day

GABRIELLA AND GRACIE DON'T SAY MUCH ON OUR STROLL DOWN Pine Street, and I'm grateful. I'm trying to get my thoughts together.

Seeing the flashback with Beckett and Clay has triggered me, and I'm trying to stop my insides from shaking.

It doesn't take long to get to the eclectic bakery-cafe and coastal store. Art, jewelry, and other knickknacks fill the front of the building. Bicycles that are statement pieces hang on the ceiling with price tags. Beach clothes fill a few racks, while every picture on the wall has a sticker that it's for sale.

The smell of fresh cinnamon buns, coffee, and other breakfast items hits me when I step inside. At the back is a counter to order. People eat and talk at tables with mismatched chairs. Those who don't have their food have metal holders with numbers on them.

Gabriella hands me a menu before we step up to the counter.

"What do you normally get?" I ask, looking at the expansive list of choices.

"Everything is good, but the crème brûlée French toast is amazing," Gabriella says.

"It's so good," Gracie boasts.

I put the menu back in the holder. "I'll have that, then." I step up to the counter and order. Gracie and Gabriella both order it as well. We pay, they hand us a number sign and coffee cups and motion to the side wall that has numerous coffee urns.

"I'll snag a table," Gracie says and hands Gabriella her cup. We pump the coffee into the cups and sit down with Gracie.

They both stare and smile at me. I shift uncomfortably, not sure what to say.

"So, where have you been hiding all these years?" Gabriella asks.

I almost claim I haven't been hiding but stop. It's what my grandparents were doing, for some reason unknown to me. "In Michigan."

The girls both look surprised. "Why Michigan?" Gracie asks.

I throw my hands in the air. "It's where my grandparents sent me."

"Where in Michigan?" Gabriella asks.

"On the Upper Peninsula."

"Who did you stay with?" Gracie asks.

"No one. I was at a boarding school run by nuns."

Gabriella gapes at me. "All these years?"

"There is a small college I went to as well."

"In the middle of nowhere?" Gracie asks.

I have to take a deep breath to try and calm myself. "Yeah, I suppose that's one way to put it."

Gracie furrows her brows. "But why did they send you there?"

"They said it wasn't safe for me to be here."

Gabriella tilts her head at me in question. "What wasn't safe?"

"I don't know. They never told me."

"And it's safe to be here now?"

Talking about the last ten years reminds me of how much of a waste my life has been. I'm suddenly angry at all their questions and butting into my life. "I don't know. Maybe you should ask your brother," I snap.

Gabriella's eyes widen.

Gracie glares at me. "Beckett's fixing your house so you can be safer. He would never harm you."

I sarcastically laugh. "Your brother killed my brother."

"No, he didn't," Gracie practically spits.

Blood boils in my veins. "He went to prison for over ten years and never once claimed his innocence."

Gabriella looks away.

Gracie says, "You were young and probably don't remember, but Beckett loved Clay as much as he loves Ryland, Hudson, or Connor or either of us." She motions between Gabriella and herself. "He would never have done that."

Heat creeps up my neck. "How dare you sit there and tell me what I remember. Almost all my memories of Clay have Beckett in them."

"So you know he couldn't have done it, then," Gabriella softly says.

"Then why doesn't he deny it?" I cry out, drawing attention from others nearby.

"We don't know. I was hoping you would tell us." Gracie scans my eyes.

I stand up, my chair falls over and bangs on the floor. But I don't care, and I don't even attempt to pick it up. I point at her. "This is why you invited me out? To claim your brother's innocence?"

Gabriella stands and puts her hand on my arm. "No. I've missed you. I'm so happy you are alive and here."

I shrug away. "Don't touch me."

She grimaces.

"You were the only one who was there that night. Don't you remember anything?" Gracie angrily asks.

All the patrons in the restaurant gawk at us.

"Beckett knows exactly what happened, Gracie. All I remember is a bonfire, my brother's cries as he took his last breaths, and Beckett yelling for me to get down. Other than that, I don't know what happened, and your brother won't tell me. Why don't you ask him, if you want the truth, and then you can fill me in."

Gracie's face lights up. "If he yelled for you to get down, then you know he couldn't have done it."

I angrily glare at her. "Then why doesn't he deny it? Why doesn't he tell us what happened?"

"Because he's covering for someone!" Gracie exclaims.

"Who?" I say, disgusted.

"I don't know, but that has to be it," she insists.

"I'm done with this conversation." I spin and leave the restaurant, but both Gracie and Gabriella follow me.

"Mia, wait up," Gabriella yells.

"Leave me alone!" I scream back, trotting down the street.

We're near my mailbox when Gracie calls out, "I didn't mean to upset you. I just want to know the truth."

I turn. "You don't think I want to know the truth? Your siblings are all alive. My only one is dead, but your brother, who's never denied anything, won't say a word about what happened that night. That's the truth."

"I know he didn't do it! He couldn't have. There isn't a bad bone in his body."

"Then why won't he talk? Why does he keep putting all of us through so much pain?"

"If you remember him as a kid, then you know what I'm saying is true," she claims.

"Gracie! What are you doing?" Beckett's voice booms behind me, and we all turn.

"I'm trying to get to the truth," she sternly says.

His eyes become slits. "Stop."

Tears fill her eyes. "Beckett, it's been ten years. It's time you told us the truth."

"Don't you ever talk about this in public again," he barks.

"Why? Talking about it behind closed doors isn't getting us any answers," she insists.

"Gracie." Gabriella tugs on her arm.

"Shut up, Gracie," Ryland calls from behind me.

Connor and Hudson approach us.

Beckett's shoulders tense. "Are you trying to get more people killed?" he quietly asks and glares at her.

"What does that mean, Beckett?" Gabriella asks.

He takes a deep breath. "This is the last time I'm going to say this. Do not talk about this ever again. Not in public. Not in our home or anyone else's. Do you understand me?"

Gracie gets in his face. "Then tell me the truth."

"Drop this," he grits out.

"No—"

"Gracie! Enough!" Hudson barks.

She points between Hudson and Ryland. "You two. You're just as bad as Beckett, hiding the truth all these years. Stop lying to us all!"

I spin to look at them, my mouth gaping open. *They know something?*

Both their jaws harden, just like Beckett's does whenever he goes around my questions. "You both know something?" I ask.

They shift uncomfortably.

I step closer. "What do you know?"

"Mia, drop it," Beckett demands.

I ignore him. "Tell me. I deserve to know the truth!"

Connor waves at Ryland and Hudson. "You two have been hiding something?"

"Keep your nose where it belongs," Hudson hisses.

Connor reddens. He pokes Hudson's chest. "Stop acting like I'm a kid."

"Step back, Connor," Ryland instructs.

"Shut up. You're just as bad."

"Connor," Beckett growls.

"Everyone stop fighting," Gabriella shouts.

"They just have to tell us the truth," Gracie puts in.

"Enough! Stop putting Mia in more danger!" Beckett shouts.

Silence.

Beckett mumbles, "Fuck."

My heart beats faster as my stomach does somersaults. "What are you talking about?"

He exhales, and his eyes harden. "Go inside, Mia."

"No. Tell me."

He clutches my arm and steers me into the house.

"Let go of me, Beckett."

When we get inside, he doesn't release me until we are in my bedroom, and he shuts the door. I expect to see his hardened eyes, but instead, I see pain and worry. He cups my cheeks. "Stop asking questions. Please."

"You have to tell me the truth."

"Please let it go," he whispers.

"I can't."

He shakes his head.

"Tell me you didn't do it, Beckett. Tell me you didn't pull the trigger."

Opening his eyes, he stares at me, saying nothing.

I grasp the sides of his head. "You couldn't have. You..." My breath shortens, and my heart pounds against my chest. A flashback of that night is clear as day. "You jumped on top of me."

Beckett blinks as tears fall.

I touch my rib cage where I have a scar from the bullet that hit me that night.

"I didn't get down. You yelled at me, then jumped on top of me. He tore you off me and shot me."

Beckett wipes his face.

"Why have you let everyone believe you're a killer?" I whisper.

He looks away from me.

I grab his chin and jerk his head back. "Tell me why."

His jaw clenches, and he takes a deep breath.

"Tell me," I demand again.

"Drop this, Mia. Nothing good can come of it," he sternly advises and turns and bolts out of the room.

I follow him. "Beckett."

He doesn't turn around.

Gracie and Gabriella are sitting on my couch. Connor, Ryland, and Hudson are installing a new window.

"Beckett!"

He opens the front door, steps out, and shuts it behind him.

In shock from the truth, I gape at the door.

Gabriella puts her hand on mine. "Mia, are you okay?"

I look at her and whisper, "He didn't do it."

Her eyes widen.

"I knew he didn't do it," Gracie cries out.

Ryland storms into the house. "This is the end of the conversation. I'm not telling any of you again."

Gracie glares at him. "But—"

"Enough! There are reasons for things. Let it lie."

Over ten years he endured prison, and he didn't do it.

Ten years stolen from him.

Ten years of experiencing only God knows what.

Beckett's voice rings through my head. "Prison is lonely."

Five. Ten. Fifteen minutes pass. I stand up.

"Where are you going?" Gabriella asks.

"To find your brother."

10

Beckett

10 Years Ago

GABRIELLA'S BEEN GETTING UNDER MY SKIN ALL DAY THEN SHE AND Mia leave the house wearing hardly anything.

And she's obviously influencing Mia who looks eighteen instead of thirteen. Mia is a nice, sweet girl, and I'm not sure why she even wants to hang out with my sister. The guys are going to be all over them tonight, and now I'm going to have to keep an eye out.

I point to them both. "Go change."

They ignore me and get into the car. I give them a stern lecture about not drinking and warn Gabriella that she needs to stay out of trouble, and she blows me off again.

I can't believe she wormed her way into our party.

The girls hop out of the car and are several feet ahead of Clay and me. I'm about to yell at him for staring at my sister's ass, but I realize I'm staring at Mia's.

Jesus. Get your head out of the gutter, Beckett. She's thirteen and Clay's sister.

I try to shove down the rage I'm feeling. "You know we aren't going to be able to go have any fun tonight, with those two running around half naked, right?"

Clay groans. "I know. I'm going to kill my sister when tonight is over for dressing like that."

"Yeah, well, at least Mia covered half her ass. Gabriella has a piece of floss covering hers."

"I think she told me her motto is, 'If you have it, flaunt it,'" Clay teases.

"When did you have that conversation with her?"

"Chill out, Beckett. I wouldn't break the bro code and touch your sister."

I sigh in frustration. "Well, those two are looking for trouble dressed like that, so don't be wandering off to get laid. You know someone's going to get handsy."

He glances at Gabriella's ass again. "I think your sister will be fine."

I growl, "Gee, thanks. Does that mean you think Mia will, too?"

He glares at me. "No. If anyone touches her, I'll kill them."

"Well, the same goes for Gabriella."

"I got it. Relax though. Well, keep an eye on them, but don't ruin the night."

"Fine."

We approach the bonfire, and the girls are on the opposite side. Clay and I position ourselves so they are in our view, but we aren't hanging out with them.

Throughout the night, girls approach Clay and me. Several ask both of us to "walk the beach" which means they want some action. But Clay and I turn them all down, keeping an eye on Gabriella and Mia.

Gabriella is flirting with a group of guys, and Mia is off to the side. Every now and then I catch her looking at me. Part of me wants to talk to her so she isn't alone, but I stay on my side of the bonfire.

I'm in a conversation when I see Clay take out his phone.

I cringe at the sight of it. Two days ago, Skates showed up at the field as we were heading to Clay's car. He demanded Clay take the mobile. Three days have passed since we met with Henry, and he still hasn't told us what we should do.

Clay rolls his eyes to the sky, sighs, and stomps toward the closed gift shop. He enters it.

The hairs on my neck stand up, and my stomach flips.

What is he doing in there?

I forget about Gabriella and Mia and follow him. When I get outside the door, I hear Henry's voice.

"You made the wrong choice, kid."

Why is Henry here?

I open the door and creep in. Blackness surrounds me, and it takes my eyes a minute to adjust.

Henry is standing next to Skates, who has a gun aimed at Clay. Clay is standing with his hands in the air.

"Henry?" I say in shock.

Henry looks at me. "I was wondering when you were going to show up."

A chill moves through my bones. "What?"

"Do it," he says, and a sick grin grows on Skates' face. He pulls the trigger and shoots Clay in the chest. Clay's blood splatters all over me, and we both scream. Skates turns the gun on me.

I'm paralyzed with grief and fear when the door opens and Mia appears.

"Get down, Mia." I shove her down on the concrete and throw my body on top of her.

I'm not sure what I'm thinking. I should have tried to get her out the door instead of on the ground. Skates kicks me off her, and before I can cover her body again, he shoots her, and her blood covers me as well.

"No," I scream, and tears begin to run down my face.

Skates empties the rest of the bullets out of the gun and hands it to me with his hand covered in a black glove.

I look at him in confusion.

"This is your murder, and I own you."

"What?"

He hustles out the back door.

"Henry?" I whisper.

Henry kneels in front of me. "You want your mom, dad, brothers, and sisters to live?"

I stare at him in horror, shivering.

Henry crouches down to look at my face. "Answer."

"You're my dad's best friend," I barely get out.

"Yes. And do you want it to stay that way?"

"I...I don't understand."

"We don't leave loose ends. So I'm going to arrest you for the murder of Clay Crimson. Mia may live or die, but you will go down for one or both. You will not deny it. If you ever deny it, I'll make sure your entire family has a harsher death than what Clay got. Do you understand me?"

How can this be happening?

"Answer me. Pick. Your life or your family's?"

My chest is so tight, I struggle to breath. "Mine."

"Good choice. You're now in debt to Skates. You and your family's life in exchange for your loyalty to him."

I am unable to talk.

"You're young. You'll still be able to have a life when you get out of prison. But you will always owe Skates and, when the time comes, you'll do what he asks."

"Henry?" I manage to get out.

"Learn your lesson from this kid. Keep your nose out of other people's business."

The rest of the night is chaos. Flashing lights, handcuffs, Gabriella running up to me and screaming my name, tears in her eyes, and my mother and father hugging me for the last time, pleading with me to tell the truth about whatever happened.

I say nothing. I sit in a trance next to Henry, who consoles my parents and keeps looking at me, saying, "Why did you do it, Beckett?"

An ocean of tears run off my cheeks.

When I get taken outside the police station and into the van waiting to take me to the county jail, my brothers, Hudson and Ryland are outside. They stare at me in horror.

Help me. Tell me how to get out of this.

I scrunch my face and slightly nod to the back of Henry's head, trying to warn them that he is part of this. Ryland catches my eye, and the blood drains from his face. It's all I need to do.

Clay and I had told Ryland and Hudson what was going on with Skates. They'd overheard our conversation and demanded to know what was going on. They know we spoke with Henry and were waiting for his instructions.

As Henry presses my head down so I can get into the van, Ryland yells out, "Beckett."

I turn my head, and he pounds his fist to his heart with tears in his eyes. It is our secret Brooks Brothers sign we created when we were children, a signal that together we stand, and alone we fall. We created it while playing cops and robbers as kids.

I look straight ahead as more tears fall. Clay is dead. I don't know if they saved Mia or not. Uncontrollable sobs come over me and don't stop until I get to the county jail where they book me for murder.

11

Beckett

Present Day

In prison, when I couldn't control the waves of emotion that popped up every now and again, I would work out. Often, it would be in my cell where I was trapped, so push-ups, sit-ups, running in place, and jumping jacks became my ritual.

No longer am I constrained, so I rip the tags off the new swimsuit my mom gave me last night at dinner. Throwing it on, I run down the street and onto the hot sand.

When the water hits my toes, I let out a breath. The last time I felt the sand between my toes or the salt of the ocean water was the night of Clay's murder.

Clay and I used to swim here all the time. It's a quiet part of the island, not a beach the tourists frequent.

I swim out farther and farther until I know it would be hard for anyone on shore to see me. I'm on the spot where the ocean meets the bay, and there is no buoy. While the island may have changed a lot, the sea remains the same, and I'm still familiar with this spot.

When I get far out, I swim as hard as I can for hours. The waves pick up with the tide, and I'm still not any more relaxed than when I got here.

No one can know. Ryland and Hudson know, and they shouldn't have the information they do.

I have to protect Mia from them. She can't ever find out the truth. Everyone needs to stop asking questions.

The current is getting stronger, and I move closer to the island, cutting through the water. My body should be tired of swimming for hours and fighting the waves, but it's full of a decade of anger and grief.

I didn't anticipate Mia. I thought she died. My attorney said the evidence from her murder was mishandled and I got lucky. I didn't understand but wasn't going to question it and have more time added to my sentence. Clay and Mia, they were all that consumed my thoughts in prison. Well, that and avenging their deaths when I got out.

The judge gave me a fifteen-year sentence. Parole seemed like a pipe dream. When I got a notification the board wanted to review my case again, I didn't think I would get released. The first time I stood in front of the parole board, I was barely twenty-two and got my hopes up. The second time, I wasn't going to set myself up.

They gave me my freedom, and the only thing I should be thinking of is how I'm going to kill Clay's murderer. I should be doing my due diligence on him.

But all I can think of is Mia. I curse myself, knowing I shouldn't have made any moves on her the previous night. I'm tainted and dark now. She's innocent and light.

And you couldn't even control yourself like a real man. You had to come all over her hand within two seconds of her touching you.

The sun is setting. No one is around. The few people who

were in my view are now gone. When I begin to make my way back to shore, I figure I must be hallucinating because Mia is running toward me in cutoff jean shorts and a T-shirt.

She dives under the water then pops back up, swimming toward me.

Oh shit. Something bad happened.

My heart beats in my neck.

"Mia, what's wrong?" I ask, standing up to my neck in water. It's over her head, so I embrace her.

She runs her fingers through my hair, and brings her lips to mine, urgently darting her tongue in and out of my mouth, breathing new life into all my cells. Her legs wrap around my waist, and the false sense once again stirs in me that everything can be all right.

You need to stay focused, Beckett. You have a mission.

"I'm not a good man, Mia," I mumble.

"Shh," she replies before grasping me tighter.

"You should stay away from me," I tell her as I slide my hands into her shorts and palm her ass.

"No."

My heart soars even though I know she's too good for me.

She pushes her forehead to mine. "You said you wouldn't leave me. I'm not leaving you." Her turquoise eyes scan mine, and every emotion I've been trying to work off comes crashing to the surface.

I sob. Hard.

She tries to wipe my tears, but they fly out too fast. My body heaves against hers as walls I've built for ten years come crumbling down.

There are so many things I did in prison to hide my pain.

I grieved daily in my mind, working out till I could hardly move at times.

I cried into my pillow for the first few weeks until I realized there was no room in prison for tears.

I talked to hardly anyone, keeping to myself, not sure who I could trust and fearing for my life. When I got stronger and was no longer a boy, it still didn't matter. You never turned an eye. Anyone could be your enemy waiting to take you down.

I learned loneliness can grip you like death itself.

The boy I was, the man I thought I would become, no longer exists. He's a faint memory I try not to remember. Instead, I'm a hardened felon, out of sync with everything that used to make sense to me, and ready to seek vengeance.

An eye for an eye, a tooth for a tooth has become my motto.

I no longer care about the consequences of my life. I will either be dead or end up back in prison when I get my vengeance. There is no way around it.

I hate my fate and everything I've become.

The most stunning woman is in my arms, and I'm sobbing, unable to control anything I've managed to in the last ten years.

"Shh," she whispers against my lips. And it's as if she's giving me kisses of redemption.

When I finally get a handle on my emotions, she shivers in my arms, and I realize it's gotten dark, and the water is cold.

"Let's go back in," I tell her.

Mia strokes my cheek with the back of her hand. "Okay."

I release her, and we swim in side by side till it's shallow. She holds my hand while we wade through the water.

When we get back to her house, the new windows are installed, and everything has been cleaned up. I punch in the code to her door, and her stomach growls.

"You haven't eaten today, have you?" I've eaten nothing either and realize I'm hungry, too.

"No."

I already know from putting ice in her freezer last night and opening up her fridge that she has no food in the house.

I sigh. I haven't started my job yet and have no money. I can't even take her out somewhere nice.

God, you're such a loser.

"Go get clean clothes on. My parents will have tons of food."

"They won't care if I'm there?"

"What you saw last night, that's normal. 'The more, the merrier,' is my mom's motto."

She nervously scans my eyes. "You won't leave me on my own?"

"I'm going to need to shower and change, but you're welcome to stay in my room when I do."

Or come in with me.

Wishful thinking, Beckett. Would you even know what to do?

"Okay." She spins to go to the bathroom and stops. Turning back to me, she reaches up to my head and kisses me.

"Or I could shower with you," I blurt.

She stares at me.

Great, now you've freaked her out.

She bites down on her lip then takes my hand and leads me toward her bathroom.

Don't fuck this up, Beckett. I say a quick prayer that this time, I won't disappoint her.

When we get to the bathroom, she turns the water on and we both freeze.

"I haven't done this before," I divulge as heat creeps up my neck.

Jesus. Shut your mouth.

A tiny smile plays on her lips. "Me, either."

I look at her in surprise. "No?"

She shakes her head.

Taking a deep breath, I step toward her and clutch her shirt at the waist then bend down and kiss her.

Her arms go around my neck, and her tongue swirls in my mouth.

I remove her wet shirt, grasping it in my palm next to her

back, stealing her lips then unhooking her bra in a swift movement.

At least I didn't lose that skill.

I throw her clothes on the floor, and she unties my swim trunks. Her hands are shaking, and I don't know if it's from cold or nerves.

I push her shorts off her, and she shoves mine off me. I stand back and look at her.

A sexy pink flush fills her face, and she bites down on her lip, anxiously scanning my eyes.

"You're gorgeous." My heart races faster.

She reaches for my hand, and we step into the shower. The warm water rolls down my back, and I wrap her in my arms.

She's cold, and I turn her in the small shower so she's under the water. Her arms are quickly around my neck, her body flush against my growing hard-on.

"You're nice and warm," she says, smiling.

"You can steal my body heat anytime."

She giggles.

I hold the sides of her head, bending down to kiss her then move her forward so the water is only on her back. I fill my palm with shampoo and wash her hair, massaging her scalp.

"Mmm, that feels nice." Her eyes are closed, and I absorb every detail of her: her lips, slightly swollen from our kisses, the long length of her black lashes, the curve of her neck, the way her chest rises and falls with each breath, the freckle below her ear.

She's beyond beautiful. How is it possible she's not already taken?

I rinse her hair and pour her body wash in my hands, turning her into me then kneading it into her shoulders while kissing her neck. My hands move down her arms and to her chest, teasing her nipples then dropping to the curve of her waist. I slide my finger over her rib and trace her scar.

Mia tilts her head and looks up at me, and I dip down to kiss her, gliding my hand farther down her, slipping into her folds, circling my finger on her clit.

"Oh..." she breathes into our kiss, and I wrap my other arm around her waist, holding her tight to me.

My erection presses hard on her back.

She grips my thighs with both hands, digging into my muscle, her chest heaving faster.

"You're exquisite," I tell her as she presses her cheek to mine, closing her eyes and her mouth forming an O.

I maintain my speed on her, not wanting to rush anything with her, desiring to keep her like this.

"Beckett," she whimpers, her legs caving and my arm fully supporting her.

"I got you, angel," I murmur in her ear, sucking on her lobe.

"Oh God...please, Beckett...oh God...oh," she cries out, quivering in my arms.

"You turn me on...so much," I mumble, increasing my speed on her and sucking on the curve of her neck.

"Beckett," she cries out, and it echoes from the tiles. Her body trembles as her eyes roll, and her face flushes.

I hold her tight to me. I'm kissing her jaw when she steadies herself and turns into me, gripping my head and guiding me into her mouth.

I wrap my arms around her. Her hard nipples slide against my chest, and she moves her hand down my chest.

I'm so consumed by her kisses, I don't realize she poured soap in her hands, until they glide over my shaft.

Don't blow your wad in two seconds this time, Beckett.

"Tell me if I'm doing anything wrong," she whispers.

Doing anything wrong?

Breathing hard, I get out, "No. Don't stop. Please keep doing what you're doing."

She resumes sending me back to paradise with her kisses, and I greedily lick her tongue between panting.

"What if I do this," she murmurs and twists her hand while shimmying it up and down my shaft.

"Fuuuuuck, that's so good," I tell her.

She bites my bottom lip.

"God, you're sexy as hell," I tell her.

Her mouth moves to my neck then my chest, and she sucks on my nipple.

I groan, and she speeds up her hand job.

Heat rushes through my body, and my balls shrivel. I put my palm on the shower wall to support me as I cry out, "Fuck, Mia," and explode.

Well, at least you lasted longer this time.

I'm breathing hard, and she pulls my head down and crushes her mouth to mine, making me feel like I'm a man she wants and needs and craves.

And my only desire is to be with her. I want to please and protect her, to make her smile, to make anything bad that ever happened disappear.

I drop to my knees.

She looks at me like she isn't sure what I'm doing. I slide my hands between her thighs then pick her up, throwing her legs over my shoulders.

My tongue swipes through her slit, and she squeaks, gripping my hair. I laugh softly then refocus and lick every inch of her pussy, teasing and taunting her so she's shaking before I even send her to her high.

Her pink paradise is my shrine that I worship and give homage to, flicking and sucking in delight.

The steam of the shower creates a gray fog, and the heat from her body penetrates me.

"Beckett," she cries out, unraveling, and shoving my face into her body so hard I can't breathe.

Her thighs squeeze my neck as she bucks into my face, trapped between me and the wall.

When I can't make her tremble anymore, I slowly let her down, rising and kissing her stomach then breasts then mouth once more.

"I think we did good for our first shower session," she murmurs.

I grin and give her another deep kiss. "I'll agree to that."

12

Mia

After we dry off from our shower, I throw on a pair of capris and a T-shirt then run a comb through my hair. Beckett rinses his swim trunks and wrings them out then puts them back on.

"Should I dry my hair, or is it okay if it's wet?" I ask.

"Whatever you want. You know island life, nothing fancy required."

Suddenly, I'm nervous. I know things with Beckett's siblings weren't the greatest today, and I hadn't seen his parents in ten years, except for his mom for a mere minute last night.

And I was drunk when I saw her.

I look down at my outfit then back in my drawer.

I seriously need to buy some new clothes. I don't have anything nice.

"What are you doing?" Beckett asks.

Shifting on my feet, I glance at him. "I don't have any clothes nicer than this, except for the sundress I wore to court."

"Mia, you look beautiful, and you don't need anything else. It's just my parents' house."

I look at him in panic.

He steps forward and wraps his arms around me. "I'm wearing a swimsuit."

"Yeah, but you're going to change."

"Into a T-shirt and pair of shorts my parents bought me as my *congrats on getting out of jail* wardrobe. Trust me, you're fancier than I will be."

I let out a breath. "Okay."

"Everything else all right?"

"I've never met or hung out with anyone's family before," I blurt out.

Beckett's face scrunches. "Really?"

I bite my lip. Heat crawls up my neck and into my face.

He caresses my cheek. "You already know my crazy family. You didn't have any problem standing up for yourself, so you'll fit right in. Don't think twice about any of them."

"But I said some not so nice things today."

"You didn't say anything wrong, and nothing will be mentioned. It's already forgotten about, I guarantee you."

"Really?"

"Yep. That's how the Brooks roll. We don't hold grudges. I don't even know who will be at my parents'. Gabriella and Connor still haven't moved out, but who knows if they are home or not. And the others all have their own places."

"Okay," I say quietly.

He leans down and pecks me on the lips. "Stay by me or go into my room at any time if you need a sanity break."

"A sanity break?"

He grins. "Yep. Try going home to that chaos after living in a six-by-eight cell that had lights out at nine o'clock every night."

The thought of Beckett living for ten years like that makes me sad. I pull him down for a real kiss, putting everything I have into it, hoping maybe I can be something good in his life.

He ends our kiss. "I'm hungry. Let's go eat."

I take a deep breath, trying to calm my butterflies.

He wraps his arm around my waist. We lock my door and stroll the few houses between his parents' and mine.

It's a warm May night. The lights are on in the Brooks house, and Beckett's parents are sitting on the back deck, drinking cocktails. The fire dances in the bonfire pit, and reggae music is playing. The pool glows pink.

"Mom, we came to clean out your fridge," Beckett announces and tightens his arm around me.

She stands up. "Let me make you—" She stops and gapes.

"Mom, Dad, you remember Mia?"

Beckett's dad stands up and turns to look at me.

Confusion briefly fills their faces, but they quickly recover.

Before I know what's happening, his mom is ripping me away from him and into a hug. "Mia, I'm so glad to see you again."

"Umm, you, too."

Then his dad kisses my cheek and hugs me, too. "Mia, sorry about the fire ants. I heard you fell into a bad nest. I spray the yard, but it's nearly impossible to eliminate them."

"No worries. I'm okay."

Their friendliness catches me off guard, and I hardly embrace them, but they don't seem to take offense.

Beckett pulls me back to him. "What did you make for dinner, Mom?"

"We just ate leftovers, but I can make you something."

"That's okay. I'll go look at what's in the kitchen," Beckett says.

She waves at him. "Don't be silly. Mia, are you allergic to anything or picky?"

"No. I'll eat anything."

"Good woman!" Beckett's dad declares. "Hudson brought

home a girl last year who would only eat rabbit food. Drove me batty."

I laugh.

We move into the kitchen. Beckett's dad drags a barstool out for me. I sit down, and he takes the one next to me. His mom opens the fridge and starts removing food.

"Do you need any help, Mrs. Brooks?"

"Call me Connie."

"And call me George," Beckett's dad says.

"Okay. Do you need any help, Connie?"

"I think I got it. You just relax."

"Want a cocktail?" George asks.

My face heats. *You were so drunk.* "No, thank you. I think I overdid it a bit last night."

George's face gets solemn. "Connor said he gave you a fishbowl. Those things are strong enough to knock me on my ass, and I can handle my liquor."

"Don't forget about Dave and his shots." Connie tsks as if she disapproves.

Beckett brings his lips to my ear. "I need to get out of these trunks. You coming with me or staying? Tap on the bar once to stay or twice to come with me."

I bite my lip and tap once on the bar. He winks, kisses my head, and says, "I'm going to change. Don't scare Mia off while I'm gone."

"Better hurry back, Son. You know how your mom loves to show everyone your baby book," George warns.

Beckett groans. "Focus on food, Mom."

His dad pulls a bottle of water out of the fridge then hands it to me.

"Thank you."

He winks, and it reminds me of Beckett's. "Does it feel good to be back in Florida?"

"I missed the warm weather."

"You were in Michigan?"

"Yes. The Upper Peninsula. It stays pretty cold all year round."

"You must have frozen, being a Florida gal," Connie chimes in.

"I wore a lot of layers. But I missed the sunshine and ocean."

Connie opens the bread box sitting on the counter and looks at me. "What do you think about California club sandwiches?"

I shrug. "I don't think I've ever had one."

"What? That's a sin. They are delicious, and Connie makes the best ones," George boasts.

"What is it?"

"Basically, it's a club sandwich but with avocado on it," Connie explains.

"I love avocados, so that sounds delicious."

Beckett comes back into the room, wearing a pair of black athletic shorts and a gray T-shirt. He smells like he put on some sort of manly cologne. A sandalwood and vanilla scent flares in my nostrils. My pulse beats faster. He sits next to me. "What did I miss?"

How does he always smell so good?

"Your mom is making California club sandwiches."

George opens the fridge and slides a bottle of beer to Beckett.

"Dad, I can't." He sends it back to him.

Sadness briefly fills George's face, but it's quickly gone. "Sorry. I forgot." He takes another water out of the fridge and gives it to Beckett.

"Thanks."

"Gabriella and Connor said the windows all got replaced in your house today?" Connie says.

My face flushes. I still can't believe they replaced my windows and door locks for free. "Yes. It was very generous of them."

Beckett puts his arm around the back of my seat.

"Ryland said you're going to need a new roof," George informs me.

Panic fills me. "What?"

He nods. "Your tiles are nearing fifty years old. Most are lucky to see forty."

How much does a new roof cost? My gut flips.

"Mia, don't worry," Beckett says.

"I don't know anything about roofs."

Connie reaches over the island and pats my hand. "Don't worry, dear. The boys will take care of it."

"What? No..." I shake my head.

George laughs. "No isn't an option. The weather looks perfect tomorrow. They will have it ripped off and put back together before sunset."

"What?" I look at him then Beckett.

"It's already figured out, don't worry about it," Beckett says like it's no big deal. "Throw extra bacon on mine, Mom."

I don't want to fight with him in front of his parents but also don't want to be a charity case for him and his family.

"So, where were you two before you came home?" Beckett's mom asks.

My face flushes again. Images of what Beckett and I did in my shower play out in my mind. I glance nervously at Beckett.

He stands up, rips a bunch of grapes off the vine, and pops one in my mouth. "Swimming," he says and throws a grape in his mouth, too. When he sits back down, he puts his hand on my leg, caressing the inside of my thigh with his thumb.

My face burns hotter as my loins throb from his touch. I pick up my water and drink half the bottle, trying to cool off.

His mom sets a plate in front of each of us. "It's a nice time of year to swim. The water is finally warm enough."

Beckett nonchalantly says, "I thought the water was warm. What did you think, Mia?"

Blood pumps through my veins. I bite down on my lip, trying to bite back a smile. I look at his mom. "Yes, the water was perfect."

13

Beckett

MIA FITS IN PERFECTLY WITH MY FAMILY. I KNEW SHE WOULD. MY parents were a little surprised when we first got here, but they both believe in my innocence. For a decade, they asked me at every visit to tell them who I was covering for, begged me to let them help, but I would just go silent and look away. There was nothing anyone could do for me while I was in prison. And I wouldn't put them at risk. If my father knew that his best friend had set me up, he would have ended up in the cell next to me, or possibly dead.

They don't question what I'm doing with Mia, and I'm grateful. I don't feel like being grilled about our relationship and what surely is going to be something along the lines of them wanting to know what Mia knows or thinks about the night Clay and her were shot.

And I'm sure that one of my siblings probably gave them some sort of information about the details of today's argument.

We're halfway through our sandwiches when Gabriella comes in. "Mia! Where did you find him?"

Mia blushes again, and I like to assume she keeps thinking about the shower.

I'm pretty sure if I asked her for a replay, she'd give me one, so my ego is feeling pretty good that I didn't mess it up.

I definitely want a replay.

"Umm—"

"Swimming," I tell Gabriella. "Where have you been?"

"On another crappy date."

"What happened?" I sternly ask her.

She rolls her eyes. "Chill out, Beckett. Nothing you need to go beat anyone up over. Just no chemistry. Friendzone forever."

"Carlo?" Connie asks.

"Sean?" George asks.

"Leo?" Connie asks.

"Jesus. How many 'friends' do you have?" I growl.

"Easy there. I'm not sleeping with them. I happen to be a nice person, and people want to be my friend," she claims.

"Sorry, sis, but dudes do not want to be your friend unless they want to get in your pants. You're twenty-three, not three."

"Can we not talk about getting into your sister's pants, please?" My dad winces as he says it.

"Sorry, Dad."

Mia excuses herself to the bathroom, and my mom shows her where the new one they just added on is.

"So you and Mia are friends now?" Gabriella asks.

"Yes."

"Guess you made your point, then." She cockily raises her eyebrow at me, and I realize that I just stepped into her trap.

Shit. Yeah, I want to have sex with Mia. It's all I can think about. The fact I just admitted it to my sister makes me nauseous. Mia isn't someone I want to fuck and be done with.

"Not the same thing." I glare at Gabriella.

"Why is that?" Gabriella smirks at me.

I stop myself from answering so I don't step into another one of her traps. She wants me to tell her how I feel about Mia, and I'm not going to. That's between Mia and me, and I'm not going to tell Gabriella before I tell Mia. And to be honest, my thoughts are all over the place about how I feel about Mia.

A few days ago, I had no one. I slept on the bottom bunk with a smelly guy on the top bed, who farted and snored all night. Last night, I slept next to Mia. Well, I didn't sleep much because I iced her arm on and off, and I kept staring at her and kissing her head.

The only person I can think of is her, and I've never felt the things I'm feeling about her about anyone else. But what do I know about this kind of stuff? And I don't want to scare her off and tell her any of this. She's probably had so many boyfriends she can't keep track of the number who have professed their feelings for her.

Mia comes back into the kitchen.

"Let's drop it," I say to Gabriella, who smirks at me again.

Mia pauses. "Did I interrupt something?"

"Nope."

She narrows her eyes.

"Mia, I'm going shopping tomorrow. You want to come?" Gabriella asks.

"Clothes shopping?"

"Yes."

Mia nods. "Yes, please. I need a new wardrobe. Most of my clothes are for cold weather."

"Well, don't throw them out. Your blood will thin quickly," my mom tells her.

"Isn't that an old wives' tale?" Mia asks.

"Not at all. You'll see. At seventy degrees, you'll be in a long-sleeved top and pants."

"Really?"

"Yes."

"All right. I won't. What time do you want to go?"

Gabriella shrugs. "Maybe after lunch? Maybe before? I can text you if you want."

Mia's face turns red. "I don't have a phone."

"You don't have a phone? How is that possible?" Gabriella shrieks.

I roll my eyes. "Not everyone has a phone, Gabriella."

She gapes. "Yes, everyone does have a phone."

"I don't," I point out.

"You just got out of prison, and Mom bought you one. You've chosen not to open it."

"What am I going to do with it?"

"Ummm...text me. Call me. Surf the Internet."

I roll my eyes again.

Gabriella looks back at Mia. "Why do you not have a phone?"

Mia shifts on her seat. "My grandparents never got me one, and I didn't have access to much money. They said I didn't need it. I had the phone in the dorm hallway for them to call me on."

"What! How did you communicate with your friends?"

Mia twists her fingers in her lap and looks down as her blush deepens to crimson.

I have no one... Mia's words from the night before make me come to her rescue.

"She isn't as superficial as you," I tease my sister.

Gabriella tilts her head and glares at me. "I am not superficial."

She throws a grape at me, and I catch it in my mouth.

"Score!" I shout, pumping my fist in the air.

Gabriella laughs. "Still got it, I see."

I cockily pat both of my shoulders.

She rolls her eyes. "Mia, why don't you take Beckett's phone, since he isn't using it, and I'll text you tomorrow."

"Umm..."

I stand up. Mia and I both finished our sandwiches, and I think it's time for a break.

"Good idea. Come on, Mia. Let's go figure out this phone."

Gabriella smirks at me and I ignore her.

Mia looks at me nervously but stands up.

I put my arm around her waist and lead her up the stairs and into my room. As soon as I shut the door, I kiss her. "I have a confession to make," I murmur.

"What's that?"

"I just wanted to get you alone. Gabriella can show you how to use the phone."

She runs her fingers through my hair. "Is this a sanity break?" She presses closer to me and darts her tongue against mine.

I tighten my arms around her. "The best one ever."

There's a knock on my door, and I groan as it opens.

Mia spins out of my arms.

Gabriella smirks. "Sorry to interrupt, but I figured you have no idea what you're doing."

"You do know you're supposed to wait after you knock for someone to respond to you before opening the door and coming in?"

She bats her eyes. "Sorry but not sorry."

Nothing has changed. Gabriella still knows how to get under my skin.

Yeah, but you missed this.

"Where's your phone?" she demands.

"On the desk."

"I'll get it," Mia says and walks over to the desk then freezes. As she stares at the phone, her face turns crimson. I'm about to ask her what's wrong, but she snatches the phone, avoids my eyes, and hands it to Gabriella.

"I got a new phone number and haven't memorized it yet. I left my phone in my purse downstairs. Let me get it," Gabriella says.

"I'll come with you," Mia says quickly and practically runs out of my room.

What just happened?

I look at the desk and cringe. The box of condoms Ryland threw at me when I first got home, with a sticky note that says, "Time to get back on the horse," was sitting right next to the phone. And it's open. I had removed one out of the package just to make sure nothing changed with condoms in the last ten years.

Fuck.

I scrub my hands on my face.

Why didn't I throw that out? The empty condom wrapper is sitting right next to the box, and the condom is on top of it.

Well, you didn't exactly expect to have Mia in your room.

God I'm a pathetic loser.

I toss the condom and wrapper in the garbage can along with the sticky note. I toss the box in the drawer.

I definitely won't be needing these now. Mia's probably not going to allow me next to her again.

Fuck.

After a few minutes of going through any possible explanation of what I could say to Mia, I decide it's pointless. I'm a loser, and there is no getting around it.

Yep. The once cool and cocky kid who could get any girl he wanted no longer exists.

Ten years have passed, and I feel less confident than a virgin. I officially have no game.

And now Mia knows it, too.

14

Mia

Ten Years Ago

The beeping of a machine rings in my ear, and the light is so bright I have to close my eyes again.

"Mia!" my grandmother shrieks.

"Shh, don't scare her," my grandfather reprimands her.

I slowly open my eyes and see them staring at me. "Where am I?"

My grandmother cups my face with both her hands, and she's crying. "Mia, thank God you're awake."

She hugs me, and I look past her at my grandfather, who is brushing his cheek. "What happened?"

"You don't remember anything?" my grandmother asks, releasing me.

I close my eyes.

The bonfire.

"I'm sorry. I shouldn't have lied to you about going to the party. Did I get drugged or something?"

Pain passes over my grandparents' faces.

My grandfather puts his arm around my grandmother, and she puts her hand to her mouth.

Why is she crying so hard?

"I'm okay. You don't have to worry anymore. Whatever happened, I'm fine," I try to reassure her.

She sobs into my grandfather's chest.

My grandfather rubs her back and hesitates but then says, "There was a shooting. Do you remember?"

"A shooting? No. Who got shot?"

He stares at me.

"I got shot?" I look down at my body, but the covers are over me, so I can't see anything.

He carefully says, "Yes."

"Where?"

"In your rib. They removed it because the bullet was lodged in it."

"They took out my rib?" I cry in panic. "Don't I need it?"

He puts his hand on my shin. "You'll be okay without it."

I release a breath.

He continues to stare at me, rubbing my grandmother's back.

"Is there something else you aren't telling me?"

My grandmother sobs harder.

Chills run through my body. "Did something happen to Gabriella?"

My grandfather shakes his head. "No, honey. She is fine. It's..."

He looks away, closes his eyes then looks back at me. "Clay got shot and died."

A pain shoots through my heart, and an uncontrollable wave of emotion hits me as my tears fall like never before. "No!"

My grandfather takes my hand, trying to console both my grandmother and me.

I cry for a long time and finally look up and manage to ask, "Who shot him?"

He blinks several times and gulps. "Beckett shot you both."

"What? No, that's impossible!" I exclaim, shaking my head.

Very softly, he says, "He hasn't denied it. Not once."

"I don't understand."

"None of us do."

"That's..."

Get down, Mia!

I jerk my head. "He yelled, 'Get down, Mia!'"

My grandmother sits back in her chair. "Mia, do you remember something?"

I try to remember, but I can't. "No. I know he yelled that to me though."

"When? Where were you?"

"I don't know. I can't see it, but I hear him yelling."

"Honey, that could have been during any part of your childhood." My grandmother pats my hand.

"Beckett would never hurt Clay, much less shoot him or me."

My grandfather grasps my hand. "I know this is confusing. It is for all of us, but we need to accept reality. Beckett Brooks is a murderer."

SEVERAL DAYS PASS IN THE HOSPITAL. WAVES OF GRIEF OVER LOSING Clay come and go. And I grieve for Beckett as well.

I don't believe he could do it. And why would he do it?

I want to talk to Gabriella, but my grandparents won't allow anyone to see me, and the phone has been removed from my room. I don't understand why, but they said that it's not safe for me.

When I'm getting released, I think I'm going home. It's not till I get in the minivan, and I look out the window and see a sign that reads "I-75 North" that I question where we are going.

My grandfather veers over to a rest area, and my grandmother gets out of the van and opens my door. She jumps in next to me and squeezes my hand. "We need to talk, honey."

Panic courses through me. *Why is she looking at me like that?*

"What?"

"The island isn't safe for you."

"What do you mean?"

"You can't go back."

My stomach flips. "I can't go back? I don't understand."

"As hard as this is going to be for all of us, we're doing the right thing for you."

She takes a deep breath. "We are driving you to your new school."

"I don't want to go to a new school."

She squeezes my hand. "Yes, I know, dear, but we need to keep you safe. The boarding school we are sending you to—"

"I don't want to go to boarding school!"

She strokes my hair. "Once you get used to it you'll love it."

"No."

"We love you, Mia. We don't want anything else to happen to you," my grandfather chimes in.

No. This cannot be happening.

"Where are you taking me?"

"There's a lovely school in the Upper Peninsula of Michigan."

My head jerks toward her. "Michigan? That's across the country."

"Yes. No one will find you there."

"No one will find me? What does that mean?"

She purses her lips and looks away.

"Tell me," I cry out.

She turns back to me. "This school will keep you safe. We love you, and this is why we are making this decision."

"I'm sorry I lied about the party. I won't ever do it again!"

"Oh, honey, this isn't about that. This is about keeping bad people away from you."

"Bad people? But you said Beckett murdered Clay. He's going to jail. There isn't anyone else to come after me."

"We're doing the best thing for you, Mia." She returns to the passenger seat.

"You can't just leave me in Michigan," I plead, but the decision has been made.

Any joy, warmth, or friendships I had before the shooting are gone. Like the snow that covers the ground most of the year, my new reality is cold, harsh, and bleak.

Loneliness grips me like a sieve, suffocating me at times. It takes any shyness I had and makes me a bigger introvert. I become antisocial and full of anxiety around people.

I hide my past from those around me. It's so sad, I can't even imagine having to explain it to anyone. So I suffer in silence as grief over Clay and Beckett, my friendship with Gabriella, and my previous life never goes away.

When I turn twenty, I try to date. I can never get past three dates, and two different times I'm kissed and want to die from the embarrassment of not knowing what to do.

They say Beckett Brooks killed my brother. I wish he had killed me, too.

15

Mia

Present Day

Gabriella gets done showing me how to use the phone. I've avoided looking at Beckett since he came back down the stairs. He's been talking to his parents across the room.

Time to get back on the horse. An open condom wrapper and condom was next to the note. I stared at it. I had never seen one before.

The anxiety I usually feel around dating is back.

Beckett and Clay during their high school years always were surrounded by girls. They talked about them. Hung out with them. Dated them.

He's been with tons of girls. I don't even know what to do.

Like in the shower—I didn't know what he was going to do to me when he dropped to his knees. He knows exactly how to touch me with every part of his body, and I don't know if what I'm doing is right or wrong. I want to make him feel as good as he makes me feel, but I don't have all his experience or even to know where to start.

Who are you kidding? You have zero experience.

I try to pay attention to what Gabriella is showing me with the phone. It seems simple enough.

You're so out of touch, Mia. You don't even know how to use a cell phone.

"Easy, peasy, huh?" Gabriella asks.

I nod. "Thanks." My anxiety isn't going away with all my thoughts racing. Every time I glance at Beckett, my pulse increases. I've never wanted anyone before. But I want him. I didn't understand what it meant when people said they have to have someone. But that is how I feel about Beckett. And I'm way out of my league.

The cell phone reads that it's past 11:00. I stand up. "I think it's time for me to go. Thanks for dinner, Connie."

Beckett stares at me, and I'm not sure how to take his look. So many notions about my lack of sexual or even dating experience have me flustered.

Connie hugs me. "Come over any time. It's so good seeing you, Mia."

"Thanks."

George hugs me, too. "We always have room for you here, Mia."

Their kindness makes me blink hard. "Thank you," I manage to get out.

Before the condom incident, everything felt comfortable and fun. I always loved hanging out with Gabriella at their house when I was a child, and nothing has changed. They are still the same warmhearted, good family.

"I'll walk you home," Beckett says, scanning my eyes.

Is he nervous? No, I must be imagining things.

"Thanks."

He motions for me to go first, and when we both get outside, we stroll side by side, but he doesn't hold my hand or put his arm around my waist like he did before.

My panic increases. He saw me staring at the condom. *Ugh.*

Neither of us says anything when we get to my house. I punch in the four digits, his inmate number, and turn to him. "I'm sorry about the code. Can we change it to something different?"

"It's okay. We can change it tomorrow if you want."

"Thanks." I step inside, but he stays outside.

He hesitates.

"Are you going to come in?" I ask him.

He exhales, steps inside, and shuts the door.

We stare uncomfortably at each other, near my front door, not moving.

"I'm sorry," he finally says.

I look at him in surprise. "For what?"

His face turns crimson. "The condoms with the note my brother put on the box."

My cheeks burn. "It's okay. It's your room."

"I just wanted to see if they were the same as ten years ago." He looks at the ceiling then back at me, as if embarrassed.

Why is he embarrassed? He isn't an awkward virgin who doesn't know what to do.

"I should apologize. I didn't mean to stare. I've just never seen one," I blurt out, and my face grows hotter.

"Since you're on the pill?"

"How do you know I'm on the pill?"

"They were on your dresser."

"Oh." I take a deep breath.

"I'm sorry. I don't mean to pry into your business," he quickly says.

"I've never had a reason to use a condom."

"Since you're on the pill?" he repeats.

"I'm on the pill because I have endometriosis."

His eyes widen. "I studied that in my nursing courses. Does the pill help?"

I look at him in surprise. "You took nursing courses?"

"Yes. I got my degree so I could work in the clinic and do something besides sit in my cell all day."

A gush of pride washes over me. "That's amazing."

He shrugs. "So, does the pill help the pain?"

"Yes."

"The guys you've been with have never used a condom?"

Guys I've been with? My cheeks are scorching, and I look away.

He steps forward and turns my chin to look at him. "Hey, I'm sorry. I'm not judging you."

I inhale deeply. "I've never been with anyone."

His head jerks back. It's not a big jerk, but it's enough, I notice.

God, this is so embarrassing.

"How is that possible?"

I look away.

He turns my face back to him again. "I mean it as a compliment."

I bite my bottom lip. My heart's racing, and my stomach is doing flips.

"You're beautiful and sexy. And I don't know how you kept all your boyfriends off you all these years."

I quietly say, "I've not had boyfriends. I've been alone."

A sad look crosses his face, one that comes from firsthand knowledge.

"You deserve more," he states.

Time stands still as he scans my eyes, swallowing hard, licking his lips, breathing harder.

"I don't know how to please you," I blurt out and instantly wish my mouth would shut up tonight.

Confusion fills his face. "What are you talking about?"

"When we're together...I don't know what to do."

The sides of his lips turn slightly up. "Yes, you do."

I shake my head, and my insides quiver.

He pushes his forehead to mine and wraps his arm around my back, pressing me to his body. His erection grows, digging against my stomach. "Do you feel that?"

"Yes," I breathe.

"You do that to me," he growls.

"Do you want all of me even though I don't know what I'm doing?"

"I want you so bad, you've consumed all my thoughts since I laid eyes on you in the courtroom."

I'm not sure if Beckett's heart or mine is pounding harder.

"I want all of you." Butterflies erupt in my stomach.

"Do you want me to go home and get a condom?"

"No."

He quickly says, "Sorry, I didn't mean to assume—"

"I meant, don't go. Let's not use one."

He blinks several times, reaches behind me, and locks the door. His lips possess mine, owning and worshiping me. He steps backward, guiding me down the hall while exploring my mouth with his tongue.

"You make my body throb," I murmur against his lips.

A deep throaty groan escapes his mouth, and he reaches down into my pants. "I love how you taste," he says between kisses, slipping his finger through my wet folds.

I whimper, clenching from his touch.

He inches in me, curling his finger and rubbing his thumb on my clit.

Heat ignites in my toes, rolling through me. I lock my hands onto his neck.

Licking me behind my ear then sucking on my lobe, he murmurs, "You tell me if you want me to stop at any time."

"No. Don't stop...don't...don't...oh God!" I cry out as he sends me flying over the edge, and I lose the ability to stand, relying on his arm around my waist to hold me up.

His lips flutter on my neck, his erection hard as steel, pulsing on me.

I greedily reach for his face, gliding my tongue in his mouth then bite his lip, gripping his skull and pressing as close to him as possible.

The warmth of his hand caressing my naked back sends tingles up and down my spine. I reach for his shirt, trying to remove it, and he fists the back of it and gracefully slides it off.

I kiss his chest as his heartbeat thumps on my lips, and reach into his shorts.

Groaning, he grabs my wrists and lifts them above my head, holding them high in the air while his other hand tugs my shirt off. He lowers my hands around his neck. "Don't ever let go of me, Mia," he murmurs then dips his mouth back to mine, kissing me with so much fire, I'm lost in everything Beckett. New nervous butterflies erupt when he removes all my clothes.

He picks me up and places me on the bed, feasting on my entire body, sucking my nipples, licking my bullet wound, tracing the curve of my waist with his finger. Every touch, every kiss brings flutters and tingles and spikes of adrenaline I've never experienced before.

For the second time today, he throws my legs over his shoulders. Turning his head, he kisses my thighs.

Energy buzzes throughout me, lighting me up and making me feel alive and wanted.

"You're perfect," he mumbles on my thigh then dips his tongue inside me before sweeping it up to my clit.

I gasp, fumbling with where to put my hands, not remembering what I did with them in the shower, wanting to grip his head but not sure if I should. I brush them across his head then on top of his hands, which are on my hips, then back and forth.

He decides for me, entwining his fingers between mine and holding them on my hips while circling his thumb on my skin.

The godliness of his tongue glides through me.

Flicking me.

Tasting me.

Igniting me.

Incoherent noises fill the room as he brings me to a peak but doesn't release me, licking and sucking with different intensities. I clasp his hands harder, begging him, while my breasts heave and my skin glistens with a sheen of sweat.

"Yes...right there...oh...yes..." I hardly get out, my voice raspy.

He moves my hands to his head and releases them. I grip his hair, forcefully pressing his face into my pussy as I buck my hips up.

He holds onto me and sucks me so hard, my head spins as my body becomes an earthquake full of tremors.

In my aftermath, my hands are still locked into his hair as I try to catch my breath. His fingers stroke mine, and I release them, locking eyes with his that smolder like a fire, ready to ignite.

He kisses my inner thighs again then releases my legs, licking my stomach, breathing his warm breath on my breasts, sucking on my neck.

My flesh hums, bubbling and scorching from what he's already given me, pulsing with anticipation of what's next, craving his cock that's hard and dripping on my hot skin.

I taste my orgasm on his tongue as he darts into me, as his hands dip down and spread my legs wider. The tip of his cock hits my sex, and a loud, throaty groan escapes him.

"Oh God," I breathe.

He clenches his jaw, his breath labored. "Do you still want all of me?" he murmurs.

"Yes."

Beckett scans my eyes while slowly inching in me.

He's hardly in and I don't know how he'll get any farther. I dig my nails into his back.

"Okay, angel?"

I whimper.

"Try to relax," he instructs me.

I blow out a breath, refocus, and he glides farther in, loudly groaning.

"Oh God, Beckett, it stings."

"Shh." He strokes my hair and stills. "It should stop in a minute."

"Okay." I breathe out.

Gently, he kisses me, parting my lips with his tongue, slowly exploring my mouth, stroking my cheek. I don't know how much time goes by, but the stinging goes away, and my fingers trail his back till I'm palming his ass.

He makes tiny thrusts inside me.

"Oh God," I pant.

"Hurt?"

"No...oh God, you feel good," I blurt out, rocking my hips into his thrusts.

He smiles and murmurs, "You feel amazing."

"Oh God. Beckett...what do I do...oh God," I cry out as he shimmies against my walls.

"Don't stop what you're doing," he pants back.

"No?"

"No. You're perfect. Yes...that, Mia...oh fuck..."

He lowers his mouth to my collarbone and sucks on it while he thrusts deeper.

Moans, cries, and murmurs fill the room. The air becomes thick with the scent of sex. Sweat on our flesh merges together. Tongue, lips, and teeth glide across skin.

"Beckett...Beckett...oh..." A rush of adrenaline bursts through all my veins, and my eyes roll as my heart races.

He laces his fingers through mine, pinning them above my head, thrusting into me faster and harder.

Like waves crashing on the shore, there's a never-ending supply of endorphins exploding and slowing, over and over.

I can't keep my eyes open. Every time Beckett pounds into me, my eyes can't focus, and my pulse skyrockets. I squeeze his hands as tight as I can.

"You're so fucking good," he pants, making my ego soar.

I lean up for his lips and suck on his bottom one.

He groans and thrusts some more. I douse him in my juices as my high hits me harder, and he pumps his seed in me, never slowing down.

Beckett collapses on me, each of our breaths labored, hearts beating, and skin drenched. Our fluids cover my sheets, soaking them in our high.

Beckett releases my hands, trailing his fingers down my arms, before rolling off me but taking me with him so we're both on our side.

Still panting hard, he strokes my cheek. "You okay?"

"Yes."

He kisses my forehead then sweetly grins at me. "You, Mia Crimson, are a gift. Thank you."

Beckett tightens his arms around me, and I sink into his chest, feeling protected, loved, and needed.

This is what life should be like. Maybe I can have a normal, happy life after all.

Beckett worships me all night, while I fall in and out of sleep, thinking maybe we can finally both be happy and put the last ten years of hell behind us.

But I should have paid attention to Beckett's comments about the possibility of being in danger and vengeance.

16

Beckett
Ten Years Ago

"BECKETT BROOKS, YOU ARE HEREBY SENTENCED TO FIFTEEN YEARS for the crime of Murder in the first degree of Clay Crimson."

The weeping of my mother and sisters echoes in my ears, and the cries of Clay's grandparents match their painful sounds. I will myself not to look at them, but I can't help it. Sitting behind my father is Henry, patting his shoulder in sympathy.

Ryland and Hudson blink back tears, their fists pounding into their hearts, their other arms each wrapped around one of my sisters who are sobbing. Connor stands between my brothers covering his face with his hands and shaking.

I've not spoken to anyone. Besides my attorney, I've not been allowed to see anyone in my family.

It's a good thing, not seeing them. The night of the murder, looking in my parents' eyes and seeing their pain about killed me.

The attorney my parents hired I wouldn't talk to. They tried me as an adult, and Henry stood up and gave a speech to the judge about remembering my age when sentencing me.

It took all I had not to yell out in court that he's a corrupt hypocrite, but watching Skates kill Clay and Mia plays over and over in my mind, and I won't have my family's fate be the same as Clay and Mia's.

I prayed Mia would make it through the shooting, but my attorney told me that she died. He said that the evidence from Mia's body was mishandled and that I was lucky to be avoiding that charge.

The county jail is a pit. I've been locked in it during my trial, which was quick as I never denied the charges.

As the officer leads me out of the courtroom, I see Clay's grandparents' eyes full of horror and grief.

They believe I murdered Clay and Mia.

You might as well have. It's your fault. If you hadn't forced Clay to pull over, and you didn't rummage through Skates' boxes and find the heroin, maybe Clay could have quit running his errands, and he'd still be alive.

Mia would be alive, too.

God, Mia. She was innocent.

Clay shouldn't have been murdered, but he chose to work for Skates. Mia didn't have anything to do with it. She was just a sweet girl—a good girl.

If you weren't so obsessed over getting laid, you would have seen Skates talking to Clay on the field after practices. You could have stopped him from taking that first job.

"Beckett," my dad shouts out as the guard is guiding me out of the courtroom. I turn and see him mouth, "I love you." I quickly turn away, blinking away tears.

Do not cry, Beckett. Be a man.

I'm going to prison. My cellmates have already filled me in on my future. The county jail is a picnic in the park. Prison is where hell is.

The first few nights in jail, I cried in my pillow, and one of the guards came into my cell in the middle of the night and ordered me out of it.

"Where are we going?"

"Just shut up, Brooks."

He led me down the hallway, through the cells, and into a small room. "Sit down, Brooks."

I obeyed, wondering what I had done wrong and what was happening.

"You need to toughen up, kid. You're going to prison. There are no tears in prison."

"I know—"

"Shut up. You know shit. You're a cocky kid who's used to being Mr. Popular. Do you know what Mr. Popular gets in prison?"

I take a deep breath as all my fears about what is going to happen to me come to the surface.

He sits down. "I'm going to give you some advice, and I suggest you take it and don't forget it."

I stare at him.

"Shut up when you get to prison. No one, and I mean no one, is your friend. That includes the guards. Do not trust anyone. Watch your back at all times. Lift weights and bulk up. You're a pretty boy, and they love pretty boys like you. Defend yourself if needed, but do not do any favors for anyone. Stay out of everyone's business. You see a fight, walk the other way. You hear an argument, look the other way. Do not drink alcohol or take drugs. Get into the programs to keep yourself busy and out of trouble. They have a GED program. Get it. They have a college course program. Take it. Keep your head up and out of trouble. Do you understand me?"

GED. I'm not even going to have a high school diploma from my school.

"Yes, sir."

He stares at me. "I don't know why you did what you did, but you're young, and I believe in redemption. I'll pray for you that you clear your debt to society. When you get out someday, I hope you become a lawful, good citizen. You'll still be able to have a full life one day down the road."

Redemption. A full life.

I start to choke up again, and he slams his hand on the table. "Do not cry. They will destroy you the first day you get there if you cry."

I take a deep breath and compose myself.

"Good. You played sports so isometric exercises can be your best friend. The cell isn't big, but use it to your advantage."

"Yes, sir."

"That's all I have to say." He stands up, opens the door, and leads me back to my cell.

That was several nights ago, and his words of advice have played over and over in my mind.

I'm put in a van and transported to prison. It's about a half-hour ride, and my stomach is churning in fear.

When I get to the prison, I spend an hour being logged into the system. At the very end, they make me strip, spread my legs, and bend over, while they do a cavity search checking for weapons and drugs. They shave my head and hose me down with cold water then hand me an orange jumpsuit.

Before I am sent off to my cell, the warden comes in. "I'm Warden Smith. You will address me as Warden."

"Yes, Warden," I quickly reply.

"Should I expect trouble from you?"

I shake my head. "No, Warden."

He looks me over and scans my eyes. "Lights are out at nine p.m. You stand outside the door of your cell for head count. When the door to your cell locks, that means no talking, no lights. You get in your bed, understand?"

"Yes, Warden."

"Six o'clock is the wake-up call. You get up, you make your bed, and stand outside the cell when it unlocks at a quarter after six for head count. You understand?"

"Yes, Warden."

He scans my face one last time. "It's time to pay your debt, inmate 4592."

I stare at him.

"You will respond to inmate 4592. Remember that is who you now are." He waits for me to respond.

Inmate 4592. That's who I now am.

"Yes, Warden."

He turns and leaves. Two guards lead me down a hallway, and a door unlocks. Both sides of the walls are covered in cells, five flights up. A common area has chairs bolted to the floor as well as the tables.

They lead me to the third level and down the aisle as the prisoners all yell and make catcalls so loud, my ears are ringing. My heart pounds, and my insides shake in fear. I stare directly ahead of me, clenching my jaw, seeing the arms in my peripheral vision reaching out through the bars, trying to grab me.

When I get to cell 345, my cellmate is in the room taking a shit on the metal toilet three feet from the bunk beds. I assume he's in his mid-forties, and he's got a beard and tattoos all over his arms, neck, and face. He grins at me. "Welcome home, inmate 4592."

Home. Home is no longer where the heart is. It's where hell resides, and all things evil come together. Hell is where I have time to think for too many hours to count about the vengeance I will bestow on both Skates and Henry.

I may have come to prison an innocent man, but in prison I will begin my journey to become the felon I'm declared to be.

17

Beckett
Present Day

A NOISE ON THE ROOF MAKES ME OPEN MY EYES. MIA IS STILL asleep in my arms.

She's probably exhausted. I kiss her head, and she snuggles into me. All night, we couldn't keep our hands off each other, and the room smells like sex and sweat. My insides go giddy at the thought.

There's a loud bang on the roof. Mia's eyes fly open, and she sits up. "What's that?"

I groan. "My brothers being clumsy."

She blinks at me.

"I think they started tearing off your roof."

Her face scrunches up. "Hey, I was going to talk to you about that."

I roll her on her back and put my mouth next to hers. "It's happening. Don't worry about it. Let's focus on other things."

"Beckett—"

"Shh." I silence her with my lips and tongue.

She starts to kiss me back, engulfing me into her sweet perfection, when the doorbell rings.

I groan, and she giggles. I mutter, "Sometimes, my family is the biggest pain in the ass."

I'm about to move off her, and she says, "Wait."

"What's wrong?"

She places her mouth back on mine. I harden against her as the doorbell rings over and over.

I collapse against Mia's neck and groan again.

"I think we need to get up."

"I am up," I cockily tell her.

She giggles. "I mean dressed."

"I prefer you naked."

"Why don't you keep me naked again all night?"

Happiness surges through me once more. "Yeah?"

She bites back a smile and nods.

"Deal." I give her one last kiss, and we jump off the bed, locate our clothes, and unlock the door.

Gabriella and Gracie are standing in the doorway, each holding a brown to-go carrier of coffee.

"Time to get up, Beckett." Gabriella cheerfully smirks at me and shoves her way into the house.

I groan and snag a cup. "At least you brought coffee with your unannounced self."

"Mia wasn't answering her cell phone."

"Shoot. I'm sorry, Gabriella. It's been turned off all night."

"You turned it off?" Gabriella asks in shock.

Mia glances nervously at her. "Was I not supposed to turn it off?"

"No. You just put it on charge next to your bed while you sleep. Then you don't miss any calls or text messages."

"While she's sleeping?" I question.

Gracie puts her hand over her mouth to stifle a laugh.

Gabriella rolls her eyes. "You need a lesson in current times, Beckett."

There's another crash on the roof.

Mia jumps, and I put my arm around her.

Gracie raises her brows at me. "You need to get your booty up there. You know how they are."

"Noted."

Gabriella smirks at me and hands me a bag. "Mom said to give you this."

"What is it?"

"Clothes, a toothbrush, toothpaste, shampoo, soap...you know, all the things so you don't stink."

I grunt. "Awesome, thanks." Looking at Mia, I ask, "I'm going to go shower if that's okay?"

"Yeah. Of course."

I go to the bathroom and take a quick shower. When I come back out to the family room, Gabriella tells her to hurry up and get ready so they can go shopping. I kiss Mia on the head and go outside.

I climb up on the roof. "Good morning," I shout to Connor, Ryland, and Hudson who are tearing tiles off.

It's a beautiful sunny day. The sky is clear. From Mia's roof, I can see the entire length of the seven mile island, all the way down to the southern tip.

Coquina Beach. I stare at the end of the island. The last time I stepped foot on that beach was the night of Clay's murder.

"Wondering if you were going to show up," Connor says, jerking me out of my trance.

"I figured once we opened up the bedroom you'd come out," Ryland teases.

"Funny," I say but feel a perma-grin on my face.

"Good night?" Hudson raises an eyebrow at me.

I ignore him, but I'm smiling so big the sides of my cheeks hurt.

Good night isn't a strong enough phrase to explain my night with Mia.

And she wants me to stay again tonight. I give myself a high five in my head.

Ryland smirks. "An extra tool belt and your shoes are in my truck. Mom said she forgot to put them in your bag."

"I see Mom hasn't changed." I descend the ladder.

He follows me. "I need one of those coffees."

"Inside."

"Backseat, you'll find your stuff."

"Got it."

Ryland goes inside.

I find my shoes and quickly put them on then the tool belt around my waist. I'm finishing when a cop car parks at the curb, and Henry gets out.

The sight of him makes my blood boil, and my pulse beats hard against my veins.

"Beckett," he says like we're old friends.

I stare at him, jaw clenched, not saying anything.

He points to Mia's house. "What's going on here?"

Ryland's voice orders the girls, "Stay inside the house."

"But that's Henry," Gabriella says.

"I'm not going to tell you again," he sternly says.

Henry raises his eyebrows at me.

I can't wait to make you pay for your sins.

Ryland is quick at my side. "Henry."

"What's going on here, Ryland? Your brother seems not to be able to talk."

"We're replacing the roof."

"Who authorized this?"

My stomach churns.

"The owner," Ryland says.

"Since the Crimsons passed, who would that now be?" Henry asks.

"That would be me," Mia says behind me.

I turn to her. "Go back inside."

She looks at me in question. Gabriella and Gracie are with her.

"Who would you be?" Henry asks.

I step in front of Mia. "No one. Leave it be, Henry."

"Ma'am, state your name for me," Henry says.

I turn to her. "Don't answer that. Go back inside."

"Beckett, do I need to remind you of your parole requirement to cooperate with law officials."

"It's Mia Crimson," she says quickly. "I inherited the property."

I close my eyes, open them then turn back to Henry.

"Mia? You're alive?"

"Yes."

My stomach is churning.

"Where have you been?"

"At a boarding school up north."

"You plan on staying on the island?"

"Yes."

Hudson comes up behind us and asks, "Henry, we've got a lot of work to do on this roof. Do you need anything here?"

Connor stands next to Hudson with a confused expression.

Henry's eyes become slits. "Nope. You boys make sure your brother doesn't disobey any of his parole requirements."

"That isn't going to be a problem," Ryland answers.

"Let's hope not," he says like he's a friend, but I know it's a threat.

He gets into the car and leaves.

Ryland turns to the girls. "I told you to stay in the house."

"Why did we need to stay in the house when it's only Henry?" Gracie asks.

He knows Mia is alive.

"You shouldn't have come out," I tell Mia.

"He needed to know who the owner was so you didn't get in trouble."

"No, he didn't," I angrily say.

"Beckett!" Hudson shakes his head at me.

Shit. Calm down.

Mia stares at me. "Beckett, what aren't you telling me?"

Don't tell her. You'll put her in more danger.

"Nothing. Let's get the new roof on, Ryland."

Mia squeezes my arm. "Beckett?"

"Go get your phone."

"Why?"

"Please, just go get it."

Her turquoise eyes turn into slits. She removes it from her back pocket.

I hand it to Gabriella. "Program all our numbers in. Call Mom and tell her to get me a second phone."

"You can have your phone—"

"No. You keep this phone. I'll get one. Gabriella, give Mia another lesson on calling and texting."

Gracie protests, "Beckett, what aren't—"

"Jesus. Can you and Gabriella for once just do what we ask of you both?" Ryland barks. "Call Mom to get Beckett a second phone and give Mia another lesson. Do it and stop asking questions."

Gracie puts her hands in the air. "Okay."

"Let's do it on the way to the shops," Gabriella says.

"No. You do it before you go out. Mia, if you need to get ahold of Beckett or anything, call my phone," Ryland says.

Mia looks at him. "Okay."

"Connor, get back on the roof. I need to talk to Ryland and Beckett," Hudson says.

"Seriously? Whatever you're going to say, I can handle it."

"Connor, get your ass on the roof," Hudson yells.

"Asshole," Connor mutters under his breath but goes back on the roof.

I motion to the house. "Mia, please go back inside and work on the cell phone."

She hesitates but finally turns. My sisters follow her.

When everyone is out of earshot, I say, "He knows Mia is alive. They will come after her."

"We need to move quickly," Hudson says.

"What about Skates?" I ask.

"Can't find him. He seems to have disappeared. The Florida State Police have a warrant out for his arrest," Ryland says.

"My contact at the courthouse said his dad was politicking to get the arrest warrant thrown out. His connections are extensive," Hudson informs us.

"How do we know Lòpez and Daniels aren't involved with them?" I ask.

Ryland and Hudson have FBI agents involved. It took seven years before they found two agents they trusted. The FBI wants to take Skates and Henry down for a long list of crimes. They've been building a case so nothing goes south, but my gut tells me that this isn't how this is going to end. Eventually, I'm probably going to have to kill both Skates and Henry. My brothers don't know my thoughts on this. They think I'm on board with the FBI, but the fact is, my confidence in the law enforcement agency hasn't been bolstered by sitting in prison for the last decade when a cop put me there.

Skates warning that he owns me for life plays in my head daily. It's inevitable he's going to come for me and when he does, there are only two endings. It's me or him.

So while I'd love to reinstate my confidence in the law, I'm not holding my breath. And I'm prepared to do whatever it takes to make sure I'm standing and Skates and Henry aren't at the end of this.

"Mia can't go by herself today. Gabriella and Gracie will be at risk, too. Now that Henry knows she's alive, he'll come after her."

Ryland runs his hand through his hair. "The girls are already asking too many questions. We can't put them on house arrest. I'll go with them and take my gun just in case. I'll call a few of the guys off another job to finish the roof."

"Give me the gun. I'll go," I tell Ryland.

"You'll violate your parole. We can't risk anything happening to you."

"Do you even know how to shoot a gun?" Hudson raises an eyebrow.

"No."

Hudson points at Ryland. "You go with the girls. I'll call the crew and send more guys over. Beckett, you come with me."

"Where are we going?"

Hudson's jaw clenches. "You're going to learn to shoot a gun. It's time we get over the excitement of you being back and do what we need to do. You have to know how to protect yourself and Mia."

18

Beckett

Ten Years Ago

The morning alarm rings, but I'm already awake. Today is visiting day, and it's a day I love and hate.

I love seeing my family.

I hate seeing the sadness and pain in their eyes.

But, for the first time, Ryland and Hudson are on the list.

Only two people are allowed, and it's only once a month. My parents came the first time. This is my second time I've been allowed to see my family. Two months of living in hell, and I sometimes wonder how I'm going to make it through fifteen years.

I've not talked to Ryland or Hudson since the day of the shooting, when they caught Clay and I discussing his situation with Skates.

I quickly make my bed, and, when a quarter after six hits, I stand outside the cell. When the guards release us from head count, I take the few shower items I have to my assigned station.

Showering is my least favorite part of the day. The water is cold, two guards stand and watch, and you get two minutes to shampoo your hair and soap your body. In those two minutes, you also have to rinse.

The first week was the worst. Since I was the newest inmate in prison, the others all did what they could to intimidate me. Comments about dropping the soap and asking if I wanted a scrub down, just to see my reaction, were plentiful.

The guards do little to control the heckling. Two minutes felt like forever the first week, but then a new prisoner came in, and he became the new target.

But I've been nicknamed, "pretty boy," and every time I hear it, I think of the guard from the county jail who gave me his lecture. Everything he said was true, and I've spent any opportunity I've had in my cell or out of it trying to gain as much muscle as I can.

I finish my shower, put on a clean orange jumpsuit, and head to the cafeteria. I stand in line, and, when I get to the counter, I pick up a tray of the same food I've eaten every day the past week. Cold porridge of some sort—it could be oatmeal, cream of wheat, or grits cooked the wrong way. I honestly can't decipher it, and I've stopped trying. There is nothing on it, and I've learned to eat it. If you don't eat, you starve, and I need to add muscle, not lose it, so I've learned to get it all down and keep it down.

During meals, you can quietly speak to your table mates, but if it gets too loud, the guards flash the lights and blow a whistle, and you have to stop talking. The same men sit at my table for every meal. They try to speak to me all the time, but I say as little as possible.

"You got guests coming, kid?" Roscoe, a thirty-three-year-old cocaine addict who got eight years for drug dealing, asks.

I grunt and focus on my bowl of mush.

"Who's on your list?"

I ignore him and take another bite of food.

"Cat got your tongue again?" Roscoe says.

"I'm eating," I reply.

"What about a girlfriend. You got a girlfriend?"

A girlfriend. I never had a girlfriend. Clay and I had so many girls after us, we decided playing the field was way better than having to commit to one girl. So that's what we did.

We got whatever we wanted—hand jobs, blow jobs, sex. It didn't matter what we wanted. Girls were more than happy to put out for us and give us whatever we wanted.

But my memories of all the girls I messed around with are starting to fade. It's only been two months, and faces are blurring. The only faces that don't are those of my family, Clay and Mia, and Henry and Skates.

I don't know if I see Clay and Mia or Henry and Skates more. The grief never goes away. My anger, hatred, and desire for vengeance grow. Henry and Skates will get what they have coming to them, even if it takes me fifteen years.

When breakfast is over, I go to the bathrooms and clean the toilets. As one of the newer inmates, I got assigned bathroom duty. In order to change jobs, you have to have a skill useful somewhere else in the prison. My first week inside, I signed up to take GED classes, and I'm on an accelerated path. The teacher for the course told me I'm smart and discussed several degrees that would help me have a different job in prison, so I plan on obtaining my nursing degree after I get my GED in the hopes I can get out of cleaning toilets for the next fifteen years.

I finish cleaning the bathroom and go back to my cell for two hours and study for my GED. The alarm rings, signaling it's time to line up for visitation.

Strict rules exist. You can't touch the visitor, or they can be removed from the list. You get thirty minutes, and that is it, not a second longer.

When I get into the room, I wait five minutes until my family are admitted. Ryland and Hudson both come in, and I clench my jaw, holding back the emotions I feel.

They are clenching theirs as well.

They sit across from me, Ryland on my right and Hudson on the left.

"You doing okay?" Ryland asks.

"I'm dealing."

"You need more money in your account?" Hudson asks.

"No. I'm fine."

"Tell us what happened," Ryland calmly says.

"I can't. You'll all get killed."

Hudson sighs. "We already figured that. But you can trust us, Bro."

Ryland looks around the room then back at me. In a low voice, he says, "The two people we discussed. They did it?"

I stare at him.

"Bro code is in play," Ryland says.

Bro code between the Brooks brothers means that whatever is said goes to the grave and is never repeated. I finally cave.

"S or H did the shooting?" Hudson says.

"Does it matter?" I ask.

"Yes. Tell us."

I take a deep breath. "S."

"Anyone else there?"

I shake my head.

They stare at me for a few minutes.

"You need to keep everyone safe," I tell them.

"We are...we will," Hudson assures me.

Ryland's jaw clenches harder. "I'm going to kill them both."

"No. It's my vengeance to take. You don't want to end up in the cell next to me. I need you both to make sure everyone stays safe. As long as I'm in here, and I keep my mouth shut, everyone will be fine. This runs deeper than only those two. Who knows how far."

Hudson licks his lips. "Then that's what Ryland and I will work on. We'll find out who else is involved in this."

"There is something else I don't understand."

Ryland raises his eyebrows at me. "What's that?"

"Why wasn't I charged with Mia's murder, too?"

They exchange a glance.

"There was a joint funeral. Clay and Mia were cremated, and her grandparents distributed the ashes in the ocean. We weren't allowed to go to it. The Crimsons specifically said to keep the Brooks away," Hudson says.

"Have you all been ostracized by everyone on the island?"

Ryland shifts in his seat. "Don't worry about that. Focus on staying out of trouble in here and watching your back."

"Okay."

"What do you know about S's father?" Hudson says.

I shrug. "Besides the normal info everyone knows, and what we disclosed to you about the packages, nothing."

The bell rings for them to leave. They stand up, and I have to stay seated.

"Hey, Beckett," Ryland says.

"Yeah?"

Ryland and Hudson pound their fists into their chests.

Together we stand, alone we fall.

I pound twice on my heart, clenching my jaw. Vengeance will be mine, and anyone who took part in Clay and Mia's murder will pay. I can only hope that a slow burn in hell before and after their death will be their punishment.

19

Mia

Present Day

Beckett is hiding the truth about the police officer from me, and I don't know why. He looks familiar, and Gabriella and Gracie said he's their dad's best friend, so I'm sure I saw him a lot when I was over at their house as a kid.

Why was Beckett so upset I told him who I was?

And now Ryland is on our shopping trip?

Ryland stands by the front door of the boutique, diligently scanning the store. Every time a new person enters, he puts his hand on his pocket. He is wearing a baggy, button-down shirt. It's the opposite of his form fitting T-shirts I've seen him wear. It strikes me as odd that he changed into it. And why is he here?

Gabriella and Gracie have stocked my dressing room with items. There's a black triangle-top bikini, a coverup, sundresses, shorts, and shirts.

I try everything on and decide to buy two dresses, a pair of shorts, and a shirt along with the bikini and coverup. When I get to the front desk, Gracie and Gabriella are coming out of the dressing rooms with a bigger pile than I have.

"Those are the only things you're getting?" Gabriella asks.

I look at my pile. "That's a lot."

Gracie snorts. "Leave her alone, Gabriella. Not everyone is a shopaholic like you."

Gabriella looks at her pile in the dressing room. "Says the queen of clothes herself."

Gracie shrugs.

They go change and I take my items to the counter. The saleslady with a name badge that says "Veronica" takes my payment then hands me a bag.

"Your tattoo is pretty," I tell her. A twisted heart in vibrant colors is inked near her collarbone.

She touches it. "Thanks."

"What made you think of that? It's really creative."

She rubs it and shifts back and forth on her feet. "Umm...just someone I know has one, and I liked it."

"Well the color is really nice, and the artist did a good job."

She peers at me. "You look familiar."

"I do?"

"Yes." She tilts her head. "Have you visited the island before?"

"I grew up here but moved away a long time ago."

She brushes strands of her blonde hair behind her ear. "What is your name?"

"Mia Crimson."

The blood drains from her face. "Mia...as in Clay Crimson's sister?"

The hair on my neck stands up. "Yes. Did you know him?"

She hesitates. "Yes. We...well, we use to hang out. I'm sorry. I thought you died in the shooting as well?"

I'm going to need to get used to everyone thinking I was dead.

"Still here." I try to sound chipper.

"When did you get back to town?"

"About a week ago."

"Oh. Umm...well, I'm glad to hear you survived," she says quickly.

Okay, this is weird.

"Thanks."

She starts ringing up Gracie's items and says, "Still can't believe Beckett shot your brother. He seemed so nice."

"My brother didn't—"

"Gracie!" Ryland calls out and approaches us.

Veronica's face flushes. "Sorry. Beckett is your brother?"

"Yes," Gracie and Gabriella both say.

"Wait a minute. So you all are hanging out?" She gazes between us all.

"Yes, you have a problem with that?" Gabriella says defensively.

She smirks. "Nope."

"I think we're done here." Gracie turns to leave.

"Agree." Gabriella follows.

Ryland stares at Veronica, his jaw clenched. I assume he's upset at her comment about Beckett as well.

"Ryland, you ready?" I ask him quietly.

"Almost. I just have a quick question for you before I go, Veronica."

She checks him out and bats her lashes at him. "Go on."

"How did you know Clay and Beckett?"

She shifts uncomfortably, hesitates, but finally says, "I met them at the bonfires. Clay introduced me to Beckett a few times."

"You and Clay, you two...dated?"

She scans his body then licks her lips while looking in his eyes. "I wouldn't exactly call it dating. More like, we had a lot of fun together, if you get my drift."

Oh gross. She fucked my brother.

At least she didn't screw Beckett.

My stomach twists.

"Gotcha. Thanks, Veronica. Nice meeting you." Ryland puts his hand on my back to lead me through the store.

"Why did you ask her that?" I ask him once we are out of the store. "And please tell me you aren't interested in her."

He laughs. "Not in a million years. Definitely not my type."

"Okay, then why did you ask her that?"

His face turns solemn. "No reason. She just looks familiar."

I don't know why, but something about it nags at me, and my gut says not to believe him.

WE GO INTO SEVERAL MORE SHOPS. I BUY ANOTHER SUNDRESS, BUT I can't get the incident with Veronica out of my mind, and Gracie and Gabriella are still steaming mad about it.

"I think we should call it a day," I suggest.

"But you didn't get that many things," Gabriella said.

How many things do I need?

"Are you serious?"

"Yes, she is," Ryland says, rolling his eyes.

"I'm happy with what I got. Plus, we can shop another day."

"I think you just want to get back and see Beckett." Gabriella wiggles her eyebrows at me.

My face flushes.

"Gabriella, stop teasing Mia," Gracie says.

She groans. "Okay. We can call it a day. Let's go see how your roof is coming along."

"The roof is coming along fine, but Beckett and Hudson aren't there," Ryland informs us.

"Where are they? They left poor Connor to do the entire roof by himself?" Gracie asks.

Ryland grunts. "No. I had a crew come over to help Connor."

"Poor Connor," I moan.

Ryland taps the wheel. "He's fine. It's good for him."

"Okay, so where did they go?" Gracie asks again.

"None of your business," Ryland says, his jaw clenched again.

A bad feeling fills my heart. He looks at me and then quickly away.

Why is he avoiding looking at me?

"Ryland, drop me off at home so I can put all my clothes in my room," Gabriella says.

"I'll go with you. I need to talk to Mom," Gracie says.

"Mia, you want to come with us?" Gabriella asks.

"No thanks. I have some things I need to do at home."

Ryland drops Gabriella and Gracie off, and we drive down the street. He parks in my driveway. Several cars are there, and a slew of men are on the roof.

"Ryland."

He looks at me. "Yeah."

"Where's Beckett?"

"With Hudson."

"But where? What are they doing?"

"You'll need to ask Beckett."

"Why did he get upset that the police officer knows my name?"

Ryland looks away.

I put my hand on his arm. "Please tell me."

He opens his mouth but then shuts it. He finally says, "Mia, anything you want to know, you need to talk to Beckett."

I look down and see the butt of a gun sticking out of Ryland's pocket. "Ryland, what is that in your pocket?"

He quickly repositions his shirt over it. "Nothing."

"Are you carrying a gun?"

"Yes. I have my concealed weapons permit. I'm not doing anything wrong."

"Why are you carrying it while we're shopping?"

"Because I felt like it."

"Bullshit."

He sighs. "Look, it's my gun, and I'll carry it where I want to."

"Do I need to start carrying my gun with me, too?"

His head jerks to me. "You have a gun?"

"Why do you look surprised?"

"Does Beckett know you have a gun?"

I don't say anything.

"Mia, why do you have a gun?"

"Why do you have a gun?"

"Answer my question, Mia."

"Why? You don't seem to answer any of mine."

Ryland rubs the heel of his hand against his forehead. "Do you really have a gun?" he asks like he doesn't believe me.

I don't say anything and get out of the truck. Ryland jumps out and follows me into the house.

"Mia. Tell me if you're serious."

I go directly to my grandparents' bedroom, open up the safe, and remove my handgun. I turn around, and Ryland is gaping at me.

"Any other questions."

"Yes. Why do you have a gun?"

"You ever been shot, Ryland? Ever watch someone you love take their last breath after being shot?"

Ryland's eyes are wide. "No."

"There's your answer. Now, why do you have a gun?"

His eyes flitter from mine to the gun. "Protection."

"From who?"

"Anyone who wants to hurt my family."

"Who's out to hurt your family?"

He looks away.

"Is that police officer out to hurt your family?"

His face hardens.

"Is he out to hurt me?"

Ryland sighs but still won't look at me.

"Ryland, where's Beckett?"

"You'll have to ask Beckett that," he repeats.

"Just tell me," I cry out.

"Tell you what?" Beckett says through the doorway, then, "Whoa. Mia! What are you doing with a gun?"

I roll my eyes. "I think you have questions to answer first, Beckett."

"I'm going to go check on the roofers." Ryland glances at Beckett and steps past him.

Beckett stands a few inches from me. "Mia, why do you have a gun?" he repeats sternly.

"Where were you?"

"With Hudson."

"Doing what?"

Just like Ryland, Beckett clenches his jaw and looks away.

"Damn it, Beckett. Tell me. I can't handle being left in the dark anymore."

"Mia, can you put that gun away?"

"Fine." I put it back and lock the safe up. "Now, stop keeping me in the dark."

He wraps his arms around me. "I'm not trying to make you feel left out."

"Then tell me what's going on."

He hugs me tighter. "I can't. You have to trust me."

"Tell me why that police officer wants to hurt your family."

He gapes. "Who told you that?"

"I guessed it, and Ryland didn't deny it."

He shakes his head. "I can't."

"You mean you won't."

"Mia, I won't put you in danger."

"Don't you mean more danger?"

Beckett closes his eyes.

I clasp his cheeks. "You have to tell me everything."

"I can't," he whispers.

I shove out of his arms and go out to the kitchen.

"Mia. Don't walk away from me, angry."

I sarcastically laugh. "I wish you would listen to yourself."

"What are you talking about?"

"I'm not stupid. That police officer wants to hurt your family. He wants to hurt me. We're all in danger, and you won't tell anyone what is going on."

"Why can't you trust that there is a reason I can't tell you. I would never do anything to hurt you. I'm trying to protect you."

I glare at him.

"A gun alone isn't going to protect you, Mia. Do you even know how to shoot it?"

"Of course I do."

He freezes.

"Give me a target, and I'll hit the bullseye."

His eyes grow wide. "When did you learn to shoot a gun?"

"At eighteen."

"Why?"

"You really have to ask me that?"

He scans my eyes. "Someone could get hurt. You could get hurt."

Anger flares in my bones. "Stop acting like I'm the thirteen-year-old girl who's innocent and doesn't know anything. I may not be interesting, or good with people, or know how to use a cell phone, but I know how to protect myself."

Beckett cocks his head to the side. "I think you're interesting, and you're good with people. I don't know why you say that."

I roll my eyes at him and ignore his comment. "I may lack social skills, but do you know what a lot of time by yourself does, Beckett?"

His eyes lock into mine. "It makes you think and obsess."

I raise my eyebrow at him, surprised. But I shouldn't be. Beckett's been alone for ten years, too.

"What do you obsess over, Mia," he says quietly.

I look away.

He steps forward and turns my chin so I'm looking at him. "Tell me."

"That night. You. Not being a victim ever again."

"I'm sorry I threw you down. I should have tried to get you out the door."

"You didn't do anything wrong. You tried to save me."

"But I didn't. And it won't happen again."

"What do you mean, Beckett?"

He looks at the ceiling.

My heart races. "Beckett, what are you planning?"

"Nothing."

"You're lying."

He cups my cheeks. "Can you trust me? Please."

As I stare into his eyes, I realize I can't. If he isn't going to tell me the truth of what happened and who's involved, then I never will fully trust him. "No. Not if you can't tell me the entire truth."

"Mia, I can't. It's for everyone's safety."

I push out of his arms and blink back tears. "Then we're done here."

"What do you mean?"

My insides quiver and a tear drips down my cheek. "I can't do this with you."

"Don't say that."

"Then tell me the truth, Beckett," I cry out.

"I can't," he quietly states.

"Then neither can I." I snatch my purse, trot into my grandparents' room, and unlock the safe. Taking the gun out, I double-check the safety is on and put it in my purse.

"What are you doing?" Beckett asks.

"Leaving."

"Where to?"

I brush past him, remove one of the new sundresses from my shopping bag, go into my bedroom, and remove my up-north warm clothes.

Beckett stares at me as I change and repeats, "Where are you going?"

I ignore him, go to the front door, and slip my sandals on.

"Mia! Answer me," he barks.

"I don't know. I need space, and there's too much going on here," I say in a loud voice.

"Why are you taking your gun?"

I spin on him. "Because there's a cop who somehow is involved in my brother's death and you going to prison for ten years. I doubt he's the only one, and word is getting out I'm back. So since you don't trust me enough to tell me, I'll just have to figure out who is good and who is bad."

"Mia—"

I open the door. "Don't, Beckett." I race to my car and get inside it.

He comes after me and tries to open the door, but I locked it.

"Mia!" He pounds on my window.

There are cars parked behind me, so I pull over the lawn and drive away with tears in my eyes. I love Beckett. I've always loved Beckett. But I don't know how I can be with him if he isn't going to tell me what happened and who's involved.

20

Beckett

"Damn it!" I kick the ground as Mia's SUV tears away from me.

I can't do this with you. Mia's words play over and over.

Ryland climbs down the ladder. "Where's Mia going?"

I throw my hands in the air in frustration. "I don't know, but she took her gun."

"What?"

"She said since I'm not going to tell her what's going on that she'll have to figure out who is good and who is bad."

"Beckett, she knows Henry is part of this."

My gut is flipping, but Ryland's words make it flip even more. "I know."

"Maybe you should tell her."

I jerk my head at him. "About what we're planning? No way!"

"No. Not that. Just what happened that night and who was part of it."

This is bad. "Mia shouldn't know anything. It's too dangerous for her."

"Maybe it's more dangerous for her not to know. Besides, it isn't like she is going to tell anyone."

The same fear I always have fills me. "I don't know."

Ryland looks around to make sure no one is around us and says, "What do you remember about a girl named Veronica?"

"Veronica?"

"Yeah. She said she was 'friends' with Clay, hung out a few times. Blonde, nice body?"

"Blonde, nice body...can you be more specific?" I raise my eyebrows. "That sounds like half the girls in our class that were all over Clay."

"Okay, killer body. Said she met Clay at the bonfires, so I don't think she went to your school."

I wrack my mind. Someone who didn't go to our school who Clay met at the bonfires.

I snap my fingers. "There was a girl right before Clay died. I only met her a few times. She hooked up with Clay, probably four or five times. I don't know much about her. Why do you ask?"

"We saw her in one of the shops. She said Mia looked familiar, and she has a twisted heart tattooed on her collarbone."

My eyes widen as chills run through me. "Are you sure it's the same tattoo?"

"Positive."

The tattoo is what Skates has on his forearm. Members of his gang have the same symbol inked on their skin to signal they are loyal to him for life.

I know that tattoo well. Several inmates had it, and over the years, more and more had come into the prison I was at. Skates' gang had substantially grown over the past decade. Gang fights in the prison were common and, as Skates' power grew, so did the pressure to join.

It didn't matter if you were in prison or outside. Skates had plenty of "jobs" for his members to do for him. Recruiting new members was part of the gangs' duty.

"She could have met Skates after everything went down. I don't remember her having a tattoo ten years ago, but I could be forgetting."

"She said she thought Mia had died. There wasn't a death announcement in the paper about Mia. It only said that she was shot. Her grandparents held the joint funeral and told everyone she died, but it was never announced."

"News on the island travels fast though."

"Yes, but she seemed flustered when Mia asked her about her tattoo and also when she found out who Mia was."

"So, you think she played a part in Clay's death?"

Ryland shrugs. "I don't know, but I think it's possible. And if she knows that Clay was involved with Skates and is part of his gang, then she'll tell him Mia is alive and back, if Henry doesn't know where he is and hasn't already told him."

"I need to find Mia. She shouldn't be going anywhere by herself."

Ryland turns and shouts, "Hudson. Connor." He motions for them to come down.

They both climb down the ladder.

"What's going on?" Connor asks.

"Need you to scour the island for Mia. If you find her, call us. We'll take the southern part. Connor, you stay here on the northern part. Hudson, you take Holmes Beach to Cortez Rd."

"Any idea where she might have gone?" Hudson asks.

I scrub my hands over my face. "She just said that she needed space, and there was too much going on here."

"My gut says to check the beaches, both intercoastal and seaside," Connor says. "That's where I'd go if I needed space."

I pat Connor on the back. "Me, too. Good suggestion. Everyone check the beach areas first."

We part. Ryland and I hop in his truck. He hands me his phone. "Try calling her. Tap that icon and type her name."

"I probably should learn to use one of these."

"Yeah, you need to."

I do as he advises. "What now?" I tilt the phone so that Ryland can see.

"Hit the phone number, and it should dial."

I tap the number, and it rings but goes to a canned voicemail message.

"She isn't answering."

"We should put a tracker on her phone. Actually, with everything that has happened today, we should make sure everyone in the family has one."

"How do you do that?"

A smug expression fills Ryland face. "It's pretty simple. I can do it, and none of them would know. I just need to get their phones in my hands."

"Okay, let's do it today."

I look out the window. The water is sparkling, and the green palm trees are softly swaying in the wind.

It's incredible how so much beauty can hold so much corruption.

Mia's words fly through my mind again. *I can't do this with you.*

"Something else going on?" Ryland asks.

"Hmm?"

"You're leg is bouncing all over the place."

I exhale. "Sorry. I think Mia's finished with me."

"Why do you think that?"

"She told me she can't do this with me anymore."

"Because you won't divulge the truth about what happened?"

"I told her it was to protect her, but she thinks I don't trust her."

"Maybe it's time to disclose things. Mia isn't going to run around talking about it."

I close my eyes. "If I tell Mia, I have to share everything about Clay's relationship with Skates. I don't want to hurt her any more than she already is by tarnishing her memory of Clay. I'm not sure what she'll think if she knows he was involved with him."

And she's sure to hate you once she knows the role you played in Clay's problems.

"Yeah, but Clay didn't know what he was getting involved in."

"I know, but still. Isn't it going to hurt her more?"

"Maybe it will help her have a bit of closure."

I snort. "Closure. There's no closure till they are all dead."

Ryland nods. "I'm with you till the end, Bro, but maybe it will be for Mia. She probably needs something. Imagine if one of us died, and you didn't know anything around it, and the person who went to prison for the murder didn't do it."

Maybe Ryland is right.

"Oh, and then you're sleeping with that person who knows the truth, but they won't tell you anything. She kind of has a right to be pissed at you."

I groan. "When did you become full of relationship advice?"

He snorts. "Don't get too excited. I think I scare off most women."

"Why do you say that? Girls always were fawning all over you from what I remember."

He pauses and glances at me quickly. "Let's just say I like all the control in the bedroom. Not every woman is into it."

"What does that mean?"

He chuckles. "Nothing, little brother. Forget I said anything."

"Are you into kinky shit?"

His jaw twitches. "Define what you mean by kinky."

"I just got out of prison. I think you'll have to fill me in."

"Some other time."

What does that mean?

We cross Cortez Road where the bridge dead ends into the island. We drive a few hundred feet and go through the roundabout, past Bridge Street, a small road with shops and restaurants butting up to the bay. "Start looking for her car." He motions to my side of the road where cars are parked to access the beach.

Since it's the off season and a weekday, there aren't as many tourists as there typically are, and the island is pretty dead looking. Parking spaces that would normally be full are empty.

We drive a few miles, and Ryland veers into the parking lot on Coquina Beach.

My heart beats faster, and my breathing becomes heavier.

"You okay?" Ryland looks at me.

Pull it together, Beckett.

"Yeah. Just a lot of memories." I spot Mia's car, which is parked as close to the building where Clay and Mia got shot as possible. "There's her car."

Ryland parks next to it. I sit in the seat for a minute, staring at the building.

"Everything looks the same," I mutter.

"Yes. They don't allow bonfires anymore, but that's about it."

No bonfires, no more murders.

I open the door. "You can go. I'll see you later. Thanks for helping."

"You don't want me to wait?"

"No. I'm good."

"At least take my phone, Beckett."

"You sure?"

"Yes. Let me text Connor and Hudson." He quickly types out a message and sends it off. "Call Hudson or Connor if you need a ride or anything."

"Thanks." I get out of the truck, passing the building where Clay took his last breath, and Mia's and my entire life changed.

Thump, thump, thump, beats my heart against my chest cavity. I should only be looking for Mia, but I can't help myself and look inside the gift shop.

No trace of that night exists. It's as if it never happened.

"Can I help you?" a woman with gray hair and a purple T-shirt asks me.

I shake my head and smile at her. "I'm good, thanks." I turn and spot Mia, sitting in the sand with the waves rolling over her feet.

No one else seems to be around. Minus a few beach walkers, the white sand stretches into the turquoise water, empty.

Quietly, I sit next to Mia and put my hand on top of hers. She turns to me with tear-stained cheeks.

"I don't want to lose you," I blurt out as a seagull lands right near my foot and chirps.

She looks at the water, and a tear rolls down her face and drops onto her thigh.

I scoot closer to her and put my arm around her and kiss her cheek. "What do you need from me? Tell me so I don't lose you."

She looks at me with sorrow-filled eyes. "The truth."

"What if it causes you more pain?"

She digs her foot into the sand. "I know how to deal with pain, Beckett. I've dealt with it my entire life."

But you shouldn't have to.

I tug her closer to me. "I'll tell you what happened, but no one can know about this conversation."

She leans into my chest, and I kiss her head. "I promise."

"I don't want you to think bad about your brother. He didn't know what he was getting into."

She tilts her head up and scans my eyes. "Okay. I won't."

"And I don't want you to hate me for my part in it, but I won't blame you if you do."

Mia peers at me. "Did you pull the trigger?"

"No."

"Then nothing you did is your fault."

I take a deep breath and look away.

She grips my face and moves it toward hers. "It's not your fault."

I nervously scan her eyes. "You haven't heard the truth yet."

"Tell me."

I try to figure out where to begin. I look around to make sure we are still alone. Even though we are, I keep my voice low. "Do you remember Casey Cline?"

"The restaurant owner?"

"Yes."

"Sure, why?"

"He has a son named Skates. Well, his name is Jimmy, but he goes by Skates."

"Did he shoot my brother?"

I swallow the lump forming in my throat. "Yes."

She blinks several times. "Why?"

"He started to come to our football practices and talking to Clay after. I didn't know. I...I..." I exhale and look away as shame fills me.

Mia puts her hand on my thigh. "It's okay, tell me."

I swallow hard. "I used to go do things with girls in the bleachers after practice. Instead of looking out for Clay, I was more worried about girls." I stare at her, waiting for her to be disgusted with me.

"That's not your fault. It wasn't your job to look out for Clay."

"He was my best friend."

"You couldn't have known anything bad was happening. You were a kid on the football field. It should have been safe."

So she isn't going to judge and hate me?

She strokes my cheek. "What did Skates want with Clay?"

"Clay started 'running errands' for Skates. He would go to the parking lot on 75th and Manatee and take boxes of napkins to the five different restaurants that Skates' dad owns."

"And?"

"One day, I was with him when he picked up an order, and I made him pull over on the causeway. I removed all the napkins out of a box, and we discovered heroin taped to each bundle."

Mia puts her hand over her mouth.

"Clay promised he would never run errands for Skates again, but Skates told him that he was in a contract with him for life. He also knew we found the heroin."

Mia takes a deep breath and bites down on her lip.

"That was mistake number two that I made...going through the box."

"Clay's death isn't your fault," Mia reiterates.

"I made more mistakes, Mia."

She looks at me in question.

"Clay and I met with Henry, the police officer who showed up at your house today. I thought because he was my dad's best friend, we could trust him. But he's on Skates' payroll. Ryland and Hudson's sources found out he makes sure nothing happens to Casey Cline or Skates on the island."

She closes her eyes. "You couldn't have known."

My self-hatred for ever trusting Henry fills my soul, gripping me so hard the air in my lungs becomes thick. "Henry told Skates we spoke with him. He was there when both Clay and you got shot."

She cups my face. "You're not to blame for Clay's murder."

Tears fill my eyes. "I am."

"No, you aren't," she cries out.

I close my eyes for a brief moment.

When my eyes open, Mia's, as turquoise as the sea, search mine. "Why did you take the fall?"

"Henry and Skates threatened to murder my entire family and in worse ways than what they did to Clay and you. They didn't want any open murder that could possibly be traced back to them. A closed case meant they were off the hook, and no one was any wiser. Henry knows my family better than anyone. He knew I would sacrifice myself to protect them."

"But you could have told another law enforcement agency."

"You don't understand," I sternly tell her. "This goes deeper than the island police. Casey Cline has deep connections throughout the state police. My entire family would have been killed."

I don't mention to Mia that Skates told me he owns me. That for over a decade I'd lived in fear Skates would demand I do something in prison. Thankfully, I never received any messages, but I know he's waiting for me. My time without being faced with that problem is running out.

The waves come up to our calves as the tide rolls in. We stay quiet for several minutes.

"Do you know why my grandparents hid me? They kept saying it wasn't safe. If they thought you did it, then why did they say that?"

I kiss the top of her head. "I don't know. They never said what wasn't safe?"

"They wouldn't tell me."

"We may never find out. If Henry or anyone ever asks, you need to say you don't remember anything."

"Okay."

"But, Mia, you can't go anywhere without me, Ryland, or Hudson. Now that Henry knows, it's not safe for you to be by yourself."

"I'll take my gun with me."

"No, Mia. We will handle this. I don't need you getting into any trouble with the law."

Her eyes turn to slits. "What do you mean you'll handle this?"

Shut your mouth, Beckett.

I quickly give her a half-truth. "Protecting you. That's all I mean."

She scans my eyes. "That's it?"

I lie to her and nod. She can't know what I will do.

It's a perfectly clear evening, and the sun begins to set. A handful of people arrive with their beach chairs and towels to watch it. I put my arm around her tighter. "I use to think about sunsets in prison and the final few seconds of light after the sun is entirely under the ocean. Clay and I used to stay out here as long as we could, sometimes in the water, sometimes just hanging out. I don't know why I focused on those memories."

"Maybe because they were happy ones."

I kiss Mia's head. "What do you miss most about Clay?"

She looks up at me with tears in her eyes. "Everything."

I blink back my own and finally manage a "Me, too." I move her onto my lap and wrap both arms around her. She rests her head in the curve of my neck.

"I keep thinking about how upset he was that I wore that outfit Gabriella made me put on for the bonfire."

I chuckle. "Remember Gabriella sitting on his lap and flirting with him?"

Mia sweetly smiles. "Yeah. You were so pissed."

"In prison, all I could think was how I would give anything to have Gabriella getting under my skin."

"I missed her, too. And I missed you."

"You did?" I say in surprise.

She lifts her head and strokes the side of mine. "Yeah. Every day."

"Why didn't you hate me?"

She puts her hand over my heart. "I know you, Beckett. In my heart, I know you couldn't have done it."

A tear drops down my cheek, and she wipes it with her thumb then brings her mouth to mine, kissing me as if I'm her everything, and together we can be whole. And I wonder if we can be.

As if she's reading my mind, she murmurs against my lips, "Do you think people get second chances for happiness?"

"I don't know, but the only happiness I've felt in over ten years has been with you."

"Me, too, Beckett." She resumes kissing me.

I want to ask her if she believes in redemption before the act. If you clear your debt before the sin, does it still count? Can you ever erase standing at the gates of hell, choosing to go in, then somehow find your way back?

But I don't. Any chance I have of keeping Mia as mine involves not dying and somehow not getting caught. And she can never know what I'm truly capable of.

21

Mia

The sun hits the ocean, sinking quickly into the sea. Beckett holds me in his arms and kisses my head. Only when it's pitch black, do we get up.

We don't say much on the ride back. When I park, lights are on inside my house.

I clutch my purse, and my pulse increases.

Beckett puts his hand on top of mine. "Mia, you okay?"

"Why are my lights on? Is someone inside?"

"Hudson put automatic timers on to help keep burglars away."

I let out a breath. "Okay." I open the door and step out of the car.

Boom!

Beckett and I are almost to the door when a crack of lightning comes out of nowhere, and I drop my bag on the ground. My gun flies into the bushes.

"Oh shit!" I fumble in the dark to find it but finally do. I put it back in my purse only to see Beckett shaking his head at me.

I ignore him and punch in the code for the lock as the rain starts to pour down.

He comes in behind me, takes my purse, and puts it on the table, then leads me over to the couch, and sits me on his lap. "I don't want you carrying a gun."

I sigh. "I know what I'm doing."

"Mia, that could have gone off and shot you when it fell."

"I had the safety on."

"It doesn't matter. It only has to fall the right way."

"How am I supposed to protect myself, then?"

"You'll be with me, Ryland, or Hudson if you go somewhere. You don't have to worry about it. We will protect you."

I straddle him, face-to-face. "It's not realistic. I've spent hours at the gun range. I'm prepared."

He furrows his brow at me. "Prepared for what?"

To kill anyone who tries to murder you or me.

"To use it if needed."

"Mia—"

I press my lips into his, digging my knees into the couch cushion, pressing as close to him as possible. "Let's change the subject," I murmur.

He groans. "Mia..." But his hands move over my thighs and around to my ass.

I slide my tongue in his mouth, flicking quickly as my panties dampen from grinding on his erection.

"You're distracting me," he mumbles.

I softly laugh. "Do you want me to stop?" I grip his hair and circle my hips on his growing erection.

"The answer will always be no to that question," he murmurs then fists my hair and gently tugs it back as his lips trail down my neck. His other hand skims under my panties and palms my flesh, pressing me into him.

Air fills my lungs in short bursts; my chest rises and falls faster along with his.

Beckett unfastens his pants and lifts his hips with me still on him, quickly shoving them down. "I like you in dresses," he growls as he moves the wet material covering my sex aside and thrusts deep in me.

"Oh God," I cry out as my body tries to accept all of him.

A deep, throaty groan escapes him and echoes in the room. He grips both my hips and thrusts my body on his girth.

The air conditioner, shut off most of the day due to the new roof, hasn't cooled the house yet, and within seconds our clothes are covered with sweat.

Beckett removes my dress then his shirt. Our flesh scorches against the other, shimmering like diamond dust, pulsing with blood and adrenaline.

"You make up for ten years," Beckett murmurs, his warm breath on my neck as he licks behind my ear.

I momentarily freeze. "I've only ever wanted you."

He scans my eyes. "Want me forever."

"I will."

He smashes his lips to mine as if he needs to convince me.

There's no persuasion needed. Beckett is my salvation from every lonely moment, sad thought, or dark time I've had in the last decade. He's the light that makes me believe in the future again.

"Always," I promise him. "Always you."

He releases my bra and sucks on my breasts.

My body hums and quivers.

"Oh God," I moan as his flesh that fills me goes deeper, thrusting into me faster, hitting me in a place I never knew I had before him.

"You feel perfect...so perfect," he says against the O of my lips.

"Oh...Beck...oh...oh...oh," I cry out as I soar into a tidal wave of euphoria, heat sweeping through my cells, crashing into his climax as he starts pumping into me hard, expanding my walls, taking me higher into my trembling state.

I collapse onto the top of his shoulder, tasting the salt of his skin as his arms wrap tight around me, and we continue to oscillate against the other.

A car alarm goes off in the distance, the rain pounds on the new roof tiles, music from the house next door beats loudly, but I still hear the thumping of my heart next to Beckett's.

As chaos blares outside, we still, catching our breath.

"I love you," he whispers, so low I almost don't hear him.

I slowly tilt my head up.

"I do. I've never loved anyone. And you don't have to say it back. I just want you to know." He scans my eyes nervously.

I brush my fingers on the side of his head. "I love you, too. I've always loved you."

"Really?"

"Yes."

He kisses me, and I put everything into it, giving him my heart, trying to show him he is all I've ever wanted or needed.

Beckett's phone rings. I roll off him, and he slides the phone out of his pants pocket. "It's my mom, and I have Ryland's phone."

"Go ahead." I motion for him to pick up.

"Mom, it's Beckett. I've got Ryland's phone." He puts his arm around me and kisses me on the head. "Let me ask Mia. I'll let you know." Beckett hangs up.

I look at him. "Everything okay?'

"Yeah. My mom said she's ordering pizza, and everyone is coming over for a family dinner tonight. They want us to come. You want to go?"

Family dinner. I remember those. A moment of nostalgia and sadness passes through me.

"Mia? We don't have to go if you don't want to."

"No. Let's go. Can I shower and change first?"

Beckett wiggles his eyebrows at me. "Can I shower with you?"

"Is that really a question?"

He cockily grins and picks me up. "Then let's start scrubbing you down."

We shower, I throw on another sundress, and Beckett removes another outfit from the bag Gabriella brought over earlier this morning.

He packs up his dirty clothes and slings the bag over his shoulder.

With butterflies in my stomach, I place my hand on his arm. "Hey."

He raises his eyebrow at me.

"Why don't you leave those here, and I'll wash them for you. Just take the bag empty and bring more stuff over." I bite down on my lower lip.

He bites back a smile. "Are you asking me to stay for a few days?"

I shake my head.

His face drops into a frown, and he furrows his brow. "Oh, sorry. I didn't mean—"

"Move in with me. If you want to," I add quickly.

A huge grin grows on his face. "Yeah?"

"If you want."

He wraps me in his arms. "That's the nicest thing anyone has ever asked me, and I definitely want to."

My insides do a happy dance. "Good."

He brushes his lips over mine. "There is one thing we're going to need to do though."

I look at him in question. "What?"

"Grocery shop. I love my parents, but I don't want to eat with them every night."

22

Beckett

MIA AND I'VE BEEN LIVING TOGETHER FOR A WEEK. I'VE BEEN working for Ryland and Hudson's construction company. Part of my parole is I have to retain a full-time job. While I would love to resume my nursing duties, I'm pretty sure the medical community isn't going to hire a felon convicted of murder, so I'm grateful to be working with my brothers.

Hudson gave me an advance so I could buy groceries and didn't have to mooch off Mia, and I worked a few extra hours a day to make up for it, so today is the first day I'm home before seven.

Ryland drops me off, and I get the mail. There's a large envelope for Mia, but she isn't in the house.

At first, I get panicky, but when I go out back, I see her lying on a sun chair next to the small pool. It's a warm, clear day, and the summer humidity mixes with the ocean breeze. The sound of the waves crashing against the shore can be heard from Mia's backyard, and you can smell the saltwater in the air. She's listening to music with her earbuds in, and I sneak up behind her and run my hands down her arms.

She practically jumps off the chair, and her eyes fly open. Pulling her earbuds out, she throws her hand over her heart. "You scared me half to death!"

I laugh and kiss her. "Sorry. I couldn't resist."

"You're home early."

"Did I interrupt your tanning time?" I lick my lips, checking her out in her black string bikini.

She wraps her arms around me and wiggles her eyebrows. "You'll have to check out my tan lines to tell me if I need more sun."

I run my finger between her skin and bikini tie, and she shivers slightly. "If I weren't so dirty, I'd assess that right now."

She scans me. "I don't think you look that dirty."

"Trust me. I'm dirty."

"I like you dirty," Mia murmurs against my lips.

I chuckle and hand her the envelope that was in the mailbox.

"What's this?" she asks.

I shrug. "I don't know. It looks important though. I'm going to go shower. Should we grill out and have a pool night?"

"Sure. I took chicken out of the freezer. I'm sure it's defrosted by now."

I peck her on the lips. "Okay. I'll be out in a few."

I don't take a long time showering. After, I throw on my swimsuit, I pick up the plate of chicken, grilling utensils, and lighter. I ignite the grill and put the chicken down. When I turn, Mia is sitting up in the lounge chair, staring at the contents of the envelope. Her face is white as a ghost's.

"Mia, you okay?"

She slowly looks up at me, as if in shock.

I sit on the lounger next to her and put my arm around her. "What's wrong?"

She hands me the papers, and chills consume my body.

There are a dozen eight-by-ten, black-and-white photos of Mia over the years, dressed in warm clothes, with snow around her. In some of them, she has a bookbag. In others, she's on campus with headphones in, oblivious anyone is watching her.

A piece of paper has typed:

MIA,

You need to go back. It's not safe for you here. Leave now.

Someone who cares

LEAVE NOW. IS THAT A THREAT?

My stomach flips. "Who knew where you were all these years?"

Her lip quivers. "My grandparents. That's it."

"Someone else knew you were there. How else did they get these pictures?"

"Beckett, I don't know."

I look closer at the envelope. The postmark says *The City of Anna Maria*. "Someone local sent you this. Who could it be?"

Her voice trembles, and she repeats, "I don't know!"

I pull her tight to me. "Okay. It's okay," I say, but I'm trying to convince myself as much as her.

"So someone has been monitoring me all these years?"

The hair on the back of my neck stands up. "Do your grandparents have any close friends on the island? Maybe one of them knew?"

She shrugs. "A lot of them were older. Who knows if they are still alive, and I honestly don't remember them."

"I wonder if my parents would know anyone they hung out with? They were close before the shooting."

Mia jerks her head at me. "Do you think Henry is trying to scare me?"

"I don't think it could be him. How would he have gotten these pictures?"

She tugs on the ends of her black hair. "Let's ask your parents."

But then they are going to ask questions.

"Wait. Let's not ask my parents."

She tilts her head at me. "Why not?"

"If I ask questions about your grandparents, they're going to want to know why I'm asking. Let's go to my house, and we can pull out their photos. See who's in the pictures with your grandparents. My mom always had her camera out when we were little."

"You think the person who sent this will be in your mom's photos?"

"I can't guarantee it, but there's a good chance there are a ton of pictures of your grandparents and whoever they were friends with."

"Aren't your parents going to want to know why we are looking at photos?"

I sit back for a moment, contemplating. I quietly say to Mia, "Let's tell them we are looking for pictures of Clay."

Mia closes her eyes briefly. "Okay."

"I'll put the chicken in the fridge."

"I'll go change." Mia stands up.

I embrace her once more. "We'll figure this out."

Her turquoise eyes fill with worry. "What if we don't? What if this is a warning?"

"Let's just take it one step at a time, okay?"

She takes a deep breath. "All right."

I turn off the grill, throw the chicken in the fridge, change out of my bathing suit and into shorts and a T-shirt. Mia throws on a sundress. We lock up the house and stroll hand in hand to my parents' house.

When we get inside, my mom is cooking dinner. She looks at us and teases, "Did you smell the food?"

"Funny. We came to look at your old pictures."

She tilts her head at us. "They're still in the family room cabinet. What made you interested in that?"

Mia squeezes my hand. "I wanted to see the pictures you might have of Clay."

My mom gives us a sympathetic smile. "Sure. Anything you want to keep, take with you."

"Really?" Mia softly asks.

My mom's grin widens. "Yes. They are yours."

"Thanks, Connie."

Mia and I leave the kitchen and quickly find the boxes tucked away in the big cabinet.

"Wow. Your mom did take a lot of pictures."

"Yep. She annoyed my brothers, sisters, and me."

Mia smiles, but it's a sad one. "I wish we had more pictures. Especially of my mom, Clay, and I together."

"Maybe we'll find one in here."

"That would be nice. I don't have any. I only have a few pictures of my mom and Clay or my mom and me. I know she wasn't around that much, but..." She looks away.

I stroke her arm. "She's still your mom."

"Yeah."

"Well, if it exists, my mom will have taken it," I joke.

We start to dig through the boxes. There are thousands of pictures my mom captured over the years. So many pictures of me have Clay in them. There are also a few with Mia, Gabriella, Clay, and me.

Photos from parties over the years and even events held at their friends' homes are plentiful as well.

About an hour in, my mom comes into the room and sets down a TV tray with two plates of lasagna and garlic bread along with two glasses of water. "Finding anything interesting?"

Mia has a stack of pictures with Clay in them, and one of Mia and me wearing pajamas is on the top. Mia and I look like we are sleeping. Her head is on my lap, and I'm lying on the pillow against the armrest.

My mom holds the picture and starts to laugh.

"What's so funny?" I ask.

"This was on your grandma's birthday. She got a little tipsy, and we said we would watch you and Clay. It was the middle of the night, and Gabriella and Clay were both asleep, and you two wouldn't go to bed. I figured you had way too much sugar. You had been playing video games and fell asleep. When I found you two, I took this picture before I woke you up and told you to get back in bed."

I snap my fingers. "I remember that! You got mad and told me that I was ten and shouldn't be keeping a six-year-old up all night."

"I remember! Beckett snuck chocolate cake out of the kitchen, too."

"He sure did. There was chocolate everywhere." My mom picks up a pile out of the box. She sorts through a few then hands them to Mia. "These are all of your mother. You look just like her."

Mia's eyes light up as she looks at the pictures. "She looks so happy in these."

"Take those if you want."

She looks at my mom and smiles. "Thanks."

"Sure, sweetie." She pats Mia's hand and stands up. "I'll leave you both to it. There's more food in the kitchen if you want seconds."

"Thanks, Mom."

I scoot closer to Mia, and we look at the pictures from the box my mom gave us. Her mother is in many of them.

Who is that with her mother? He looks familiar.

"Can I see those for a minute?"

"Sure." She hands me the pictures.

Is that...no, it can't be. But it is. It's him.

He's younger, and I haven't seen him in over ten years, but sure enough, it's him. Picture after picture of Mia's mom also has Casey Cline. Her mom looks almost identical to how Mia looks now but slightly younger. I'm guessing she isn't even in her twenties. Casey, with his salt-and-pepper hair, seems to be nearing fifty.

Why do they look so cozy?

"What are you looking at, Beckett?"

I scan Mia's eyes. "Is it just me, or do your mom and Casey Cline seem kind of cozy?"

"That's Casey Cline? As in Skates' dad?"

I swallow hard. "Yes."

Mia sifts through the pictures and angrily says, "Why is he in all these pictures with my mom?"

"I don't know."

Silence fills the room. She finally says, "My mom died from a heroin overdose. Casey Cline is a heroin dealer. Do you think he was her dealer?"

"There's a good possibility."

She blinks tears. "So Casey Cline not only murdered my brother, but he also killed my mother?"

"I don't know, but it's possible. But, Mia, don't you think we should ask my mom about their relationship? See how your mom is focused on him in this picture. And he seeems like he's flirting with her in this one."

"Okay, that's gross. He has to be double my mom's age."

"Let's go talk to my mom." I stand up, take her hands, and tug her up off the ground.

Mom and Dad are finishing up dinner when we get into the kitchen.

"Mom, what can you tell us about Mia's mom and Casey Cline?"

My mother chokes on her food. After coughing like a maniac, she takes a big sip of water.

"Why are you asking this?"

"All these pictures of Mia's mom have Casey in them, and they look pretty cozy." I lay the pictures out on the table.

My parents exchange a glance. I've seen it before. It's the *oh crap, the kids know something we don't want them to know* glance.

Do my parents know Casey is involved with heroin? It's common knowledge Mia's mom died of an overdose, but no one I'm aware of knows about Casey's drug business.

"Please tell me whatever you know," Mia quietly asks.

My parents look at each other again.

"Mom!"

She jerks her head at me. "What?"

"Tell us what you know."

She sighs and drags the chair next to her away from the table. "Sit down, Mia."

Mia looks at me, almost scared, but sits. I take the seat next to her and put my arm around her. She leans back against my chest. We wait for my Mom to talk.

She fidgets with her hands, which is what she does when she's nervous. My dad's leg is bouncing under the table, which is what he does when he's anxious.

What do they know about their relationship?

"Mia, your mom and Casey...well..." She blows out a big breath. "They had a secret affair."

"Secret affair?" Mia mutters.

My mom nervously glances at my father again. "Your mom was only in high school and got pregnant. She wouldn't tell anyone who the father was, and between Clay's birth and yours is when those pictures were taken. I think your mom might have been eighteen or so..."

Mia looks at me with the color draining from her face.

"Your grandmother figured it out from these same photos and

confronted your mom and Casey. They denied the affair, but then your mom got pregnant again about a year later with you."

"Wait. Are you saying that Casey is Mia and Clay's father?"

My mom only stares at us. My dad's leg bounces faster.

"No," Mia whispers.

My mom holds her hand, and I tighten my arm around Mia.

"Your mother never confirmed it. There is no evidence to prove that, and Casey has always denied the affair," my dad tells us.

"But you don't believe that? You think they had an affair?" I ask.

My mom takes a deep breath. "I think the chances are high."

"You think he's my father?" Mia asks.

My parents look at each other, and my mom quietly says, "I think it's very possible."

Mia turns slightly green and suddenly jumps up and runs to the bathroom. I run after her and hold her hair back as she throws up in the toilet.

When she's done, she washes her hands and rinses her mouth out and spins. Her eyes are bloodshot from being sick, and a few tears fall down her face.

I hold her in my arms.

"Do you know what this means if he's my father?" she cries.

"Yes."

I don't need to say anything more. Casey Cline played a role in the murder of his own son.

"Skates is my half-brother," Mia whispers then turns and starts throwing up again.

23

Mia

I'M TRYING TO LOOK AT JOB OPENINGS, AND ALL I CAN THINK about is the possibility I'm related to Skates and Casey Cline. I finally shut my computer and remove the photos out of the drawer that I brought from the Brooks' house. A picture of my mother and Casey sharing what they probably thought was a secret glance makes my stomach churn for the millionth time.

My entire life, I've wanted to know who my father was and if he even knew I existed. *If he did know, would he want a relationship with me? Was there still time to have one?*

The idea Casey Cline could be my father makes me wish I was still in the dark.

How could she have been with him? He was so much older than her.

The eight-by-ten photos that were anonymously mailed to me are sitting on the counter, and I pick up one that has me in it when I was around the same age as my mother in the photos. I lay them side by side.

My mother and I look almost identical. There is no resemblance to Casey that would give me any clue if he really is my father.

Do I look anything like Skates?

I don't remember the face of Skates when he shot me. The dark room made it hard to see. I remember his blue eyes, but that is it. My mother and Casey both have blue eyes.

I open up my laptop and go to Instagram. I don't have an exciting account and didn't have a phone to be able to post anything, but I created it to try and figure out how to apply makeup and look at what current fashion trends are, which I was able to view on my laptop. It didn't help me, and I still am clueless when it comes to that, but nonetheless, I have an account.

I type in the search bar @skates, and after about a half hour of searching, I come across it. His id is @skatesami, and as soon as I see him, I know it's him. He has the same eyes as in my memory. A scar runs down his cheek. Unlike Clay and me, he has blond hair, just like his father.

The chill that runs through my body intensifies when I see the tattoo on his forearm—a skateboard with the twisted hearts gang symbol above it.

Veronica's laugh and, "I wouldn't exactly call it dating. More like, we had a lot of fun together, if you get my drift," plays over and over in my mind.

I look back at the tattoo on the Instagram picture. It's the same.

It can't be a coincidence. *When did she get involved with Skates? Was it before or after my brother's death?*

I continue scrolling through Skates' feed, and my pulse increases. Veronica is in multiple photos over the years with Skates, kissing him, making faces with him, doing other things that people who are romantically together do.

Tapping on one of the photos, I see she is tagged, and I click on it. Her feed displays more pictures of Skates and her. It takes a lot of time, but I finally get to the bottom of her feed. Her entire timeline has Skates in it, but she posted the first photo eight years ago.

They could have gotten together before or after Clay died.

You need to find out.

Despite my promise to Beckett to stay at the house or only go somewhere with him or his brothers, I remove my gun out of the safe and toss it in my purse.

It doesn't take long to drive to the shop where Veronica works. I'm pretty sure she is there because her Instagram story had a video of her complaining she had to go into work with a hangover.

With a racing heart, I pull into the parking lot. I get out of the car and go into the shop.

It's a large store, but no one seems to be in it except Veronica. Since it's off season, it isn't abnormal. When I walk in, she has her back to me and is singing to the music, putting sale stickers on some T-shirts.

I slowly make my way to the other side of the rack, and she jumps.

"Jesus, Mia! You scared me!"

I don't say anything and stare at her.

What now, Mia? You should have planned this better.

"Can I help you with something?"

"What was your relationship with my brother," I blurt out.

She rolls her eyes. "We had fun together."

"What does that mean?"

She looks me up and down. "I think you can use your imagination."

My stomach flips.

"Did you love him?"

She laughs so hard tears come out of her eyes. Wiping them away, she says, "Of course not. We were teenagers, and I'm pretty sure we both were seeing other people."

So she could have been seeing Skates then. "How did you meet him?"

"At a bonfire. Why do you want to know this?"

I shift back and forth on my feet but finally say, "I'm trying to figure out more things I didn't know about him."

"Why?"

"Because he's my brother."

Veronica peers at me. "We had fun. It wasn't serious. I can't tell you much more than that." She turns and strolls toward the counter.

"Were you sad when he died?" I blurt out again.

She keeps moving, and nonchalantly says, "Sure."

Wow. That sounds convincing. She was sleeping with him, and it sounds like she didn't care about him at all.

"Were you there the night it happened?"

She spins back to me. "No."

"Why not? If you and Clay were seeing each other, wouldn't you have been there?"

Veronica steps closer to me. "I told you we weren't serious. And what does that have to do with anything?"

My pulse inches up. "I don't know. I'm just curious. So, why weren't you there?"

"How would I remember? It was over ten years ago."

You would remember where you were the night someone you were sleeping with got murdered, even if it was casual, wouldn't you?

"Really? You don't remember why you didn't go?"

Her eyes become slits. "Whatever you're trying to dig up, I'm sure doesn't exist. Beckett killed Clay. No one knows why, end of story."

So, she does know something.

"Who said I was trying to dig something up?"

She tilts her head at me. "Aren't you?"

"No." I try to sound convincing and decide to change the

subject. Her tattoo is half covered with her shirt. "How long have you had your tattoo?"

"A long time."

"Did you have it when you knew my brother?"

Silence ensues as we look at each other.

Focus Mia.

She peers at me. "Why are you asking me this?"

"Curious, that's all. My brother didn't date any girls with tattoos as far as I can remember."

She twists her hair. "I got it shortly after he died. And we fucked, we didn't date. Stop acting like we had a relationship. It was fun, that's it."

Shortly after. So she could have known Skates when she was with my brother.

Another customer enters the store.

"If you'll excuse me, I need to get back to work." Veronica turns and leaves me.

I pretend to look at a few articles of clothing, sneaking glances at her. She's behind the counter, turned slightly away from me, brows furrowed, and seems to be in a text conversation with someone.

Another co-worker comes in, and Veronica starts talking to her, giving her instructions on what needs to be done for the day.

She must be getting off her shift.

When I leave the store, I park in the lot adjacent to the shop. Within fifteen minutes, Veronica steps outside, and a man driving a black convertible Porsche pulls up to the curb. He has gray hair and is wearing sunglasses. I can't see the front of his face very well, but she gets into the passenger side, and they leave.

The island traffic is sparse, so I'm able to stay back and easily watch where they go. He drives down Gulf Drive and out of the city of Anna Maria and into Holmes Beach, stopping at the marina. I drive past it and veer into a parking lot catty-corner to it.

Both Veronica and the man get out. I'm several hundred yards away, so my vision isn't totally clear, but they go directly to a dock that has a brand-new boat with several cabins in it. It's not a full yacht, but I'm guessing it's worth at least several million.

The cabin door opens, and Henry steps out. I catch a glimpse of a man with blond hair inside, but I can't see his face.

I'll bet it's Skates.

Henry exchanges words with Veronica and the gray-haired man, and then he climbs out of the boat, onto the dock, and heads to his police car I hadn't noticed. He drives in the opposite direction.

Veronica steps into the cabin and passionately kisses the man standing inside, while the gray-haired man turns and gets back off the boat. As his Porsche passes me, I duck down in my seat and tug my cap over my eyes further. He's at a stoplight, and I catch a glimpse of his face. He's older than the pictures, but it's definitely Casey Cline.

The light changes green, and he speeds off. I turn to look back at the boat, but it's already left the dock.

I can still see Casey's Porsche, so I follow him.

Why are you following him, Mia?

I continue to drive down the island, barely noticing the blue of the ocean through the houses and condominiums fronting it. The Porsche maneuvers down a side street, and I neglect to notice I'm getting closer, when I need to stay back. We go down several residential roads, and I'm so focused on the Porsche that I miss the *dead end* sign.

At the end of the street, Casey pulls into a driveway, quickly reverses then passes me and turns his car in the road so it's blocking any chance I have to turn and leave.

My pulse beats in my neck, and my stomach flips. I try to hide under my hat again, but it's no use.

Shit, shit, shit! What am I going to do?

He gets out of the car, angrily knocks on my window, and tries to open my locked door. Out of fear, I yell, "Stop." He freezes as the blood drains from his face. "Mia?"

I don't say anything, just stare at him. *How does he know who I am?*

"Mia," he says louder then tries to open my door again.

"Move your car," I order him.

"Open the door, Mia."

"How do you know my name?"

"Open the door," he repeats, trying the handle again.

"Stop! You're scaring me," I cry out.

He releases the handle, takes a step back, and puts both hands in the air. "I'm not here to hurt you. Unroll your window at the very least."

I take a deep breath and pick up my purse, putting my hand inside it and on my gun. With my other hand, I put the window halfway down.

"Don't come any closer," I tell him with a shaky voice.

He nods. "Okay."

I scan his eyes.

"Why were you following me?" he asks.

I don't say anything.

He closes his eyes. "You know, don't you?"

"Know what?"

Opening his eyes, he scrubs his face. "You look just like her."

"Don't talk about her," I snap at him with tears in my eyes.

"Mia, park in the driveway, and let's go in my house and talk." He points to a large house, overlooking the bay.

I shake my head.

"I loved her," he says, almost absentmindedly.

Disgust seeps through me. "You loved her? She was a child!"

He looks away. I think it's shame, but he turns back. "Age doesn't mean anything. We both loved each other."

I blurt out. "Are you my father?"

"Yes."

Tears fall down my cheeks. Years of anger, sorrow, and grief fill my lungs, suffocating my airways, thicker than the humidity that stifles the summer air.

He steps closer, and I clutch the gun inside my purse. "I wanted to tell you. But your grandparents—"

"My grandparents knew?" I gape at him.

His chest rises and falls as he inhales a deep breath. "We were good friends. They didn't want me around after they discovered our affair."

"So you let my brother and I be fatherless...parentless, even after she died?"

He closes his eyes as if in pain. "I did the best I could."

"The best you could? You did nothing for us," I cry out.

He steps right next to the window. "That's not true! I protected you all these years!"

I clutch the gun harder, my thumb on the safety, wanting to shoot him. Disgust consumes me, ripping through my core and crushing any sense of right versus wrong. "You protected me? How exactly is that? Everyone on the island believed I was dead!"

Casey nervously scans my eyes. "That was my doing."

My gut drops lower. "What?" I whisper.

"Mia, come inside the house."

"You sent me away?"

"It was for your safety."

"My safety?"

"Mia, please, just come inside," he tries again.

All the years of grief shatter me all over again, and it's as if I finally have someone to blame. My mother's drug addiction and overdose had to be connected to him. Clay's murder, at the hands of his son and my half-brother, leads to him. The confusion and blame I felt toward Beckett, who lost over ten years of his life and is still looked upon as a murderer, involves him. A decade of sorrow and loneliness I endured, creating the antisocial outcast that I feel like, is because of him.

I whip off my seat belt, throw open the door and jump out, as my purse falls to the ground. Aiming the gun, with tears falling down my cheeks, I glare at him. "Whatever you are going to say, you can say it right here."

His eyes go wide. "Mia, what are you doing with a gun?"

"Stop asking me questions," I yell and step closer to him.

He takes a step back and puts his arms out to the side. "Okay."

"Did you send me the pictures?"

He looks away.

"Answer my question," I scream.

"Yes."

"Why?"

"It's not safe for you to be here."

"You're the cause of everything."

"What does that mean?" he asks.

My chest heaves with sobs. "You killed her. You murdered him. Now you want to do the same to me."

"What?" He looks at me in surprise. "No, Mia. You have—"

"Mia!" Beckett's voice tears through the air. I turn my head. Ryland's truck is behind Casey's Porsche, and Beckett is jumping out.

I shake the gun at Casey. "You deserve to die."

"Mia!" Beckett yells again, but I don't look at him this time.

"You don't know the truth."

"You're a liar," I seethe.

"Mia, give me the gun," Beckett says.

As if in a trance, I don't look at him. "No."

Casey's blue eyes drift from Beckett to me. "She has it wrong."

"Don't tell me I have it wrong," I scream.

Beckett's arm goes around me, and he tugs me into his chest. "Give me the gun, Mia," he murmurs in my ear.

A lifetime of pain overcomes me, and I sob harder. "He deserves to die," I cry as the gun shakes.

"Shh." He runs his hand down my arm until it's covering mine that's holding the gun. "I've got it. Let me have it," he quietly says, wrapping the other part of his body around me, so my face is in his chest.

"I'll take it," Ryland's voice says, as the weight of the gun leaves my hand, and Beckett holds me tight as I weep harder.

"Shh," he whispers over and over, kissing the top of my head.

"Everything's his fault," I bawl.

I don't know how long I stand in the street, crying in Beckett's arms. When my tears slow, Beckett leads me to the passenger side of my SUV. "Let's go home."

Somewhere during my outburst, Casey moved his Porsche, and Ryland turned his truck around and is standing outside his vehicle, watching over us.

Beckett belts me in my seat and gets in the driver's side. He turns the car around and passes Ryland, who gets into his truck.

During the ride home, Beckett holds my hand. We don't say anything, and I stare out my window.

When we get home, Ryland parks next to Beckett's side of the car. I go into the house and curl up in my bed, trying to comprehend what would have happened if Beckett hadn't shown up.

How did he even know I was there?

My head is buried in my pillow when Beckett comes in. He sits on the edge of the bed and strokes my hair. I roll over to face him.

His hair is blonder from working in the sun, and his skin is as bronze as when we were kids. Eyes that can morph between hardened and warm are now full of worry and sympathy.

"You've always been beautiful," I blurt out.

A small smile plays on his lips. He brings them to mine and kisses me, pulling me into our world of peace, understanding, and love. It's the place where everything's right and nothing wrong exists, where unspoken promises are created and hope lives.

Beckett pushes his forehead to mine, slowly opening his eyes. "Mia, we have to talk."

I put my lips back on his. "Let's not."

He groans but stops my kisses and positions me on his lap. "You need to tell me everything that happened."

I sigh. "I don't want to talk about it."

He brushes my hair behind my ear. "I know, but you have to, so start talking."

24

Beckett

DARKNESS SETS IN AS MIA FINISHES TELLING ME WHAT HAPPENED. She's been sitting on my lap for over an hour, and, from time to time, tears fall down her cheeks.

I'm trying to stay calm knowing that Mia's spoken with Veronica and that she's probably in bed with Skates.

But now we know Skates is hiding on his dad's boat out in the ocean.

As much as I want to call Ryland and Hudson and put my plan in motion, I don't. Mia needs me right now.

"You promised me you wouldn't go anywhere without one of us. If Ryland hadn't installed the tracker on your phone, who knows what would have happened," I softly scold Mia.

"He did?"

"Yes. He put it on every phone my family owns. Don't be mad. It's for everyone's safety."

She hesitates but then says, "I'm not mad. I understand. But I took my gun."

How do I get it through to her that she shouldn't be carrying a gun?

"Which I also asked you not to do," I remind her. "You could have been shot or arrested today."

She closes her eyes, and another tear escapes. "I'm sorry. Once I discovered Veronica's Instagram with Skates, I wasn't thinking. Don't be mad at me, Beckett."

"I'm not mad at you, but promise me you won't do that ever again."

Hesitantly, she finally agrees.

"I mean it, Mia. I don't want you in prison or dead."

More tears fall. "Okay."

I sigh and hold her closer to me. "Are you all right? That was pretty intense with Casey."

She takes a shaky breath. "Everything is his fault. He may not have pulled the trigger on Clay and me, but he's just as much to blame. And now he's trying to scare me enough to leave with those pictures."

Something hasn't been sitting right with me since Mia told me Casey sent the pictures and how Casey claimed that Mia had it wrong.

"Mia, why do you think Casey sent you to Michigan? If he wanted to hurt you, he would have done it instead of sending you away."

She snaps her head away from my chest and glares at me. "He did hurt me. He ruined my life by sending me there." Her turquoise eyes, full of pain, stare at me.

I stroke her cheek. "I know you hated being there, but if he wanted you dead, you would be. It doesn't make sense to me."

She looks away. "Why does he have to be my father? And that makes Skates my brother." A new round of tears flies out of her eyes. "I have their evil blood in me."

I turn her chin toward me and sternly say, "No, you don't. There's nothing about you that's evil or bad."

"There has to be. He's my father." Her face crumples in pain.

I cup her cheeks. "It doesn't matter. You're warmth and light. Everything good in life is in you."

She sniffles. "It can't be."

"Nonsense." I lean into her and firmly hold her head, parting her lips with mine, trying to show her nothing she is thinking is true.

"How can you still want to even be near me?" she whispers, her lips trembling against mine.

I push my forehead against hers. "You're my everything. "

"It's their fault you lost ten years of your life."

"That has nothing to do with you."

"How can it not?" She closes her eyes in pain.

"It doesn't. You aren't them."

She opens her eyes as drops of tears turn into streams again.

I quickly turn and flip her onto the bed. My face hovers over hers. My hands grip the sides of her head. "Listen to me, Mia. You are innocent of all their decisions. Nothing they have done is your fault. When I say that you're my everything, I mean it."

She takes a shaky breath and sniffles. "I hate myself right now, knowing I'm part of them," she whispers.

"Shh, don't say that. You aren't part of them."

"I am. You can do better than me."

My heart breaks, seeing the pain she's going through. She's already been through a lifetime of sorrow, and she shouldn't think any less of herself based on who her DNA comes from.

I brush my lips against hers and stare into her ocean-colored orbs. "That's not true. I need you like the air I breathe. When I'm away from you, all I can think about is you. Nothing will ever change that." I crush my mouth to hers, ravaging her tongue, stealing her warm breath, taking all I can but giving everything I have to her.

Her hands grip my shoulder muscles, and her legs widen until my growing erection is pressing into her heat.

With my blood pumping in all my veins, I lick behind her ear, then suck on her lobe before murmuring, "You make me forget bad exists."

"Make me forget, Beckett," she sniffles out.

The rising and falling of her chest presses into mine. I quickly remove her clothes as she releases my shirt and pants.

Her hard nipples and the fullness of her soft breasts smash my pecs as my lips and tongue glide down her neck. "I love everything about you," I mumble then flick my tongue on her nipples before tracing the edge of them.

How did I ever exist without her?

She begins to whimper quietly, gripping my hair and widening her legs into a V and bucking her hips.

I flip on my back, rolling her on top of me and guiding her down so I slide through her tightness.

I groan as her wet heat surrounds me, and her walls grip me in pleasant torture.

"Oh God," she whispers as she always does whenever I first thrust inside her, her eyes briefly closing as her mouth forms into a shaky O.

I clutch one of her hips and circle her clit with my other hand, watching the flush grow throughout her face.

"Beckett," she breathes, her chest rising and falling quicker, palming my stomach.

"I got you, my angel," I murmur, mesmerized by every breath, sound, and facial expression she makes.

She's so beautiful. How did she become mine?

"Please...oh...oh..." She tilts her head back; her soft black hair brushes my hand that's on her hip.

My thumb circles faster and harder.

"Don't stop...oh God...Beckett," she cries out as her body convulses on top of me, clutching my cock, shooting currents of heat through every cell in my body.

"Fuck, you feel good," I growl at her.

Her eyes roll, and she cries out, oscillating harder.

When her climax passes, I sit up, cupping her head and urgently sticking my tongue in her mouth.

She wraps her arms around me, and I'm in the place I love most—flesh to flesh, limbs pretzeled, the smell of sex and Mia's scent flaring in my nostrils.

"Hold me tighter," I murmur between kisses, never wanting her to let me go and caressing the soft skin on her back.

Mia grips me harder and grinds faster.

"Yeah, angel, do that," I praise her as my heat burns hot throughout me.

"This?" she whispers, gyrating.

"Oh, fuck. Yes. Do that."

How is it possible she was a virgin before me?

Mia knows just how to ride me. My memories may be faint from anyone before her, but no one ever made me feel the way she does. She has no idea how much she turns me on. And that's before she shatters on me. Nothing on earth is better than her unraveling.

Salt from her skin hits my tongue as I lick and suck on the curve of her neck.

"Oh God...Beckett...oh..." she moans and arches her back into me, slowly, then with more intensity, spasming on my cock.

My balls shrivel and nerves sit on the edge of euphoria. I grip her hips and frantically thrust faster. "Come with me, angel," I growl, trying to hold out until she unhinges completely.

She cries out my name, and her eyes roll before she buries her face in my neck. I pump hard into her, groaning as adrenaline bursts all my atoms, sending me flying into paradise.

As we still in the aftermath, trying to fill our lungs with air, I don't loosen my arms around her. Her nails are still digging into my back muscles, and I stroke her head. I raise my head out of her neck. Staring into her eyes, I tell her, "You're mine, and I'm yours, Mia. Every part of you, I want. Your blood, my blood, it doesn't matter. What matters is us. Together. Do you understand me?"

Her eyes fill with tears. "Yes."

"Good." I kiss her some more. "I don't want you going anywhere without me, Ryland, or Hudson. At least not until I say."

"Why? What are you going to do?"

"Nothing," I lie. "Just promise me."

She bites her lip.

"Promise me, Mia."

"Okay. I promise."

"And no more carrying your gun. Put it in the safe and keep it there."

She closes her eyes and sighs.

I cup her face. "Mia, nothing good is going to come from you carrying your gun. I don't want you in prison or dead. Promise me."

"Fine. I promise."

"Thank you." I return to kissing her but can't ignore the uneasiness in my gut. Casey and Henry know that Mia is fully aware of how Clay died and that is dangerous.

I look Mia in the eyes. "You can't tell anyone else that you know how Clay died."

She looks at me in panic. "I-I'm sorry. I didn't think."

I pull her into me, stroking her head. "Shh. I know. It's okay. It'll be okay." But I know it's the furthest thing from the truth.

Forever. I want her forever, and I need to figure out how to end the danger that's surrounding us without going back to prison or getting killed.

25

Beckett

RYLAND ARRIVES TO PICK ME UP FOR WORK.

I dip down to kiss Mia. "Remember your promise to me."

"I know. I'll stay here and work on my tan, promise."

Licking my lips, I grin at her. "I'll make sure to check your tan lines out tonight."

She laughs and presses her warm lips against mine once more.

I remove my lips from hers. "I've gotta go."

"Should we grill out tonight?" Mia asks.

"Sure." I kiss her on the head and leave.

When I open the door, the thick summer air hits me in the face. I get in Ryland's truck, and he hands me a cup of coffee.

"Thanks."

"How's Mia?" he asks, concerned.

I sigh. "Not great but better than last night. She's sick over Casey being her father and is struggling. I made her promise to keep the gun in the safe and not to go anywhere without one of us, but that's only going to work for so long. I don't like her being by herself while I'm working, either."

He arches his brows. "Understandable."

I blurt out, "Skates is hiding out in the gulf in one of Casey's boats."

Ryland scrunches his face. "How do you know?"

"Mia saw him at the marina yesterday."

He takes a big breath. "That will be good information to get to Lòpez and Daniels."

"Sure."

"Why don't you sound happy about that?" Ryland looks back at the road.

I sigh. I can't tell Ryland I believe this is only going to end with Skates and Henry dead, or me, or all three of us, so I tell him a half-truth. "It's been three years since you started working with them. I don't have a lot of faith in their abilities or the law that didn't protect me."

Ryland shakes his head at me. "Beckett, Henry's corrupt. That doesn't make the law corrupt."

"No, but there are more people involved than just Henry who have the law on their side."

"And that is why it's taking time."

I angrily say, "We are running out of time. Casey and Henry both are aware that Mia knows the truth. How long do you think it's going to be before they try to harm her?"

Ryland's jaw clenches. "Let's hope that doesn't happen."

"Well I need more than a 'let's hope.'"

"There isn't anything we can do besides what we're doing unless you send Mia away."

Send her away as Casey did?

"She wouldn't do that. And that is another thing I can't—" I stop talking. Ryland parks on the job site. Casey is standing outside his Porsche, leaning against the door.

"What's he doing here?" I mutter and glare at him.

"Easy there, Beckett. You need to stay calm," Ryland advises.

Before the vehicle has stopped, I'm jumping out of the truck. "What do you want?" I bark at him.

He puts his hands in the air. "I just want to talk."

"Why?"

Ryland has parked and is quickly at my side.

Casey looks at Ryland then back at me. "Can we talk privately?"

"Whatever you're—"

"Go, Ryland. I got this."

"Beckett—"

I spin on him and point to the house we are working on. "Go." I don't need Casey to be aware that Ryland knows what happened that night.

He hesitates but goes into the house.

When he is out of earshot, I quietly say to Casey, "You need to leave Mia alone."

His face falls. "I would never hurt her."

I look at him in disgust. "And why would I believe you?"

"I kept her safe all these years."

"And why was that?"

"She's my daughter."

"And Clay was your son," I fire at him.

He blinks back tears. "Yes, I know."

Why is he getting emotional as if he cares?

"You made Mia's grandparents send her away?"

"Yes."

"Why?"

"So she could be safe, and she needs to leave. It's not safe for her here."

"Because you don't want anyone around who knows the truth of what you are involved in."

Shame fills his face and catches me off guard. "I never meant to get involved in that."

I scoff at him. "Then why are you?"

Casey closes his eyes as if in pain, slightly bobbing his head. When he opens them, he stares at me. "I didn't have a choice."

My blood boils. "You didn't have a choice? We all have a choice."

"My son—"

"The one that's alive or dead?" I angrily sputter as all the years of pent-up grief and rage boil within me.

Once again, he looks remorseful. "Alive."

I glare at him.

"He started selling and running things through my restaurants. I didn't know it was happening until it was too late, and I either had to comply, or I wouldn't be standing here."

What a coward.

"Skates would have killed you?"

He looks at the sky then back at me. "No, the drug lord he worked for at the time."

"At the time?"

He hesitates but quietly scans my eyes and says, "He took care of him. It's why the Twisted Hearts have multiplied so quickly."

Skates killed the drug lord he worked for? Holy shit.

"Mia's mom and brother are both dead, and you're as much to blame as them."

He sighs. "I know. Every day I think about it."

Does he want me to feel sympathy for him?

"What's the purpose of this visit?"

He shifts. "Mia needs to leave. She's all I have left that's good."

My pulse shoots up, and I poke him in the chest. "Mia is not yours. She never has been and never will be. Do not ever claim her as yours again."

He sighs and puts his hands in the air again. "Okay. But you need to get her away from the island."

"What are they planning?"

"I don't know. But it isn't safe. You and I both know that."

I hate him and everything he stands for, but he is right. Mia isn't safe here.

"Then you need to find out what they are planning."

"I can't. They don't tell me anything until after the facts."

"You're such a coward."

He glares at me. "Do you think I like having to live like this?"

"Honestly, I don't know how you live with yourself. You fed Mia's mom drugs and she overdosed, you—"

"Is that what Mia thinks?" he gasps.

I jerk my head back and furrow my brows at him. "Of course. She knows the truth."

"That's not the truth."

"Then what's the truth?"

He looks away, closing his eyes.

"You better start talking," I sneer at him.

He turns back to me with tears in his eyes. "Mia's mom and Skates were the same age. They went to school together and were friends. Skates got her into using and then dealing. I loved her. I tried everything I could to get her off that junk, but she couldn't stop. I even paid for her to go to rehab several times."

As I look at Casey Cline, I realize he's a pathetic waste of space. The man I feared for so many years is nothing but a coward who cares more about his own safety than the people he supposedly loves.

I lean into his face, and his eyes turn to fear. "You're a sad existence of a man. How many people have died because of what you turn an eye to or enable by helping out your son who is a murderer?"

He doesn't deny it. "I know I am," he mumbles.

"Stay away from Mia. Unless you have any information to give me to help protect her, other than telling me to send her away, don't come near me ever again." I storm away from him and into the house where Ryland and Hudson are both waiting for me.

"What happened?" Hudson asks.

"Not here." I nod to the crew that's working around us, and I go into the kitchen so I can help install the cabinets I started working on the previous day.

The rest of the day, I work in silence as anger and sadness flood my soul. So many lives destroyed when it didn't have to be that way. And now the one person outside my circle who claims to care about Mia and could find out what Skates is planning for her won't put himself in any danger to find out.

Around noon, I take out my phone and pull up Mia's tracker. I see she's still at the house and send her a text.

"How are the tan lines?"

"Lol. You'll have to find out tonight."

Don't worry, sweet girl, I will.

"Looking forward to it."

"Everything okay? You've never texted me before."

"Yep. Just thinking of you."

"Well, I'm always thinking of you."

"Ditto. I have to get back to work. See you tonight."

"Okay. Love you."

"Love you, too, Mia."

I put my phone away and pick up my measuring tape to mark where the bolts will be placed, and one thing is very clear. I need to get to Skates and Henry before they get to Mia.

For several hours I work in silence. I'm lost in my thoughts when a bolt of lightning cracks through the sky, shaking the house and causing me to jump.

Within seconds, rain is pouring down hard, and the house becomes dark. Lights blink on and off, and the power goes out.

"Shit," I hear Hudson and Ryland say almost simultaneously.

It's so dark, work can't continue. Flashlights from phones are soon lighting up the house.

Thirty minutes pass, and Ryland mutters, "Crap."

"What's wrong?"

He holds his phone out to me. "An electrical line went down. Power is going to be out probably until tomorrow."

The air fills with groans and comments about the heat, no air-conditioning, and obscenities.

"Pack it up. We're done for the day. Report back tomorrow at seven. We'll get the generators out of storage," Hudson yells out.

As best as possible, the crew puts tools and materials away. Within fifteen minutes, everyone minus Hudson and Ryland has left.

"You want to tell us why Casey was here?" Ryland corners me as another bolt of lightning cracks across the sky, shaking the oversized chandelier the crew installed earlier today.

I fill them in on my conversation with him.

"Maybe Mia should go back up north. Just till things calm down," Hudson suggests.

I jerk my head at him. "She's not going to go, and I'm not sending her anywhere on her own."

"Go with her."

"You know I can't leave the state."

He sighs. "Sorry. I forgot about your parole."

"I'll get ahold of Lòpez and Daniels today and update them. Let's see if any of this can help them find Skates and get him locked up," Ryland says.

I snort. "I won't hold my breath. Can one of you take me home? Mia's there by herself in the dark."

"Yeah, let's go. Can you lock up?" Hudson asks Ryland as he opens the front door.

"Sure. I'll let you know when I talk to Lòpez and Daniels."

"Thanks." I still don't have any faith the FBI is going to do anything quick enough for my taste.

The rain is falling in sheets, and thunder rolls. I run to Hudson's truck and hop in. He starts the engine and wipers, but they can't keep up with the amount of rain.

"I can't see. We're going to have to sit here for a moment," Hudson says.

I sigh and take out my phone out. I dial Mia, but her phone goes to the generic voice message.

My gut flips. "She isn't answering."

"She probably doesn't have her phone on her," Hudson says calmly.

I dial again but get no different results. "Something isn't right."

"You don't know that," Hudson says.

I pull the tracker up, and it blinks that her phone is at the house.

"See. Mia's there. Stop worrying." Hudson points to the phone.

As the green light flashes over and over, the pit in my stomach grows. I call again, but there is no answer.

I turn to Hudson. "You need to get me home. Something is wrong."

"Beckett, you need to calm down. I can't see to drive."

"Then get out and let me drive," I yell at him.

"Calm down!"

I jump out of the car and open up the door to Ryland's truck.

"Beckett!" Ryland and Hudson both call out.

"Give me your keys!"

"Beckett! Get back in, and we'll go," Hudson yells through the rain.

I slide back in the truck and slam the door. "Go."

Hudson grumbles something incoherent but starts to back out. The roads are already flooded, a common problem on the island when it rains, and Hudson is moving slow.

"Can you go any faster?"

"Jesus, Beckett! Do you want to get there alive or dead?"

I don't say anything. My heart is racing, and I feel panicky. I keep trying to call Mia, but she doesn't answer. "Pick up," I yell out.

"You need to calm down," Hudson says again.

It seems to take forever to get home, and before Hudson parks, I'm jumping out of the truck.

I don't need to enter the house to know that they have her...the door is hanging wide open, and Mia's phone is lying in the dirt.

26

Mia

It's a gorgeous, sunny day, and I'm lying out listening to music. My headphones are in, and I have my eyes closed. I'm trying to get into the music and forget about what happened with Casey.

I can't believe he's my father.

And Skates is my brother.

My stomach flips again at the thought. A self-loathing I've never experienced before yesterday takes over, and I try to push it out of my mind, but I can't.

I wish I could go backward and be in the dark about Casey being my father. And it makes me dislike my mother.

How could she have been with him?

She was only sixteen when she had Clay.

He was an adult.

And he claims he loved her.

A cold shiver runs through me, thinking about my mother as a teenager while a forty-year-old man stole her innocence.

He fed her heroine and got her hooked on it. It's his fault she died.

Suddenly, I realize the warmth on my skin hasn't just changed from my disgust, and I open my eyes to see black clouds everywhere.

I snatch my towel and get inside when a bolt of lightning cracks in the sky, causing me to nearly jump out of my skin.

Shutting the slider door, I lock it, go into my bedroom, and am almost changed when the power goes out. Blackness surrounds me, and I reach for my phone and turn on the flashlight so I can find a shirt to throw on.

When I finish changing, I go into the kitchen and put the hamburger meat I pulled out of the freezer in the fridge. I know the power is out, but I don't know when it will be on next. The air has already shut off, and I can tell the difference in the temperature.

Is the power out all over the island? Will Beckett be home soon?

I almost text him to ask, but I don't want to bother him while he's working.

As soon as I sit on the couch, my thoughts revert to Casey, my mom, and Skates.

I need to get a job.

The money my grandparents left me is still substantial for my meager spending habits, and Beckett insists that his check will pay for groceries and utilities, but I need to get a job to occupy my time. Otherwise, these thoughts about my family are going to drive me insane.

I turn on my laptop that's on the coffee table only to realize no power means no Internet.

"Great," I mumble as another bolt of lightning crackles through the sky, shaking the house.

Picking up my phone, I hit the hot spot, hoping I can connect my laptop to the Internet and pass the time while I'm waiting for Beckett to arrive home.

More thunder rolls, and I almost mistake it for the sharp knock on the door.

Beckett. I wonder if the lock is out from the power?

I run to the door, don't look at who is on the other side, and throw it open.

"Beck—"

Henry shoves his way through the door and grabs my arm.

"Ow! You're hurting me," I cry.

"Let's go." He drags me through the doorway and into the pouring rain.

My adrenaline kicks in. I try to fight him off, but it's no use. I'm powerless in his grip, and my phone falls on the ground.

He manhandles me to his truck. It's not the police car but his personal vehicle. With a harsh shove of my head, he forces me into the passenger seat and shuts the door.

As he's racing over to the driver's side, I try to get out, but I can't. He's done something to the door. I'm unable to open it. Before I can try his door, he's inside and sitting next to me.

"Let me out," I demand.

He roughly grabs my face. "Shut up. You're not in charge here. I am. You're going to shut up and sit still, or I'll have to get forceful. Do you understand me?"

I see it isn't a threat. He will hurt me. So I sit back and look out the window at the rain coming down so hard, I can't see anything but water and try not to cry.

Why did I open the door without looking out first? Beckett told me to be careful.

My gut flips as the car starts to move, but it's nearly impossible to see out the window. The wipers are working hard, but it's a monsoon.

Where is my gun when I need it?

I look over at Henry, who is concentrating on the road. His gun is in a holster.

What would it take for me to unlatch the holster and get it out?

As I contemplate my options, he looks at me for a brief moment, his eyes in slits. "You shouldn't have been prying."

I turn away from him, shuddering.

He turns onto Gulf Drive. "You and Beckett. Can't keep your noses out of other people's business."

I close my eyes, damning myself for going to see Veronica and asking her questions as well as Casey. I'm sure he told Henry about our encounter. This is my fault. Beckett warned me, and I didn't keep my promise to him.

How am I going to get out of this?

The remainder of the ride is in silence. I can hardly make out where we are due to the weather, but we finally park in the marina.

I snap my head at Henry. "What are we doing here?"

A sinister smile forms on his face. "We're here for you to meet your maker."

Meet my—oh God. They are going to kill me.

Of course, they are. What did you expect, Mia?

A new wave of fear washes through me, and a tear drips down my cheek. I quickly wipe it away as Henry grunts.

Pull it together, Mia. Don't start crying. Think.

Henry gets out, runs around the car, and opens the door. I try to stay inside, but he yanks me out and practically carries me down the dock and onto the boat I saw Veronica get on the day before.

My stomach drops, and I swallow down the bile rising in my throat.

I almost slip on the wet floor, but Henry has a strong hold on me and shoves me through the cabin door then leads me through several rooms.

We get to a living area where Skates is sitting on a couch, making out with Veronica on his lap.

"Sorry, boss, didn't mean to interrupt," Henry says.

Skates breaks his kiss, turning his head to look at us as

Veronica moves her lips across his jaw and to his ear, giggling softly and sucking on his lobe.

I stare at him, and a flashback from the night he killed Clay becomes clear.

He's aged ten years, but it's him. The same eyes, scar, and sinister expression are on his face.

"Hello, Sister," he says in a sarcastic tone filled with hatred.

My lip shakes, and I will it to stop so he doesn't see my fear, but it's useless. "What do you want from me?"

"I should have shot you so you died. That was my mistake. It won't happen again."

Goose bumps pop out on my skin, and Veronica stops kissing him and looks at me, raising her eyebrows.

Any sense of rationale has left me. I blurt out, "How can you be with him after what he did to my brother?"

They both look at each other and laugh.

"She's stupid, isn't she?" Veronica says to Skates like I'm not even in the room.

"Must have her mom's brain," he says, smiling and brings her back into him for a deep kiss.

I try to lunge at them, but Henry holds me back.

"What do you think you're doing?" he asks.

They pull out of the kiss. Skates turns his head with his eyebrows raised. "You think your brother meant anything to Veronica?"

I gape at him.

"All Veronica had to do was let him have one taste of her, and he was hooked. He would have done anything she told him to. Just like your mom and her heroine."

"What?" I whisper.

"Addicts. Clay was addicted to Veronica. It only took one comment from her to make him decide to work for me. All it took for your mom was one hit, and she was mine, too."

Tears fall. I can't contain them.

They both set Clay up. Skates gave my mom heroin, not Casey.

"Why?" I choke out. "Why would you do that to them?"

Veronica whispers something in his ear.

"Okay, baby." He winks at her, and she gets up and leaves.

"Tell me why," I cry out.

Skates stands up and struts over to me. He puts his finger over my shaking lip, and I try to step back, but Henry is behind me. "I dated your mother first. But she wanted my father's money. A user and whore...that's what she was. And when she realized that she would never be able to really be with him, she came to me, crying and upset."

I stare at him, trying to comprehend that my mother first dated him.

He arches his brow and smugly stares at me. "She would do anything for heroin. *Anything.*"

I close my eyes, not wanting to know or think about what Skates put her through. I open them when he tilts my face to look at him.

"Your brother could have had a nice life, working for me. But he couldn't mind his own business or keep it to himself. It looks like you have the same traits."

I try to look away from him, but he keeps his hand tight on my chin and snickers.

"I'm going to have fun with you. Your death is going to be like hers. Slow and painful over time. And you're never leaving this boat again." He licks his lips, and a twisted smile crosses his face.

What is he talking about? Slow and painful? He's going to torture me?

He lets go of my face and steps back. "Put her in the third bedroom."

Henry roughly steers me through the cabin and into a small bedroom. He quickly shuts and locks the door.

I try to get the door open, but it's no use. I'm trapped. The boat is dark from the storm, the window covered with a drape.

As my eyes adjust to the darkness, I look around the room. I see nothing but a bed, an empty closet, and a nightstand. Peering closer at the nightstand, I see a silver plate with something on it.

Sitting on the bed next to the nightstand, I look closer, and horror fills me. A rubber band that a doctor would use to draw blood, a needle, and a small packet of fine white powder along with a spoon and lighter lay next to it.

I've never seen drugs. My life has been sheltered, but since it killed my mother, I've researched heroin. I know everything there is to know about it, except what it feels like to use it. And I never wanted to. I am fully aware it's one of the most addictive substances on earth.

And this heroin, as white as it is, I'm pretty sure is the purest form you can get.

Slow and painful. It now makes sense. Torture in the usual sense isn't in his plan. For fun, Skates wants to turn me into one of his junkies just to watch me slowly die.

An addict like my mother.

You're never leaving this boat.

While fear is abundant, I also feel something else. Something scarier. Mixed in with all my emotions is a sense of curiosity.

Pain is something I've felt my entire life. Mental anguish and sadness from being so alone have played a constant role. Loneliness, something I thought I wouldn't have to feel anymore, having Beckett in my life, reignites in my belly, strengthening and gripping me harder than ever before.

Before, I didn't know what it was like to love and be loved. But now, since Beckett, I do. And the thought of never seeing him again, of never being in his arms, crushes my soul.

I need to get out of here.

I try to open the door again, but I can't open it. The only thing that has changed is that the boat begins to move. A new wave of panic overcomes me, and I collapse on the bed with tears.

When I try to pull myself together, I look over at the silver platter.

Maybe masking the pain and loneliness is better than feeling like this?

Is that what she thought?

It doesn't matter how much I've vowed to be different from my mother. I may just become her.

27

Beckett

DRENCHED FROM THE DOWNPOUR, I RACE IN THE HOUSE AND punch in the code to the safe.

Fuck. Why did I tell Mia not to keep her gun on her?

I grab the pistol, stick it in the back of my belt, and run out to Hudson's truck.

"What's going on?"

"They have her."

"Oh shit."

Think Beckett. Think.

"Start driving," I yell at Hudson as my pulse beats harder in my neck.

"Where?"

"I don't know. Just...just go down Gulf Drive while I think."

He throws his phone at me. "Call Ryland. I can't while I'm driving through this."

I hit the button.

"Hudson—"

"They have Mia," I cry out.

"What?"

"The door was open. Her phone was on the ground. They have her."

"Okay. Stay calm. Where do you think they could have taken her?"

"I don't know," I say, tugging at my hair.

"Beckett, we should call Casey. He knows where Skates is hiding out."

"That's it. The marina." I turn to look at Hudson. "Go to the new marina on Holmes Beach."

The rain starts to lighten up, and the sun peeks behind a cloud, shining through all the drops.

"Hurry up. The weather is changing. They will go out to sea."

"I'm going as fast as I can," Hudson claims but speeds up.

"I'm calling Casey. Keep me informed." Ryland hangs up.

I throw the phone in the cupholder and scrub my face.

They'd better not hurt her.

You should have killed them when you got out of prison.

Mia's face fills all my thoughts, and new rage and fear moves through me. I try to stop all the notions of what could happen to her and how scared she probably feels.

We round the corner, and Hudson scowls. "Look! It's Henry's truck."

Hudson turns into the parking lot, and I jump out before he comes to a complete stop. A boat, no doubt Casey's, is coasting through the canal.

"Fuck!" I scream and hit my hand on the hood.

Hudson sticks his head out the window. "Get back in, Beckett."

As I do, the phone rings. Hudson puts it on speaker.

"Casey said to meet at his house. Skates isn't getting off his boat while his arrest warrant is out. That's where he thinks they would take Mia."

"The boat just left," I say in a panic.

"He knew that. He has a tracker on the boat. Meet up at Casey's, and we'll go out in his boat. He's getting it ready now."

"On our way," Hudson tells him and hangs up.

"I should have killed them," I growl.

He doesn't say anything.

I snatch the gun out of my back pocket and flip the safety on and off. I've only shot when Hudson and I went to his land the prior week, but I won't hesitate to kill Skates or Henry. For ten years, it's all I've thought about, and now that they took Mia, there isn't anything I won't do to get her back.

"Put the safety on and away," Hudson tells me.

"I shouldn't have told Mia not to keep her gun on her."

Hudson sighs. "Let's not go down the *what I should have done* road. Let's focus on getting Mia back and not all winding up dead."

"I can't lose her," I choke out, looking out the window.

"I know, Bro. Don't go down this path right now. You gotta stay strong."

I take a deep breath, trying to get a handle on my rage. The sun is fully out now, the sky clear of any clouds. Besides the flooded roads, there is no sign that any weather besides a great beach day ever existed.

"There is no wind. The sea is calm now. They are going to be able to move faster."

"I'm sure Casey's boat goes fast," Hudson says as he maneuvers the truck into the driveway next to Ryland's.

Instead of going into the house, we make our way down to the dock where Casey's boat already has the engines stirring up the water.

The boat is smaller than the one at the marina. It holds one cabin and has three engines on it.

Ryland is on the vessel. Casey is standing at the wheel. Hudson and I unhook a rope and jump on.

"What are they planning?" I hurl at Casey.

"I don't know. They don't tell me anything."

"Liar!" I grip him by the throat.

"Beckett! This isn't going to help," Ryland growls and tries to pry my hand off Casey's throat as his face turns purple.

"Damn it, Beckett. This isn't helping Mia!" Hudson yells.

I release Casey, and he coughs. When he can speak, he says, "I know you don't believe this, but I love Mia. She's my daughter. I don't want anything to happen to her."

"Did you love your son, Clay?" I spit at him.

Pain crosses his face. "Yes."

I shake my head at him and sarcastically glare. "And do you love Skates?"

He closes his eyes as if in more pain. "Yes."

Disgusted, I scoff at him. "Just drive." I turn and make my way to the front of the boat.

Within a few minutes, Casey is driving at top speed, and I'm holding onto the rails, with saltwater flying at me, trying to see if I can spot the yacht Skates is on.

Casey slows the boat, and I look back at him. "What are you doing?"

"You need to get back here. It's going to get rougher, and you can't stand there."

"I'm fine. Drive."

"No. It's not safe."

"You seriously—"

"Beckett. Get your ass back here," Ryland barks at me.

He motions for me to sit next to him. I begrudgingly take the seat.

"What are we going to do once we get there?" Hudson asks.

"I'm going to kill them and end this once and for all," I confidently say.

"Beckett—"

"Hudson, don't give me your holier-than-thou shit. They

killed my best friend. They shot Mia. Now they've kidnapped her. I went to prison for ten years—"

"Yeah, and you don't need to go back," Ryland barks.

"Would be worth every second."

"What's Mia going to do then?" Hudson raises his eyebrows.

I look away from him. The thought of Mia not being with me and on her own is too much to bear.

"We should call the FBI," Ryland says.

"No. They will get Mia killed," I argue.

My phone rings. I look down and see an unknown number. I send it to voicemail. It rings again. After four times, I answer it.

"For ten years, I've waited to make this call. Time to pay the piper," Skates' voice comes through the line.

"Where is she?" I growl at him.

"You did well, not talking all those years. I've got to give you credit for that. But one whiff of pussy, and you can't shut your mouth. You're just as bad as Clay."

My gut drops. I should never have told Mia. He knows I told her.

"What are you talking about?" I try to play dumb.

"It's time to remind you where your loyalty lies. Tell my dad he's coming on the boat, too."

"What?" I glare over at Casey, who's clueless about the conversation I'm having. With the wind and roar of the engines, he can't hear.

"You don't think I know about your little rendezvous with him? I've got a tracker on his boat. I know you're coming."

The pit in my stomach grows. *It's a trap. We're walking right into his trap.*

A sinister laugh comes across the phone. "I'll see you soon, pretty boy."

"Damn it!" I throw the phone on the floor, and it breaks.

"Beckett. What's going on?"

In a quick movement, I'm behind Casey, gripping his neck again. "Did you set us up?"

The boat takes a sharp turn, and he grasps for the wheel. Hudson races over, prying my fingers off him. "Stop it, Beckett! This isn't helping."

Casey coughs again, slumping in the driver's seat.

"It's a trap," I yell. "Skates knows Mia and I have spoken with you. There's a tracker on this boat. He knows we're coming."

"What?" The color drains out of Casey's face.

"He said to tell you that you're coming on the boat, too."

Casey shakes his head. "Oh God. He's going to kill me."

"Stop the boat," Ryland yells.

I spin on him. "We aren't stopping."

"Beckett, stop the boat. We can't just walk right into his trap. We should have made a plan before we left."

"If we stop, Skates will know we've stopped," I bark.

"Then slow it down," Hudson chimes in.

Casey grips the throttle and slows the boat down so it's still moving forward against the waves but not fast.

"What do you think Skates is planning?" Ryland asks Casey.

"I don't know. Honestly. It could be anything. Shooting her and dumping her at sea. Not shooting her and dumping her at sea. I don't know."

I stare at him in horror, swallowing down vomit. "This is the son you love?" I growl.

"You don't understand, but he's my flesh. It's my fault he's like this."

"How?" Hudson asks as I glare at him.

Casey looks away then back, slowly opening his eyes. He stares at me. "I took Mia's mom away from Skates."

New disgust fills me. "Mia's mom dated Skates?"

He nods.

"You forgot that little detail this morning, didn't you? What else haven't you told us?"

Casey looks to the sky then back at me. "He thinks she left him because of my money, but that isn't true. She loved me. I loved her. He hated her for it. He hated Clay. He hates Mia."

He hates Mia. Meaning he wants to hurt her.

I jerk my head at Casey. "Did he set Clay up?"

Tears fill his eyes. "Veronica's initiation into the Twisted Hearts was to sleep with Clay and convince him to work for Skates."

"No," I barely manage to get out.

"He wanted to own Clay. But then he talked. And now, I don't know what he will do to Mia." He breaks down and starts to sob.

I glance at Ryland and Hudson then back at him. "You need to get your shit together. It's time to stop being a coward and do what's right. And that is saving Mia, no matter what happens to Skates."

He looks up in agony but slowly agrees.

God, I want to punch him then throw him off this boat.

Later, Beckett. Get Mia first.

"Casey, tell us about the boat," Ryland says.

He takes a deep breath. "There are three cabins with a central living area and kitchen. You can drive from inside or climb up to the top. The captain is one of Skates' men, and another man is on board as part of the crew."

"Don't forget Henry. His car was at the marina," Hudson pipes up.

"Do you have a gun on you?" I ask Casey.

"No. They won't let you on without a pat-down anyway."

I look at Ryland and Hudson. "Do you have your guns?"

"Yes," Ryland says.

Hudson sighs. "I don't have mine on me."

I hand Hudson Mia's gun. "Take this. You two get in the cabin when we approach so they don't know you're here."

"He's going to kill us," Casey states.

"You're going to tell him you've been playing Mia and me. Get your story together because he needs to believe that you're on his side and only talked to us to find out what we knew. He needs to think you brought me here to have me killed."

Casey's head jerks. "Skates won't hesitate to shoot."

"Yes. I know that. I saw him murder Clay and shoot Mia."

He looks away.

I turn to Ryland and Hudson. "You need to get Mia out of there. Leave us if you have to, but whatever you do, get her to safety."

Their jaws clench, but they nod.

"Where would they have Mia?"

"The bedroom, but you have to go through the main cabin to get to it," Casey says.

Shit. "Then we need to get everyone out on the deck."

"How?" Casey asks.

What leverage do I have on Skates?

A few minutes pass then it hits me.

"I know how to make Skates come out."

"What are you going to do?" Ryland asks.

"Hit him where it hurts the most."

If there's one thing I know about Skates from being incarcerated, it's that loyalty is everything to him. I know a lot about who's loyal and essential to him from the ten years I've spent in prison. And while I may need to kill Skates with my bare hands, I'm pretty confident by the time I spew my story, Henry's going to be begging for his life. Skates isn't going to appreciate what I tell him. I turn to Casey. "Speed up. We need to get there before something happens to Mia."

Please, God, don't let anything happen to her.

28

Mia

It feels like we've been at sea forever. In all reality, it's probably only a few hours, but when you're all alone, and there's nothing to do, your mind plays tricks on you.

Time is something that can go slower than normal.

I've sat on the bed. I've laid on it. I've paced the edge of the bed. Anything to stop looking at the plate of heroin as too many thoughts plague me.

If I'm going to die, maybe this is a better way?

Will it make me pass out and not know I'm here?

If I can't physically escape Skates, will this allow me to escape him mentally?

A battle follows every thought.

That's what she did.

Don't be her. You're better than her.

Why are you even thinking about this?

I've never considered or desired to take drugs. I hardly drink alcohol. Contemplating this is a surprise to me.

I stare at the white packet and syringe then pick up the powder, inspecting it carefully. I'm not sure what I'm looking for, as the contents are just small, white grains that look like sugar.

The sound of footsteps outside the door near, and I drop the packet and sit on the end of the bed, in front of the door.

Veronica's laugh and Skates' voice fill the air, and my pulse increases.

The doorknob turns, and Skates enters.

He never takes his eyes off me and picks up the platter of heroin. Veronica stands in the doorway, smirking.

God, I hate them both.

Skates sits next to me with the drugs.

I want to crawl out of my skin, and he wraps his arm around my shoulders. I squirm to get out, but he sternly says, "Stop moving."

I stop. My heart is beating so hard I'm sure he can hear it.

He puts his lips near my ear. His breath is pulsing against my skin, creating chills from my toes up. "Looks like you need some help. Let's get a little taste, shall we?"

I try to stand up, but he shoves me back down.

Veronica laughs, and I wish I could shut her up.

I blink back tears as he yanks me into him more. "You're going to do what I want, or the minute Beckett gets on this boat, I'm tying an anchor around his neck and letting him die a slow death. Do you understand?"

I jerk my head at him in surprise. *Beckett is coming? He knows where I am?*

He brushes his finger down my cheek. "Oh, dear sister. Did you think I wouldn't let him witness this fun?"

A tear falls off my face and lands on my hand. "Why are you doing this? We have the same blood."

He fists my hair and tugs it back so I'm looking in his eyes. "We share half our blood. You shouldn't have been born. If your mother weren't a whore who sank her teeth into my dad, you wouldn't be here."

"She was a child," I cry out.

"She was a whore," he sneers and pulls my head back farther. "A weak, addicted, whore."

"I'm sorry, but I'm not her," I choke out.

He lets go of my hair and arches his eyebrows. "Aren't you?"

"No. Please leave me alone," I cry out.

Skates sticks the packet of heroin in front of my face. "You didn't wonder what it would be like to try it out?"

I hesitate, and it's all he needs. "No."

His eyes become slits. "You're a shitty liar. Your mom and brother were, too."

I close my eyes, willing myself to stop crying and come up with a game plan to fight against him. But it's nearly impossible. The dam has broken, and the more he laughs, the faster the river flows.

"It's tasting time," he whispers in my ear.

My eyes fly open. Veronica stands over us with her fingernail covered in the white powder. I swallow the knot in my throat.

"Sniff it." She wiggles her finger at me.

I shake my head and try to pull back, but Skates has my head on lockdown, and his other hand has restrained mine.

Veronica's fingernail comes closer to my nose.

"No!" I stomp on her bare feet as hard as I can, and she steps backward in pain. The white powder falls to the floor.

Instead of being mad, Skates is amused. "Didn't realize you were so feisty."

"You bitch," she screams, holding onto her foot and bouncing up and down.

"Skates," Henry's voice calls out. "They're here."

Skates stares at me and he rubs both hands together. "It's showtime."

I furrow my brows in question, and he yanks me up. "Let's go."

Veronica is still whining, and Skates drags me through the cabin and into the main room. He shoves me onto the couch and wraps the bag of heroin in my hand. "Feel free to start the party. If you move off this couch, your boyfriend dies. Do you understand?"

More tears well and my insides shake harder.

He squeezes my hand and releases it, leaving me clutching the heroin. I can hear men talking from outside, but I don't move for fear Beckett will get shot.

For a brief moment, I'm glad to be alone to collect my thoughts and try to figure out what my next move is, but it doesn't last long. Veronica enters the room carrying the silver platter filled with the syringe, rubber band, and lighter.

Grinning, she says, "Let's just do it the right way this time."

I stare at her.

She places the platter on the table and stretches the rubber band.

"Why are you doing this?" I spout at her.

She looks at me like I'm her best friend. "You really are naive, aren't you?"

"What do you mean?"

She brushes the back of her fingers down my cheek. "You're going to be fun to play with."

Chills consume my body. "Why are you doing this?"

"I'm doing this because Skates told me to."

"That's it? Because he told you to?"

A sarcastic laugh fills the air. "Yeah. When Skates talks, you listen. And honestly, I'm rather enjoying watching you squirm."

I glare at her. "Why? I've never done anything to you."

"No? Is that what you think?"

I furrow my brows at her. "What? What have I done?"

"You're just another rich island kid who has had everything handed to them."

"No, I haven't."

She laughs. "Please. Don't even try. You, Clay, Beckett—you're all spoiled island kids who never had to fight for anything."

She hates me because I grew up on the island?

"Skates grew up on the island."

Veronica snorts. "Skates built his empire. What have you done?"

I glare at her. "Skates may have built his empire, but it's one of destruction."

"Skates built an empire of loyalty, trust, and honor. Something you know nothing about."

I gape at her, not sure how anyone could believe in what Skates has created.

There's a loud commotion outside, and Veronica throws the rubber band on the platter and leaves the room.

I'm about to stand up but then freeze, remembering Skates' warning of throwing Beckett overboard with an anchor attached to his neck.

Chills run through me as I realize I didn't do what Skates wanted in the bedroom when he made that promise.

I stand up and look out the cubbyhole. I faintly see Henry, Skates, Casey, and Beckett. Veronica is standing next to Skates.

Casey? What is he doing here?

It looks like Casey and Skates are arguing, and Beckett is watching the conversation. Two other men stand behind him with guns aimed at his back.

Beckett. Oh God. Please don't let anything happen to him.

Veronica starts to turn, and I duck down and sit back on the couch, my heart racing, trying to figure out how to help Beckett.

I scour the room and realize that I'm still clutching the packet of heroin. I look down at my hand and then back up, and that's when I see it.

In the chair next to the couch, in the side between the cushion and the seat, the butt of a gun is sticking out.

Quickly, I grab it and sit back down. I check that it's loaded and the safety is on, place it behind my back, and lean against it.

Veronica enters the room and picks up the rubber band. "I think it's time we finish what we started."

I scan her eyes. "Okay. Can I go to the bathroom first?"

She rolls her eyes.

"I haven't gone all day."

"Fine," she huffs. Turning her back to the door across the room, she points. "It's over there."

Standing up, I grab the gun from behind me, flip the safety, and aim it at her.

She turns back to me with wide eyes.

"Don't say a word. Move." I motion with the gun for her to go into the bedroom I was in earlier.

"You won't shoot me," she challenges.

I don't flinch. "I'm a marksman. You want to test my skills out?"

Her eyes widen. "Skates will kill you."

"Not if I kill him first. Anyway, you can either be alive or dead to watch. Choose."

She narrows her eyes. "You wouldn't. You're too innocent."

"I have Skates' blood in me. Innocence is just a mirage. Now, move."

She hesitates, and I motion again. She finally moves, and I put her in the room she locked me in. Before I secure the door shut, I tell her, "Don't say a word, or I'll come back and kill you. And I don't give second warnings."

I'm not sure where this is coming from, but I can only assume it's the years of having such a big hole in my heart. Maybe it's the practice I got the day before with Casey, but I have no doubt that if she tries to harm me again or Beckett that I will shoot her.

I shut the door and lock her in, making her a prisoner the same way she made me, and stick the gun in my shorts.

I need to get Beckett and me out of here in one piece.

Loud voices fill my ears, and I look out the window and see that the conversation on the deck now has Henry looking like he is defending himself.

One man is now behind Beckett with a gun, and one is behind Henry, and they both look like they don't know where to aim. Skates yanks the gun out of the hand of the guy nearest Henry. He waves it between Beckett and Henry.

"He's lying," Henry cries out.

"Eight times in the last year alone. Did you know about any of those?" Beckett asks Skates.

"That's not true," Henry claims.

Beckett points to Henry. "He's playing you."

Henry suddenly spins and tries to punch Beckett, but Beckett's too fast and ducks down. Henry's punch lands on the man holding the gun behind Beckett, and several shots ring through the air before the man flies over the side of the boat and falls into the water.

Henry and Beckett are both on the deck, and blood is seeping across it.

"Beckett!" I yell as I no longer try to figure out what to do, and run out of the cabin and onto the deck.

Skates, Casey, and the other man with the gun turn toward me.

"Mia, get back inside," Casey yells.

Tears are streaming down my face. "Beckett!"

The pool of blood is growing on the deck, and neither Henry nor Beckett is moving. Henry is on top of Beckett, and I can't tell who's been shot.

"Beckett!" I cry out again, and Casey holds me back.

"Stop, Mia!"

I shake out of his grasp. “Let me go.”

Skates laughs. “Let her go, old man.”

He releases me, and I run over to the pile of men covered in blood, rolling Henry off Beckett, who lies in the pool of red with his eyes shut.

29

Beckett

Ryland and Hudson move into the cabin as Skates' boat comes into view. We're so far out at sea that no one is around within eyesight, and all you can see is water.

Casey's face has no color in it. "Are you going to be able to do this so Mia doesn't get killed?"

He takes a deep breath. "Yes."

I shake my head and look forward, seeing red. All the years in my cell of plotting out different scenarios and ways I could avenge Clay's and Mia's death never involved a boat or Mia being a hostage. Mia was always already dead.

Already dead. I shudder at the horrible realization Skates could have already hurt or murdered her.

But he wants you to watch.

The sick thought keeps my mind from spinning down the rabbit hole of what he might have already done to Mia.

Stay focused, Beckett. This isn't the time to get weak.

We approach the boat, and I eye Ryland and Hudson in the cabin. Ryland taps his fist on his heart. I replicate his actions.

Together we stand, alone we fall. I hope we're all standing after this.

Casey drifts up next to Skates' yacht. Skates' two goons tie the boats together while Henry waves a gun at us. "Out, now," he demands and motions the gun for us to get onto their vessel.

I glare at him. I'm no longer the naive kid I was a decade ago. I've lived in hell and experienced evil. Henry doesn't scare me. He's a sad waste of space, and he may be holding a gun, but it doesn't intimidate me.

"Got something you want to say, Beckett?"

"Yeah. How do you sleep at night?"

He grins. "I sleep just fine. I open my balcony and listen to the waves roll."

Disgust fills me. *How many lives have been ruined so he can have his beach house?*

"Skates. They're here," Henry calls out as one of Skates' men pats me down and the other one does the same to Casey.

"Where's Mia?" I ask Henry.

He laughs. "You couldn't save her last time. What makes you think you can save her this time?"

Rage takes over, and I lunge at him, but the meathead who checked me for weapons holds me back.

"Easy there, kid. You might end up in the ocean with an anchor around your neck," Skates warns, coming out of the cabin. "Now move." He motions to the front of the boat.

As we're walking to the front, I look at him. "Where's Mia?"

"Oh, she's reliving her mother's days."

Tilting my head at him, I ask, "What are you talking about?"

He snickers. "The apple doesn't fall far from the tree."

My blood boils. "What have you done to her?"

Skates' cocky expression sends more adrenaline pulsing through my veins. "Given her options."

"Options?"

"Jimmy, what did you do?" Casey demands in a more authoritative voice than I've ever heard him use.

Skates turn toward him. "Well, aren't you suddenly willing to stick your neck out. Didn't know you had any balls left, Pops."

Casey swallows hard, and guilt crosses his face.

Veronica comes out, and I feel like I'm seeing a ghost. She's only aged a little in the last ten years, and the day Clay introduced me to her on the beach flashes in my mind.

Now that is the type of girl you go back for seconds with. The memory of me telling Clay that makes me shudder and wish I would have told him to stay away, knowing what I do now. *How does a girl like her get hooked up with a guy like Skates?*

She leans against Skates and bats her eyes at me with a big smile. "Beckett. I didn't think I would ever see you again."

I glare at her.

Veronica puts her lips near Skates'. "Everything okay out here, baby? Can I get you anything?"

He palms her ass, kisses her, and says, "I'm good. You go back inside the cabin and take care of our guest."

She saunters off, and he slaps her ass.

"Hey, Veronica," I yell after her.

She stops then turns.

"You hurt her, and I'm coming after you."

She looks at me then Skates then throws her head back and laughs. Turning back, she goes into the cabin.

"I think it's time to prove your loyalty," Skates says to me.

"Yeah, I can do that," I nonchalantly say.

His head slightly jerks.

Yeah, you aren't expecting me to agree, are you?

He waits.

"You know what I learned to do in prison?"

Skates raises his eyebrows.

"Listen. Observe. Put two and two together."

He licks his lips.

I gaze at Henry. "You seem to have a lot of faith and trust in the wrong person."

Henry's sneers. "Son, I don't know what kind of story you're trying to create, but you can stop right now."

"Don't ever call me son again. And I'm not creating any story. I'm only relaying what I saw over the last ten years."

"What's that?" Skates asks.

"Nothing. He's lying," Henry blurts out.

I raise my eyebrow at Skates. "Phillmore, Conceed, Triker." I name off the top three guys in Skates' gang who were in prison with me.

"What about them?"

"Henry sure does visit them a lot."

Skates' eyes turn into slits.

"That's a lie. I've never visited anyone in prison," Henry cries out.

"Too many times to count over the last decade." I'm lying. Henry knows it. I know it. Skates doesn't know it.

Skates says nothing and continues to glance between Henry and me. Suddenly, he seizes the gun the guy near Henry holds and waves it between Henry and me.

"He's lying," Henry cries out.

"Eight times in the last year alone. Did you know about any of those?" I ask Skates.

"That's not true," Henry claims.

I nod to Henry. "He's playing you."

Henry suddenly spins and tries to punch me, but I duck. Henry's punch lands on the man holding the gun behind me. Several shots ring through the air, and the man flies over the side of the boat, hits his head, and falls into the water.

Henry lands on top of me, and blood seeps across the deck.

"Beckett!" Mia yells from somewhere, but Henry's body lies heavy on me.

"Mia, get back inside," Casey yells.

"Beckett!" I hear her yell again.

I try to get up, but Henry's body is on mine, and the deck is slippery with blood. I shut my eyes because the sun shines directly in them.

"Beckett!" Mia cries out again.

"Stop, Mia!" Casey says.

"Let me go." I hear her say.

Skates snickers. "Let her go, old man."

Suddenly, Mia is hovering over me, rolling Henry off me. I feel her tear hit my cheek. I open my eyes, and she cries harder.

"Beckett!"

"Shh." I stand up and pull her with me and feel something hard in her back, so I quickly turn her against me.

Where did she get a gun? There is no doubt a pistol is pressing into my torso.

Another thing prison taught me to do is assess a situation quickly. Skates is aiming the gun at us. His only remaining ally besides Veronica is standing next to him, weaponless. I'm pretty sure I could take him if I needed to. The fact Mia is standing in front of me with a gun in her back tells me Veronica won't be interrupting us.

"Jimmy, put the gun down. It's time to stop this," Casey tells Skates.

He glares at him. "Not sure who you think you're ordering around, but I make the demands, remember?"

Casey glares, and a tear falls out of his eye. "I'm sorry I took her from you. I didn't know you were together. You never told me."

Skates scowls. "You think I care about her? I don't care about her. This is about tying up loose ends."

Sadness and pain pass across Casey's face. "You don't have to do this."

Skates sticks the gun in Casey's face. "You don't tell me what I get to do or not do. I tell you."

Casey holds his hands in the air. "Okay. You're right. I'm sorry."

Skates scans his eyes. "If I didn't need you for the restaurants, you'd be dead."

Casey closes his eyes and sighs.

In the corner of my eye, I see Ryland in the back of the boat with his gun in his hand.

I murmur to her, "When I say run, you go."

Mia's body tenses against mine, and I take her gun and step in front of her, keeping the weapon between us so no one can see.

Suddenly, there is a banging from inside the cabin. Skates looks down at the cubbyhole window, and Casey reaches for his gun.

The next few minutes are chaotic.

"Run," I whisper to Mia, push her off me, and step toward Casey at the same time Skates' goon does as well.

Skates' thug sees my gun and lunges at me, and the pistol flies out of my hand. We wrestle for it, but he gets to it first and holds it to my head. Several shots follow, and I'm once again lying in a pool of blood, but this time, there's moaning.

Within seconds he's rolled off me. Ryland yanks me up, and Casey is standing on the side of the boat with Skates' body against him, his head drooping. Casey is shaking, and red is all around their feet.

Hudson is in the back of the boat with Mia in his arms.

I stare at Ryland, trying to comprehend what just happened. The muzzle of his pistol is hot. His hand shakes harder as his eyes flick from the dead body to me and back again.

"I killed…oh fuck…" I remove the gun from his hand and pull him into me. He begins to cry.

"Shh. I'm sorry I got you in this. Everything will be okay." As I say the words, I wonder if it will.

He sobs and I blink back tears, not having seen Ryland cry since we were little kids. I hear a loud thud as Skates' body drops on the deck, and Casey falls to his knees, crying loudly over his body.

I don't know how long the waterworks last, but there is a moaning that gets louder, and I realize that it isn't any of us.

I release Ryland and go to where Casey shot Skates. I look through the hole and see Veronica lying in a pool of blood on the floor.

I maneuver my way through the cabin, but by the time I get there, she's taken her last breath. Her blonde hair is covered in blood, and her blue eyes are frozen.

Swallowing hard, I stare at her. I'm standing in a blood bath. I look down at my hands and realize my entire body is coated in blood. It's been ten years, but death once again surrounds me.

Hudson comes in. "Come sit in the main room, Beckett. We need a plan."

I stare at him and finally nod. When I get there, Mia comes flying over to me.

"Are you okay? Did he hurt you?" I ask her.

"No. I'm okay."

I hold her the tightest I ever have and stroke her hair.

"We need to sink this boat, and everyone needs to remove their clothes and wash up before getting on Casey's," Hudson says.

Ryland jerks his head. "Shouldn't we call the police?"

"No. You might go to jail. It wasn't self-defense," Hudson tells him then turns to Casey. "And you might over Veronica's death. I think Beckett did enough time for everyone."

Ryland and Casey sit next to each other, staring as if in shock. They stare at Hudson but don't say anything.

I suppose that's how I looked when Clay was shot.

Hudson goes into the bathroom and Skates' bedroom. He chooses clothes, towels, and extra blocks of soap. "Clothes stay on the boat. Mia, you go first."

She pulls out of my embrace and doesn't ask any questions.

She quickly showers and comes out in a towel. Hudson throws her a dress he found that must be Veronica's. She goes into the bedroom and comes back out while Casey is in the shower.

One by one, we all scrub the blood off us. We put on Skates' clothes, and when we're done, Hudson comes back into the room. "On the boat. Make sure you aren't stepping in any blood or making any blood marks before you get on the boat. Mia, Ryland, Casey, you go now."

I follow them, making sure no bloodstains are being tracked anywhere into Casey's boat then help Mia onto the boat. Once Ryland and Casey are also aboard, Hudson puts two pairs of Skates' sandals next to where Casey's boat is parked and tells me to follow him.

When we get to the bow of the boat, gas cans are waiting.

"Everything gets covered," Hudson instructs.

Together, we douse the boat, including the inside of the cabin. When we get to the back, we throw the cans down and switch out of our shoes, careful nothing is on the sandals Hudson left for us to get into before getting on Casey's boat.

"How are we blowing this up?"

Hudson doesn't flinch. "Flare gun."

I stare at him.

"Get on the boat, Beckett," Hudson instructs, and I obey. He follows me.

Ryland and Casey untie us from the yacht. Hudson takes the wheel, and I sit with Mia on my lap, next to Ryland, who keeps mumbling, "I don't know his name."

When we get about eight hundred feet away, I still can't see land or anything except water. Hudson digs the flare gun out of the case.

"Wait," Casey says.

He looks at him.

Casey walks over to him and holds out his hand. "Give it to me."

Hudson hands it to him.

Casey takes a deep breath, and, as more tears roll down his face, he positions the flare gun straight at Skates' yacht and pulls the trigger.

The light travels through the air, and the instant it hits the boat, an explosion takes place. Hudson hits the throttle, and we drive away as millions of flaming pieces are flying in every direction. Within minutes, smoke fills the air where the yacht sat, and no outline of any boat or its pieces can be seen.

We ride the rest of the way mostly in silence. Mia is curled in my lap. Ryland and Casey both stare off into space. From time to time, Ryland mumbles the words *killed, name, shot.* Hudson drives the entire way and we exchange glances, both worried about Ryland. By the time we get to Casey's dock, it's dark out.

No one speaks. We tie the boat and go directly to our vehicles. When we get to the driveway, Casey calls out, "Mia."

Mia freezes then slowly spins out of my arm that is around her shoulder.

"Do you think we could talk sometime?" Tears fall out of his eyes again.

I protectively wrap my arm around her again.

She stares at him. "I…I can't answer that right now."

I didn't think he could look any sadder, but he does. "Okay. I'm here if you decide you want to."

I help her into Ryland's truck and take the keys from him.

He looks at me like he doesn't understand what is going on.

"I'll drive you home and pick you up tomorrow. Unless you want to stay at our place?"

"What was his name?" he mumbles.

"I don't know."

Hudson gives me a worried glance. "You two go. Ryland can come to my place tonight."

"Okay. Call me if you need anything."

Hudson guides Ryland to the truck.

I stare at Ryland, who's mumbling to himself as Hudson walks around the truck. As they drive away, I wonder if Ryland is ever going to be the same, but then I curse myself. I already know he never will.

Death has a horrible way of defining you.

My brother killed a man to save me. I vow to do everything in my power to save him from the guilt that is sure to eat away at him.

Together we stand, alone we fall. I won't let him fall, but I'm not sure what he needs right now, and that scares the shit out of me.

30

Mia

We haven't said anything. The ride on the boat and in the car was silent. I spent the hours in Beckett's arms, or holding his hand, but not speaking.

Is it really over?

My brain is grasping at thoughts and revelations and trying to make sense of the day's events.

When we get inside the house, Beckett locks the door, and I take his hand, and lead him to the bathroom. We showered on the boat, but the stench of death and the grime of it hasn't left me. And I need to rid myself of it.

That, and the realization I'm much more like my mother than I ever thought possible. But I don't know if I can, or even should, forget that. *Does forgetting make you a more susceptible target?*

And I don't know if I should be more upset that I'm not as affected by death as I am regarding the knowledge I was so close to taking heroin.

I wanted to know what my mother felt when she took it and

why she couldn't let it go. To see if it would mask pain in a way that made life seem bearable when everything appeared impossibly bleak.

Looking at Beckett, shame fills me. I have him, and he would die for me. I knew it when he shoved me down and threw himself on top of me ten years ago, and I know it now. And I love him. Life without him wouldn't be living.

We strip out of our clothes, not saying a word. Once we're in the shower, we scrub each other with soap, and Beckett washes my hair. He rinses it and bends down and kisses me. I start to sob. Hard.

"Shh." He wraps his strong arms around me. After a few minutes, he turns off the water, dries me off then himself, and leads me to the bedroom. He opens the drawer and removes a pair of pajama shorts and a shirt for me and throws on a pair of his boxers.

Beckett goes into the bathroom and comes out with the clothes we wore home. "I'm going outside to the bonfire to burn these."

"Okay." I follow him outside.

He throws the clothes in the bonfire container and lights it. Choosing a lounge chair, he scoots it over, sits down then positions me so I'm sandwiched between his legs and lying on his chest. He wraps his arms around me then murmurs in my ear, "Tell me what happened."

Shame is a horrible feeling, and it consumes me. I bury my head into Beckett's neck. "Skates said I was like my mother. They locked me in a room with heroin."

He says nothing, but air fills his lungs, and he holds it in, waiting for me to continue.

I bite my lip and slowly look up at him.

He turns his head, and his lips are inches from mine, but I see him swallow hard. He gently asks, "Did you think about doing it?"

Closing my eyes, I breathe a few times. When I open my eyes, Beckett is cupping my cheek, patiently waiting for me to speak.

I slowly nod, staring into his eyes that are flickering along with the glow of the fire.

He kisses the top of my head. "Did you think it would take away your pain?"

I jerk my head at him. "Yes. How did you know?"

Beckett scans my eyes. "Prison makes you want to do a lot of things you never thought you would do."

I tilt my head. "Did you try it?"

"No. But that doesn't mean I wasn't tempted a lot."

"Really?"

His fingers brush my cheek. "Yes."

"I've never wanted to do anything like that before. When I was locked in the room, and there was nothing to do or even look at except it, I...I..."

Beckett kisses me briefly. "You thought it might be easier?"

"Yeah."

He caresses my cheek with his finger.

I bite my lip, staring at him.

"What else?"

"Am I like her?"

"Yes and no. Not the bad parts. Only the good parts."

"How do you know?"

"I remember your mom."

I gape at him. "You do?"

"Yeah. And she was kind and sweet. She was a good person."

A tear drips down my cheek, and he swipes it with his thumb.

"Do you think something is wrong with me when I'm more affected about being a possible addict than what happened today?"

"You're not an addict. Any of us, at any time, can become an addict. Being tempted and doing it are two different things."

"But I don't care they died. I mean, I do care in the sense that

I'm glad they died—all of them. I have no remorse over their deaths. Doesn't that make me a bad person?"

Beckett sighs. "I feel the same as you. The only remorse I have is that Ryland shot someone, and I didn't. Now he has to deal with that guilt."

"He looked shocked. I'm worried about him."

Beckett's eyes turn darker. "I imagine that is how I looked the night of Clay's murder...maybe even days after."

I stroke the side of his head. "I'm sorry. I don't remember much."

His jaw clenches. "I'm not. I don't want you to remember it."

"What was it like?"

He raises his eyebrows.

"Having your life ripped away."

He blinks a few times. "I think you know what that's like."

"But it isn't the same."

"Isn't it?"

"No. Not the same."

He holds me tighter. "When your grandparents dropped you off, were you scared?"

"Yeah."

"Sad?"

"I felt like my heart had been ripped out of my chest, and I couldn't breathe."

He kisses my forehead. "Did you feel depressed, lonely, and like your life was over?"

"Yes."

"Then you know exactly how I felt."

Silence ensues and lasts for a few moments, except for the crackling of the fire and the croaking of the bullfrogs.

"Are they really dead? Is it really over?" I quietly ask him.

Beckett looks at me. "Yes."

"Do you think we can ever forget about the past?"

"Probably not forget. But we can move forward without fear."

I take a deep breath. "Do you think I should talk to Casey?"

His body freezes. He thinks for a moment then says, "I don't know. I think that's something you have to decide, and whatever you decide is the right answer."

"You're lucky you have the family you do."

Beckett nods. "I am."

"Do you think we can have our second chance now?"

A smile forms on Beckett's face. "I got my second chance the minute I turned around in that courtroom and saw you."

I lean in and kiss him, and he wraps his arms tighter around me, making me feel safe and loved. It's a world I never knew before Beckett.

"I want you forever, Mia," he murmurs.

"I want you forever."

"Then marry me."

My heart pounds harder, and I pull back and stare into his beautiful brown eyes.

His eyes scan mine. "I don't have a ring, or money, or status. I only have me. But I promise I'll give you all of me—every day. And I'll put you first and love you and protect you the best I can."

My eyes well with tears. "Really? You want to marry me?"

His face is solemn. He cups my cheeks. "Yes. I want us forever."

I crush my lips against his, putting every ounce of love I have for him in it, knowing he is all I've ever wanted. And he kisses me back, showing me I am his everything, that we are meant for each other and no one else.

"Mia, will you marry me?" he asks between kisses.

"Yes. Yes, I'll marry you."

He kisses me more then says, "I think our second chance for happiness has already started."

31

Mia

TINGLES RACE UP MY SPINE. HIS WARM BREATH ON MY NECK TEASES me further.

"Good morning, future Mrs. Beckett Brooks." He nibbles on my earlobe.

I giggle and rollover. "So you haven't changed your mind? Last night wasn't a fluke?"

His grin widens. "Nope." He kisses my nose then lips. "I won't take the chance and ask if you want to back out."

I cup his cheeks. "I'll always want to be with you, Beckett."

Fire fills his eyes. "And I, with you."

The alarm beeps.

"Nooooo. Too soon," I whine.

Beckett picks up his phone and turns it off.

"Maybe you should skip work today? We can play in bed all day and hang by the pool. You can rub my body in lotion all day." I suggest but already know the answer.

He groans. "I can't. I need to make sure Ryland is okay."

I run my finger through his hair. "I'm really worried about him. Ryland is always so strong and in control. Seeing him in shock yesterday..." Ryland's face when we left him last night plagues me.

"The only thing I can compare it to is how I imagine I acted the night Clay got shot."

Sadness fills me. "Will it ever get easier to remember Clay? Now that we know the truth?"

Beckett sits up. "I don't know. I hope so."

Emotion suddenly overpowers me. I tear up.

Beckett pulls me on his lap. "What's wrong, Mia?"

"I wish Clay and my grandparents could be at our wedding. I don't even have anyone to give me away."

"Me too. Maybe we shouldn't think about our wedding how everyone else thinks about theirs."

"What do you mean?"

"Whatever you want for the wedding, I'll do. But there isn't anything normal about how we got here, so what if we just threw everything out the window about what you're supposed to do or not do for a wedding and do what we want."

"Ohhhh. I like that idea. We can be the big rebels that we are," I tease.

"Tell you what, why don't you make a list of whatever you want and we can talk about it tonight."

"Okay."

"And I need to get you a ring. But I'm a total loser and have no idea what you want, and I'm not asking my sisters. They will take over, and I'll end up getting you a ring they want and not what you want."

I get out of bed, go to my jewelry box and open it up. I pull out three simple rings and hand them to Beckett. I swallow the thick knot forming in my throat. "These were my grandparents'."

He takes the small diamond ring and band that was my grandmother's and slides them on my finger. "It fits perfectly."

I pick up my grandfather's ring and slide it on his. "It's an exact fit for you too."

He brushes my hair off my face. "Is this what you want?"

"If you're okay with it?"

"I am. I only want you to have what you want, Mia."

I cradled his head in my hands. "As long as I have you, I have everything I could ever want or need."

He gives me a toe-curling, panty-melting, torch my insides with flames of lust, kiss.

The alarm beeps again, and his stomach growls.

"Go shower. I'll make you some breakfast."

"Can you make it to go? I'm going to be late."

"Sure."

He pecks me, takes a shower, and I make him an egg, bacon, and cheese sandwich.

"Hudson and Ryland are going to be jealous," he says.

I hand him two other sandwiches.

"Now you're just trying to show off."

"I have to keep my future in-laws happy."

"When do you want to tell my family? My parents left for their European vacation last night."

"Why don't we wait until they get back, so your mom isn't upset?"

"They are gone a few months."

"I can keep a secret. Can you?"

He chuckles. "Did you seriously just ask me that?"

I wince. "Sorry. Forgot for a brief moment you were the keeper of secrets."

He pecks me, then palms my ass. "Write out your list, and we'll talk tonight."

"Come home for lunch with your brothers. I'll make sure you're all fed. Plus, I want to see Ryland."

"Will do." He leaves.

I grab a cup of coffee, notebook, and pen, and lay down on a lounger by the pool.

What do I want for our wedding?

Should I ask Beckett's dad to give me away?

Casey is your birth father.

For over an hour, I go back and forth about whether I even want Casey at the wedding.

No. You only want people who are good there. He hid Clay's murder and kept Beckett in prison for over ten years.

I finally decide there is no way I want Casey anywhere near our happy day. All I feel when I'm around him is pain. He's a reminder of all I have lost...of all Beckett has lost.

I scratch Casey's name off the list.

The only people I have on it are Beckett's siblings and his parents.

Those are the only people in our lives we care about.

Not that I even know anyone else on the island anymore.

Beckett's parents are friends with everyone. Are they going to be angry we aren't inviting them?

Beckett said we should do what we want.

Still...

I make a note to talk to Beckett about it.

There are certain things I don't even question whether Beckett will want it or not.

It's definitely going to be on the beach.

The beach I kissed him on when I ran into the water with my clothes on.

What kind of dress should I wear?

I don't want anything fancy. I want something simple like my grandparent's rings.

I glance at my finger and smile. It makes me feel like a part of them is still in my life. They had a healthy marriage, especially considering everything they went through with my mom and Clay, and I want my life with Beckett to be just as strong.

But with hotter sex.

Oh, gross, why am I even thinking about my grandparent's sex life?

I shudder.

Back to the list.

I write down, *Party*.

Do we have to have one? Can't Beckett and I just say our vows in front of his family and spend the rest of the day wrapped up in each other?

Hmmm. Talk to Beckett, I write.

I glance at my watch and am shocked by the time. Beckett and his brothers will be home for lunch soon.

I make sandwiches and cut up some fruit then text Beckett. “Everything is ready for lunch. Any chance of private appetizers?”

He replies, “You just made me super horny.”

“What are you going to do about it?”

“You'll find out tonight.”

“What if I'm desperately in need during the lunch hour?”

“My balls are officially blue.”

I put on a pink sundress Beckett loves and wait for them to arrive.

Beckett walks in first and checks me out. Heat fills his eyes and he hugs me and murmurs in my ear, "I didn't know you were such a tease."

I giggle, but my giddiness ends when I see Ryland. I tightly embrace him. "Are you doing okay?"

"Yeah. All good."

No, you aren't.

BECKETT

. . .

LAST NIGHT, BOTH MIA AND I AGREED WE SLEPT LIKE BABIES FOR the first time in over ten years, knowing that Skates was dead. We thought we had nothing to worry about and were going to be able to somehow, maybe, put all of this behind us.

We were wrong. I should have known that things are never that simple.

Ryland is still in shock, and when the FBI came to our job site this morning, he didn't snap out of it. Agent Javier Lòpez worked with Hudson and Ryland trying to take down Skates. When Mia was kidnapped, Ryland called and left Agent Daniels a message, but the storm cut the message up. This morning, Agent Chloe Drake arrived to replace Lòpez's partner Daniels, and she wasn't satisfied with the answers we gave them.

Not that we really answered their questions. And Ryland acting all spacey didn't help. Agent Drake is insisting Ryland meet with her.

With the FBI poking around, I thought it was best to warn Casey. Based on how we left him last night, I'm not sure if he's going to be any better off than Ryland was this morning.

Mia's face pales as we arrive at Casey's house. I squeeze her hand. "Are you sure you want to do this? It isn't too late to change your mind. You can stay in the car."

She takes a deep breath, then exhales. "No. I'm okay."

I lean over and peck her quickly. "If you want to leave at any time, just say the word."

"All right."

When I volunteered to talk to Casey, Mia said she wanted to go with me. I'm hoping she doesn't regret it.

We get out of the car, and I hold her hand and kiss the back of it while we're waiting for Casey to answer the door. After several attempts, we walk around the house. He's sitting on his deck with the bonfire still smoldering.

"Casey," I bellow out, but he doesn't seem to hear me.

Mia puts a hand on his shoulder, and he looks up.

A moment passes before he seems to register it's her.

"Mia?" he whispers.

She sits in the chair next to him. "Have you been out here all night?"

He glances around then back at her. "I...I think so."

I hope the FBI doesn't visit him today.

The smoke from the fire is thick, and I pick up the lid to put it out.

"Did you burn the clothes?" I ask.

Casey's blue eyes gaze up at me. "Yes."

Mia takes his hand. "Can we go inside?"

"Of course." He rises and motions for Mia to go first, and we follow her.

Once we're inside, we sit in the family room, overlooking the bay. He stares at Mia.

"You look so much like her."

Mia's eyes widen and become wet.

Not here for family drama.

"You need to get your act together. The FBI is sniffing around," I sternly blurt out.

His head turns toward me. "What? Why? How would they know?"

"There is a new agent in town. She replaced Agent Daniels."

Casey snorts. "Hopefully, she isn't any smarter than he was. Agent Lòpez was the one who had brains out of those two."

"Lòpez is still here, and the new woman, Drake, she didn't seem like an idiot to me."

Casey sighs and waves his hand. "I'm not scared of the FBI. I've had enough dealings with them. I'll get you all attorneys if you want."

Anger and heat rise through my chest and into my face. "You think lawyering up is going to be a good idea? This isn't something we want to appear as if we have anything to hide."

"What do they know?" Casey asks.

"Nothing. But they're poking around. You and Ryland aren't acting like yourselves, and they are on a mission to find Skates."

At the mention of Skates' name, Casey tears up.

Rage is like a lightning bolt hitting me. *He still is upset that his piece-of-shit son, Skates, is dead.*

"Are you going to cry every time his name is mentioned?" I snarl at him.

"Beckett," Mia quietly says.

My emotions win, and I lunge at Casey and tug his shirt. He looks at me in fear.

"Beckett!" Mia cries out.

"Leave town."

"Leave town?" Casey asks, eyes wide.

"Yes. Leave town and don't come back until you can stop crying at the mention of Skates, Veronica, Henry, and whoever else was on that boat. The FBI is going to question you. It's inevitable." I release his shirt.

"We have nothing to be worried about."

"Murder occurred. We covered up a crime. You blew a boat up," I hurl at him.

"That isn't—"

"If you care at all about Mia, then you'll leave until you have your emotions under control."

He looks at Mia, who is blinking hard, then back at me. "Okay. I'll head out of town for a while."

"Go somewhere where you have a legit alibi."

"I'll go check on one of my restaurants in Orlando."

"Now. Go now." I point to the door.

"Right this minute?"

"Yes."

"Can I pack at least?"

"Ten minutes then you get off this island. Let's go, Mia."

"Beckett," she quietly says. "Can I talk to Casey privately for a moment?"

My insides bubble. *He's her father.*

I take a deep breath, then kiss her head. "I'll be outside."

She smiles at me, and, as soon as I get outside, I call Ryland.

"Hey," he answers.

"All done," I inform him.

He exhales and stays quiet.

"You pulling it together?"

"Yeah. All good. I'm confirmed to meet Agent Drake tonight."

"Maybe you should meet her in a few days," I suggest, not confident he's back to normal.

"I'm fine."

No, you aren't. I know you, Brother.

My heart races. "Ryland—"

"I gotta go. Materials are arriving."

"Okay. Call me if you need me."

"Will do."

We hang up. There isn't an ounce of belief in me that he's okay. And as I wait for Mia, the twists and turns of my stomach remind me of when I sat in court, waiting to hear my sentence after being convicted of killing Clay.

Please, God, let this be over. Let my family have happiness and be safe.

There's no mercy in the world. You know better than that.

When my beautiful Mia gets in the car, all I can think and feel is that I have to protect my family. It ricochets through my cells, echoing in my mind.

Together we stand, alone we fall.

The most disturbing thought I can't seem to shake is, *this is just the beginning.*

Mia

. . .

There is so much I hate about Casey. But he's also my father, whether I like it or not. And he was distraught yesterday. If I have his blood, I hope there's some good part of him.

I don't blame Beckett for his ill feelings toward Casey. Casey deserves every emotion Beckett is feeling.

Beckett hesitated when I asked to speak to him alone, but finally left. And now Casey patiently waits for me to speak.

After several minutes of silence, he pleas, "Mia, please tell me we can have some sort of relationship."

"I can't agree to what you want right now. I'm sorry, but I need time to process all this."

Casey's eyes water and he reaches out and clasps my hands in his.

Part of me squirms inside, but another part doesn't make me pull away.

"I understand you don't agree with your mother's and my relationship. And there are things I wish I could do differently regarding her, and Clay, and you. But I want you to know how much I loved her."

So much of their relationship makes me ill. And it's confusing to me. My mother was only fifteen, and Casey was almost fifty when they first got together. He should be in jail for statutory rape.

"I don't understand how you could prey on a fifteen-year-old girl when you were an almost fifty-year-old man," I say.

He sighs and closes his eyes. "No matter what I say, Mia, you'll never understand it. And I won't go into all the details about how your mother and I fell in love. I tried to stop it, but fate wouldn't have it any other way. But we were in love. Both of us were in love."

"Then why didn't you claim Clay and me as yours? Why did you let her be a teenage mother all on her own?"

"I could have gone to jail. My businesses could have suffered."

So much anger boils in my blood. I rise. "That's your reasoning? Money? I see where Skates got his greed from." I move toward the door.

"Mia, wait."

I release a big breath of air and turn. "What?"

"I'm still your father."

I snort.

"When I return from this trip, can we talk again? You're my only child left. I want to get to know you."

I don't know why I agree. He doesn't deserve to know me. But it must be the fact that no matter how much I try to erase him as my blood, I can't. "I'm not going to commit to having a relationship with you, but I'll agree to one more meeting when you return."

"Thank you. That's all I ask."

"Bye, Casey. Have a safe trip." I leave and get into the SUV.

"Mia, you all right?" Beckett asks.

"Yeah. Let's go home."

32

Beckett

"We need to search harder. There has to be someone who can marry us. Three months is too long to wait," I tell Mia.

She bites back a smile. "It's not that unrealistic. We did get engaged yesterday. In the long term scheme of things, three months will be a blink on our radar."

"I'm ready to marry you now."

She rises then straddles me on the chair. "Your parents aren't even here."

I take a deep breath. "I want to move forward with our life."

"We are."

"But married."

Her lips twitch.

"Are you laughing at me?"

She shakes her head but has a harder time hiding her grin.

"You are."

"I thought I was supposed to be the bridezilla, not you."

"I am not a bridezilla. I don't care what we wear or where we get married. The only detail I care about is making sure you show up."

"Why wouldn't I show up?"

"You better show up!"

She pushes her fingers through my hair and kisses me. "I'm showing up. If you're this worried, we could go to the courthouse."

I tug her body closer to mine. "No. You want to get married on the beach."

She shrugs. "It isn't a deal-breaker."

Stop being a freak. You don't want Mia sacrificing the few things she wants for the wedding.

"No. We're getting married on the beach, in the spot you decided you were going to fall madly in love with me."

"I already was madly in love with you."

"And I, you."

Mia's blue eyes light up. "Let's go shopping."

"Shopping?"

"Yes. For our wedding outfits."

"I'm not supposed to see your dress before the wedding."

"I thought we weren't doing things how everyone else does."

"Then why don't you wear a white bikini and I'll wear my swim trunks."

She playfully swats me. "No way. You're wearing clothes."

I dip down and kiss the curve of her neck. "What about before and after."

"Optional." She pulls back. "Let's go shopping."

"You're serious?"

"Yep. If I don't go with you, I'll have to go with your sisters, and then I'll be forced to get something that stresses me out."

I tuck her hair behind her ear. "What would stress you out?"

"The big, white dress."

"What do you want?"

She winces. "A simple, white sundress?"

I kiss her. "Then a simple, white sundress you should have. Let's go."

She rises. "Gabriella said they just got a huge shipment in at her store."

"I thought you didn't want to tell my sisters?"

"Yeah, but if I tell her I only want a sundress, she won't question anything."

"And why am I getting something I would never buy?"

"Hmm." She twirls her hair, around her finger, then snaps. "You're taking me out to a fancy dinner. And then we're going to get pictures taken on the beach."

"Like the tourists do?"

"Mm-hmm."

I grab the keys off the counter. "All right."

It doesn't take too long to get to the boutique Gabriella works at. When we walk in, she says, "What are you doing here?"

"We need outfits," Mia says.

"For what?"

"Beach pictures."

"Like white clothes and linen?" Gabriella asks.

"Yeah."

Gabriella tilts her head at me. "You're going to wear a tourist outfit?"

"I lost a bet."

"What was the bet?"

"None of your business."

Gabriella rolls her eyes. "Whatever, Beckett. Mia, tell me about this bet."

Mia pretends to zip her lip. "Sorry. I promised I wouldn't tell."

"Fine," she grumbles. "The new stuff is over here." She flicks her wrists through a rack of pants and hands me a pair of khaki-colored ones.

"Thanks."

"I will not allow you to wear white on white."

"Is that against the law?"

"It's so early 2000."

"Whatever you say. These are fine, but what do you think, Mia?"

"Good. Try them on."

"They should fit."

"Too bad. Try them on. And get him a shirt, Gabriella," she sweetly says and smiles.

"You're awfully bossy right now."

She winks.

She looks so happy right now.

I lean down to her ear, "You can boss me around as much as you like. Bring it on, my sexy lady."

She elbows me. "Stay focused, Beckett."

Gabriella hands Mia a white bikini. "You should try this. Get some pictures of you, not in tourist gear. Beckett can wear this one, too." She holds up a white speedo.

"Absolutely not."

Amusement crosses Gabriella's face. "Why not? Worried about showing off your legs?"

"Funny."

Like my package would even fit in that thing.

The door chimes and Connor walks in.

"What are you doing here?" I ask.

"Me? What are you doing here? And why do you have tourist clothes in your hands?"

"I lost a bet. Mia and I are getting beach photos."

He grunts. "Sorry about your luck." He hands Gabriella a lunch sack. "You forgot this at home."

"Thanks."

"Connor, Beckett and I were debating something," Mia says.

"What's that?"

"Flip flops or bare feet?"

"For your photos?"

"Yes."

"You're really getting beach pictures?"

"Yes. I want them."

"Barefoot."

"That's what I said," I tell him.

We fist bump.

"Beckett, you need a pedicure if you're going barefoot." Gabriella wrinkles her nose and points to my feet.

"What is wrong with my feet?"

"You're toenails aren't polished."

"I am not wearing toenail polish."

Gabriella puts her hands on her hips and sighs. "Not toenail polish, polished. You need those callouses shaved off, your cuticles pushed back, and nails perfectly trimmed."

"I am not getting a pedicure."

"Why?"

"That's for girls."

"No, it's not."

"I'll get one with you. You should let Mia finish shopping, and we'll go next door and get one," Connor says.

"You get pedicures?"

"Dude, a lot has changed since you were freed. No girl wants to touch a guy who has nasty feet. Plus, they have chairs that massage your back while the hottie pedicurist puts all her love and attention on your soles."

"My feet are not nasty."

He looks at them. "No, but you could do way better."

"Mia—"

"You should go," she says.

"What? We're here to get clothes."

"I know, but I'll surprise you."

"I thought—"

Her eyes widen.

She doesn't want me to see her dress.

Good. I don't want to before our big day.

I turn to Connor. "You really want to go?"

"Yeah. Let's go."

"Fine." I turn to Gabriella. "Make sure you wrap Mia's dress up so I can't see it."

"Why?"

"She can surprise me on the day of the photos."

"You didn't try on a shirt or pants."

"He can try it on at home," Mia says.

I kiss Mia. Connor and I go next door to the salon. "Still can't believe I'm doing this."

"Dude, chill. You're going to love it."

"Hey, Connor," a blonde bats her eyes.

"Hi, Chelsea. This is my brother Beckett. We're here for pedicures."

"Oh! You're the one who just got out of prison, right?"

My gut flips.

"Chelsea!" Connor scowls.

"It's fine," I grumble. "Yeah."

She rubs my arm. "Why don't you follow me and I'll fix you right up."

"Are Donna and Louise free right now?" He points to two older women sitting at a manicure table and talking.

"Yep. We've been dead."

"Good. They can do our feet."

Her face falls. "But I—"

"Sorry, we want them."

She stomps off to get the other women.

"What a joke," Connor mumbles.

"It's going to happen. You can't avoid anyone who mentions my prison stint."

"Watch me."

Donna comes over. "Hi, Connor."

"Hey, Donna. This is my brother, Beckett. Can we get two pedicures?"

"Sure." She sticks her hand out and shakes mine, then leads us to the pedicure area.

They fill the tubs.

Donna says, "We're slow, and Connor is such a good client, I'm going to add on a special toxin removal for you both, free of charge." She points to the tub. "Soak your feet, and I'll be back after ten minutes."

"Thank you," we both say.

I turn to Connor. "How often do you come here?"

"Ryland and I come every week. Sometimes Hudson joins us."

I gape. "Ryland and Hudson do this too?"

"Yeah. You'll be a fan after today."

"If you say so."

Connor pushes a button, and my chair starts moving.

"What the—"

He laughs. "Sit back and relax."

I obey. "Okay. I'll take one of these chairs."

"Told you."

"So what's new little brother?"

"Nothing new. Bartending, working out, clubbing."

"You like bartending?"

"Yep. It's fun. I make good money too."

"Want to tell me why you won't come work with us?"

He groans. "Not you too."

I hold my hands in the air. "I'm not judging you. I'm just curious."

"I don't want to get into this."

"Oh, come on."

His face hardens.

"Tell me."

"Fine. All I do is get told what to do—Hudson, Ryland, and you too. I don't need it all day long. And none of you tell me anything and treat me like a kid, so I'll make my own way without anyone's help."

"Didn't say you needed help, bro."

He grunts. "No, I don't."

"But we're family."

"So? I don't need Hudson barking at me all day."

"He means well."

"You say that, but you don't know what it's like."

I snort. "Sure, I do."

"No, you don't. And they tell you everything. I don't get privy to any info. I'm just the loser little brother who isn't trustworthy."

"No one said that."

"They didn't have to. Actions speak louder than words."

"I trust you."

"Sure," he says like he doesn't believe me.

"I'll prove it."

"How?"

"I'll tell you a secret, and no one except Mia knows."

"What?"

"Tell me it's between us first."

"I know how to keep my mouth shut."

I look around to make sure no one is near. Island gossip can be lethal. "Mia and I are getting married."

He grins and leans over and hugs me. "Congratulations. That's awesome."

"That's why we were in the store."

"Gabriella doesn't know?"

"No way. She would tell Gracie, and both of them will have the wedding planned and Mia stressing."

He chuckles. "Yes, they would."

Silence.

"So I'm the only one who knows?"

"Yep."

"Thanks for telling me."

"Don't ever tell Mia or anyone else I told you. I need you to act surprised when we tell everyone."

"When are you doing that?"

"When mom and dad are back."

"Okay. My lips are sealed."

Donna and Louise come back into the room. "Detox is over, boys."

"You're going to love this," Connor reassures me.

"Whatever you say, little bro."

33

Mia

Beckett and I just left a meeting with his siblings. The FBI agents, Chloe Drake and Javier Lòpez, were also there. Beckett told Gracie, Gabriella, and Connor the truth about why he was in prison for ten years and never claimed his innocence, but all it did was anger them further.

"I can't believe they got mad at you. You only kept things a secret to protect them. How can they act like that about the truth?"

"You were upset with me," Beckett says.

"Not once you told me the truth. I understood why you did what you did."

"They need time to process. It'll all blow over in a few days."

"How do you know?"

He grunts. "We're blood and live on a seven mile long island. They don't have a choice."

"That's not funny."

He tugs me on his lap. His warm brown eyes twinkle. "You're going to be stuck with me too."

"Is that what you think?"

"Nope. It's what I know." He lowers the spaghetti strap of my tank top and kisses my shoulder.

Like anytime Beckett touches me, my body lights up.

His lips inch lower. "I think it's time I show you my new skills."

"New skills?"

"Mm-hmm." He lowers my bra and teases my areola with his tongue.

"Have you been studying pornos or something?"

He freezes. "Pornos?"

"Yeah. New skills?"

"Nope. Ryland told me about something."

My mouth hangs open. "You had Ryland give you sex tips about me?"

"No. Yes. I don't know." He laughs then lightly sucks. "You don't want to know what he said to do?"

I avoid the question. "I'm not sure. What kind of stuff is Ryland into?"

"Not answering that."

"Ummm..what does that mean?"

"I have to show you. Pretty sure you'll like it." He moves to my other breast.

My butterflies skyrocket, and my breathing picks up.

"Well? Should I show you or no?"

"Yes," I whisper.

He lifts his head. "What do you want the safeword to be?"

"Safeword? Why do we need a safeword?" I shriek.

He softly chuckles. "So I stop if you want me to."

"Why can't I say stop?"

"Mmm...not sure, but Ryland said we can't use the word stop. It has to be something you would never say during sex."

"What exactly is your brother into?"

"Let's not talk anymore about anyone in my family." He nibbles on my lobe and murmurs, "Concentrate, Mia. Pick a safeword."

Something I wouldn't say during sex...

I look at the counter. "Peanut butter."

Beckett busts out laughing. "Peanut butter?"

"What?"

"How did you come up with that?"

I point.

He snorts. "Okay. Peanut butter it is."

"Is that not a good safeword?"

"How do I know?"

I twirl my hair around my finger. "Should I pick a different one?"

"No. Peanut butter is the safeword. Now let's get down to business."

My stomach flips. "Should I be nervous? I'm kind of nervous."

"Don't be nervous."

I exhale. "Okay."

He rises with me in his arms and steps toward the bedroom.

"Peanut butter, peanut butter, peanut butter," I yell out.

He freezes.

"Just checking," I chirp.

"Mia, you cannot abuse our safeword."

"I did not abuse it."

"You did. You didn't show it any respect."

"Our safeword needs respect?"

He tries to keep a straight face. "Yep."

"Okay. I will not disrespect our safeword again." I zip my lips and pretend to throw away the key.

He carries me into our room and sets me down. "Strip."

"Like sexy strip, or quick strip?"

He steps back and crosses his arms. "Let me see the sexy strip."

"Can I get some music?"

He taps a button on his phone, and hip hop blares out. He sets it on the dresser.

Okay. If I was a stripper...

I push Beckett on the bed and crawl up his body while removing my clothes. The heat in his eyes that I love comes to life, and he licks his lips.

I twirl my bra in my hand and let it fly into the air while straddling him and grinding on his erection.

As soon as I'm naked, he spins me on the bed, so I'm face down. "Don't move, Mia."

"Okay."

"Shh." He turns the lights out, lights a candle, and turns down the music. "Close your eyes."

I shut them. After a few minutes, something silky covers my eyes before Beckett grasps my wrists, puts them over my head, and ties them with something similar to my blindfold.

"You okay, my Angel?"

"Mm-hmm."

"Good. Get on your knees and spread your legs."

I obey.

Something races down my back, and I shiver from the sensation.

"What's that?"

"Shh." He does it again, and again, while playing with my pebbled nipples until my lower body is pulsing and I'm moaning like a porn star...or what I imagine a porn star sounds like since I've never seen one.

His lips brush against my neck, near my ear. "You're making me so hard, my Angel."

"Good. I'm ready for you," I pant.

"Patience," he whispers, and moves his lips down my spine, on my ass cheeks, then spreads my legs further. His fingers graze my sex, and I whimper.

He softly chuckles before sliding under my body and gliding his hands on my thighs and up to my hips.

"Oh, God!" I cry out when he slowly makes me his dinner.

I can't see. I try to move my hands, but all I can do is grasp onto the silky material.

His fingers dig into my hips, and he pulls my body as close to him as possible while making every cell in my body combust.

I spiral, screaming out his name, trembling on his face, surging with so much adrenaline I turn dizzy.

And he doesn't stop. Over and over, I fly. Before I come fully down, he brings me back up in a sea of shattering bliss.

The moment he releases me, he slides his hard cock in me, filling my body.

"Beckett, oh God, Beckett!"

He doesn't show me any mercy. His hand wraps around my waist, and he circles my clit as he pounds against me, holding onto my hip with his other hand.

"I love you, Mia," he murmurs in my ear, leaning his warm, rock hard torso on my back.

"Yes...oh...yes...love...oh Beckett!" I cry out as endorphins tornado through my body.

"I can't wait till you're my wife," he continues.

"Yes...oh..."

His lips are an electrical current on my neck and cheek until I turn enough into him and our tongues connect in a raging inferno of lust, and need, and love.

He thrusts harder and cries out my name, stretching my spasming walls and toppling me over the edge once more.

I'm still shaking when he collapses on me, wrapping his arms under my body, breathing into my neck.

"Peanut butter," I whisper.

He laughs, removes my blindfold, and unties my wrists.

I spin on my back. "What else does Ryland say we should do?"

EPILOGUE

Beckett

The Next Day

MIA IS ASLEEP, CURLED UP IN MY ARMS. WE WERE UP LATE TALKING and giving each other orgasms.

She's so stunning.

No matter how much I look at Mia, I will never get over how beautiful she is, or sweet, or sexy.

And after so many years of emptiness, I finally feel whole again.

I kiss her head and stroke the soft flesh on her ass.

Her eyes flutter open. "Hey. What time is it?"

"It's around nine."

She yawns.

"Sleep more if you want. It's Saturday."

She rolls into me further. "What are we doing today?"

"I thought I would lick some peanut butter off you since you kept talking about it last night."

She straddles me. "Funny."

I push her hot sex down over my erection. "If you're going to sit on me, do it the right way."

"Mmm." She kisses me, and we begin to thrust, but my phone rings.

I reach over and turn it off while still kissing her.

A few seconds later, Mia's phone rings.

She pulls back.

I groan. "Ignore it. I bet it's my family."

She glances at the nightstand then reaches for the phone. "It's the wedding officiant."

I snatch the phone out of her hand and put it on speaker. "Hello."

"Is this Beckett?"

"And Mia," she calls out.

"Good morning. This is Cheryl."

"Hi. Did someone cancel? Can we get married sooner?" I ask.

Cheryl laughs. "What about today?"

"Today?"

"Yes. I have a bride with food poisoning. I know you were upset about the three month wait. Any chance you want to get married today?"

"Yes," I blurt out.

"Beckett, your parents aren't in town."

"What time?" I ask.

Mia's eyes widen. "Cheryl, can we call you back in five minutes?"

"Sure. It would be at four."

"But we'll take it," I tell her.

"Thanks." Mia hits the end button.

"Your parents are in Europe. They will be really upset."

"They can deal."

"Beckett—"

"I've waited long enough for you. I want you to be my wife."

"You aren't going to regret not having your parents there?"

"If they were here, I would want them to join us. But they aren't. I don't want their vacation to stop us from moving forward."

"But—"

"Mia, if my parents were here, would you marry me today?"

She cups my face. "Yes."

"Good. We're getting married today."

"You sure?"

"Yes."

Her eyes fill with tears. "Okay."

"Yeah?"

"Yeah. I can't wait to be Mrs. Beckett Brooks."

I kiss her, and we start to thrust again.

"Crap. We need to call Cheryl back."

Mia hands me the phone and pushes me down on the mattress. "You do it." She circles her hips on me.

Instead of calling Cheryl, I text her. “See you at four.”

She replies, “Sounds good. Same place we discussed?”

“Yep.”

Mia rides me faster and I groan her name.

She widens her eyes and gives me her innocent look. "Sorry, do you remember our safeword?"

"Yeah, why?” I grunt. “Don't stop doing what you're doing."

She reaches for the blindfold I threw on the table the previous night and ties it around my head.

I reach out for her, and she slaps my hands.

"Ouch."

"No touching, Mr. Brooks. I'm in charge now."

"Yes, ma'am.”

She grabs my hands and ties them to the headboard, then whispers in my ear, "Now, tell me how hard you want your soon to be wife to ride you."

As soon as we get done having sex, I text my siblings. Hudson seems to be freaking out about my parents missing our wedding, but I tell him what I told Mia—they will get over it.

Gabriella and Gracie call Mia on a three-way call, and within an hour, the two of them are at our house.

"What are you doing here?"

"Picking up the bride." They both give me hugs.

"What are you picking Mia up for?"

"To help fix her up," Gracie says.

"Mia does not need to be fixed up," I bark.

"Don't be silly, Beckett. She needs her hair and make-up done."

"Mia doesn't wear make-up, and she is awesome at doing her hair without your assistance."

"Oh my God, Beckett. It's your wedding day. You shouldn't even have seen her." Gabriella rolls her eyes.

"We aren't other people."

"Beckett, who are you..." Mia comes out of the bathroom with a towel around her hair and body.

Gabriella jumps up and down, clapping, and Gracie pulls Mia into a hug.

"What are you doing here?" Mia asks.

"Taking you away from Beckett until your wedding," Gabriella replies.

"But—"

"No buts. Grab your dress. Let's go," Gracie orders.

"You do not have to go, Mia," I tell her.

"Stop ruining the fun, Beckett," Gabriella glares at me.

"Mia doesn't need to be stressed out by you two."

"What? How is doing her hair and make-up going to stress her out?" Gracie demands.

"She's perfect the way she is, and you're going to try and make her all fancy."

"You're a moron. It's your wedding day. It's called normal procedure, Beckett," Gabriella claims.

"Tell you what, when you—"

"Stop," Mia yells.

We all turn toward her.

"I'll go with the girls."

"Mia, you don't—"

"I want to. I don't know anything about make-up or hair. You know that."

"Because you don't need it."

She smiles and pulls me down for a kiss. "Call your brothers and do whatever it is guys do. I'm going with your sisters."

I exhale. "Okay. But if you want them to stop at any time—"

"I'll say peanut butter." She bites on her lip, trying not to smile.

I softly laugh. "Okay."

"Why would you say peanut butter?" Gracie asks.

"Yeah, that makes no sense," Gabriella adds.

"None of your business." I kiss Mia again. "What time should I come get you?"

"No, no, no, Beckett!" Gabriella reprimands. "We will bring Mia to you."

I groan.

"Where is your dress?" Gracie asks.

"In the spare bedroom closet. I'll get it." Mia leaves the room.

"Please don't cover her in a bunch of heavy make-up. She doesn't need it."

"Do you really think we would do that?" Gracie glares.

"Yes."

"Wow. No trust in our skills."

"Sad, just so sad," Gabriella chimes in.

Mia comes out. "I'm ready." She kisses me and spins to leave.

"Are you sure—"

Gabriella and Gracie pull Mia out the door.

They better not make her look like someone else.

I go into the kitchen and grab a bottle of water out of the fridge. I lean against the counter. The peanut butter stares back at me, and I chuckle.

I'm lost in thought, thinking about how I get to marry Mia today, but also getting a bit nervous.

They better bring her on time.

What if she changes her mind and doesn't show up?

There is a knock on the door.

Before I get to the door, Connor walks in. "Heard you were here by yourself."

"Did the girls send you?"

"Yes and no."

"At least you're honest."

"Let's go."

"Where are we going?"

"Paddleboarding. It's perfect out."

"I'm getting married today."

Connor crosses his arms and arches his eyebrows. "It's ten-thirty. Your wedding is at four. You'd rather stay here and do what?"

"Good point. Let me put my suit on."

Connor and I spend the day paddleboarding, hanging out in the water, and grabbing a burger for lunch. When it's three, we go back to the house.

"Thanks for hanging with me today," I say.

"It was fun. You nervous?"

"Little bit."

"You know mom is going to have a fit, right?"

"Hudson has already sent me fifty text messages freaking out about it."

Connor snorts. "Sounds like Hudson. Well, get ready. I'll meet you at the beach."

"Sounds good."

My nerves increase the closer I get to four. As soon as I get to the beach, Connor arrives. The officiant gets out of her car, and we go over where Mia and I will stand, as well as my siblings.

Ryland and Hudson show up.

"Nice outfit. Very touristy," Ryland teases and winks.

My stomach flips. "I shouldn't have texted Gabriella and Gracie."

"Why?"

"They have Mia doing God knows what and took her away from me all day."

"It's your wedding day. You're not supposed to be together," Hudson states.

"Yeah, well, if you haven't noticed, nothing about Mia and me is the normal way."

Ryland chuckles. "Maybe it's a good thing your wedding is."

"Gabriella better not try to change how she looks," I grumble.

"Relax. She's beautiful," Connor says.

"You saw her already?"

"Sure. Gabriella's door was open. They were doing her hair and make-up."

Beckett groans again. "They better arrive soon."

"Chill out. She'll be here," Ryland says just as a horn beeps.

Gabriella and Gracie get out, and they open the door, and Mia steps out. She's wearing a white, sleeveless sundress and has pink flowers in the side of her curled hair.

My heart flips.

Oh my...she's stunning.

And going to be my wife.

Ryland pats me on the shoulders. "Told you."

When Mia's blue eyes lock into mine, and she smiles, it's as if the earth comes to a complete stop. Everything about her lights up my life, and no one else matters. I blink hard from emotion. When she approaches me, I grab her hands and murmur in her ear, "Whatever you do, please don't yell peanut butter during our vows."

She giggles.

The officiant tells everyone where to stand, and the ceremony begins. Like everything Mia and I do, we keep it simple. There's no fluff, or show, or ego in our vows. It's just our promise to each other.

As I vow to love, protect, and worship her to the best of my ability, I also give her all of me—every morsel, every crumb, every molecule of my being.

We've done the impossible. We've gotten here. And as long as I'm alive, no one will ever come between us.

The officiant says, "You may kiss your bride."

I pull her in my arms, stare into her turquoise eyes that match the sea, and put everything I have into sealing our vows.

I may have gone to prison for ten years, even though I didn't kill Clay Crimson, but every second of pain, and guilt, and shame of not being able to protect him and Mia that night, lies within me.

And in our kiss and promise to each other lies total redemption.

SINS OF JUSTICE BLURB

TOGETHER WE STAND SERIES - BOOK TWO

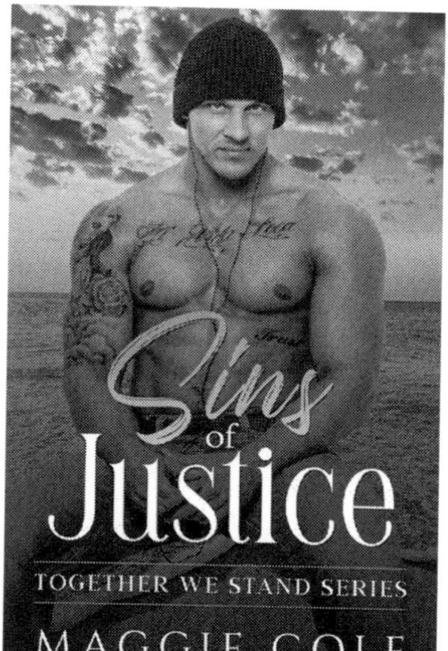

You think you know who you are. That if the time comes to take action, you'll take it, and if it's justified, there won't be any guilt. But I was wrong. Dead wrong.

~ ***Ryland Brooks***

Agent Chloe Drake ~

I'm unprepared for Ryland Brooks.

My job is to take down the Twisted Hearts..not get involved with anyone who is part of the case.

After all, my vendetta against the gang is personal.

But Ryland's like a magnet drawing me to him.

And once I cross the line there's no going back even though he's hiding something from me.

The more I dig I find...and everything points to him.

It's illegal. The laws are unjust. It's a gray area.

So I grapple with what to do and figure it out...until my boss calls for a search that might destroy everything.

Will the Twisted Hearts ruin my life again?

(*Sins of Justice* is the second installment of the *Together We Stand* series. It's an epic journey of one family's struggle of forgiveness, hope, and new beginnings amidst dangerous situations. Each story intertwines and focuses on a new sibling trying to find their Happily Ever After.)

Read SINS OF JUSTICE, book two of the TOGETHER WE STAND series - click here.

SINS OF JUSTICE SNEAK PEEK

PROLOGUE

Ryland

One aim. One pull of the trigger. One bullet. That's all it took to end a man's life. My reaction was quick, merciless, and final. I don't even know the name of that man. All I see now is his face, frozen in death. His body lies in a pool of his own blood.

For ten years, I owned a gun. Every week I went to the shooting range and practiced. My aim became so good that I could hit the bullseye every time.

You think you know who you are. That if the time comes to take action, you'll take it, and if it's justified, there won't be any guilt. But I was wrong. Dead wrong.

My family's protection drove me to buy a gun, learn how to shoot it, and finally use it. When I aimed, I aimed to kill. I did it to save my brother. I would do it again to save Beckett or anyone in my family, but the repercussions of knowing I'm a murderer are harsher than I can bear.

And I'll never know his name. We blew all the evidence up. Any scrap that could have been in the explosion is certainly at the bottom of the sea, lost forever, buried in the sand.

After the explosion, I don't remember the rest of the boat ride back to the island. I woke up at Hudson's and vaguely remember him telling me that he gave me a melatonin to sleep.

"Ryland?" Beckett's voice tears me out of my thoughts.

"Hmm?"

"Agents Lòpez and Drake are here."

Who is Drake? Where is Daniels?

"Drake?" I turn and see an angel in front of me. Fiery red hair that brushes her shoulders, green eyes with flecks of light, and luscious, heavenly lips.

She holds her hand out. "Agent Drake."

Agent Drake. Nothing is registering.

She's dressed way fancier than what you usually see on the island and definitely on my jobsites. The navy dress hugs her curves, and my eyes drift to her pert breasts, curvy waist, and perfect legs.

Even her kneecaps are sexy.

Agent Drake. Oh shit. Pull it together, Ryland.

I lock eyes with hers and shake the hand that she's offering me.

"Ryland." Javier sticks his hand out, and I slowly release hers, breaking eye contact with her.

"What are you doing here?" I ask.

Javier peers closer. "The storm yesterday interfered with our cell phone service. I didn't get your message until this morning. Is everything all right?"

"Is everything all right?" *I don't know. Is it? Will it ever be?*

Hudson steps closer to Agent Lòpez. "You shouldn't be here. We had a deal with Daniels."

Javier nods. "Yes. Of course. It's just that Ryland sounded desperate to speak with us yesterday. He didn't answer his phone when I called several times this morning."

Desperate to speak with them.

I gaze at Beckett as if he can somehow make sense of all this.

Yesterday. Everything happened yesterday.

"Can we talk privately? This really isn't a good place," Hudson says to the agents in a low voice.

Yesterday, when I made that phone call, I wasn't a murderer. I clench my jaw and blink hard, trying not to cry.

Agent Drake is holding something out to me. "Here's my information." I reach for it and lock eyes with her.

Do you know I'm a murderer?

God, I have to get out of here.

I turn and walk away, not able to be near anyone so beautiful and angelic when I'm a cold-blooded killer.

Read SINS OF JUSTICE, book two of the TOGETHER WE STAND series - click here.

MORE BY MAGGIE COLE

Together We Stand Series

Kiss of Redemption- Book One
Sins of Justice - Book Two
Acts of Manipulation - Book Three
Web of Betrayal - Book Four
Masks of Devotion - Book Five
Roots of Vengeance - Book Six

It's Complicated Series

Crossing the Line - Book One
Don't Forget Me - Book Two
Committed to You - Book Three
More Than Paper - Book Four

All In Series

The Rule - Book One
The Secret - Book Two
The Crime - Book Three
The Lie - Book Four

The Trap - Book Five
The Gamble - Book Six

ACKNOWLEDGMENTS

To my friends who read several drafts and kept pushing me to make this novel better, I thank you!

To my editors, cover artists, beta team, launch team, and author friends who shared so much wisdom with me, I thank you!

To my readers; from the bottom of my heart, I thank you! I sincerely hope you loved this novel. I can't wait to share all the new stories and characters I've been creating for you!

ABOUT THE AUTHOR

Maggie Cole is the pen name of a multi-faceted woman. She's an entrepreneur at heart and loves writing contemporary steamy romance novels that help her readers feel lots of different emotions. Sometimes you'll laugh, sometimes you'll cry, sometimes you'll have little flutters racing through your veins...and that's Maggie's biggest wish for you when you read her novels.

Maggie loves to interact with her readers in her Facebook Romance Addicts group so click the icon below and join!

She's a wife, mother, and lives in the sunshine, where she can often be found staring off into space while creating new scenes in her mind.

Printed in Great Britain
by Amazon

48162374R00168